DON'T FEED THE VAMPIRE

COASTAL CREATURES
BOOK 1

GRAE BRYAN

Cover designed by MiblArt.

No part of this book was produced using AI.

Content warnings: erotic blood play, stalking, child abduction (past, off-page), explicit sexual content, kidnapping

PROLOGUE

RILEY

The two vampire ladies were talking a lot.

It was mostly to each other—quiet murmurs and little laughs coming from the car's two front seats—but sometimes they spoke to Riley too. They didn't seem to mind that he usually didn't answer.

For people who sucked out human blood, they were pretty nice.

Riley could have maybe answered them if he'd wanted to. They'd fed him bags and bags and bags of blood—those were gross but also delicious, and the mix of feelings Riley had around it all was confusing—and the new voice in Riley's head had quieted down now that they were full for once.

Riley always meant to ignore the voice. He really did.

He just got so hungry, was all.

The voice sounded like nonsense until Riley was starving, and then the words it said were all he could think. *Feed. Bite. Drink, drink, drink.*

It was creepy. *Riley* was creepy.

That was why they were driving and not flying to their new home, even though it meant days in the car. Riley couldn't be trusted on a plane. Or he couldn't be trusted with so many warm, human bodies all crammed into one place. The plane might land at their new destination and it would be like a horror movie, the doors opening up to blood splattered everywhere and no one but him and these two vampire ladies left alive.

Riley's new moms were who they were, the two ladies. If he wanted them to be. They were trying really hard not to be too pushy, Riley could tell. Because he'd only lost his *real* mom a little while ago. When he'd bi—

But no, Riley didn't want to think about that.

He tapped his finger on the car window, tracing a leftover raindrop down to the bottom. It had been drizzling for the last hour, but it wasn't anymore. Now it was just cloudy and gray, and the trees around them were so, so green.

The desert could get green sometimes, after a good monsoon. But nothing like this.

The quiet murmuring from the front of the car stopped, and then Daphne—one of the vampire ladies—let out a gasp, clapping her hands together. "Here it is!"

Riley leaned forward in his seat, trying to see something besides forest out the front window. Just leaves and green and then there—a break in the trees.

Their new house.

It was big, a lot bigger than the two-bedroom Riley had shared with his mom back in Arizona. It looked huge and kind of gloomy, with dark wood and a steepled roof and a huge porch that wrapped all the way around. Big trees surrounded it, pressing in from all sides.

No neighbors though. Not another house to be seen.

They'd passed a small town on the coast before turning onto

the road that led into the forest, but that had been ages ago, it felt like.

They were going to be all alone out here.

But that was how it had to be because Riley was a monster now. And monsters didn't get to be around other people. Monsters had to be left alone in the woods, with nobody else for miles and miles.

Riley's eyes were stinging, but he wasn't going to cry. Maybe later, when he was alone. If the voice in his head stayed quiet enough to let him.

But for now, the two vampire ladies who had been so nice to him parked the car and turned in their seats to smile at him, and Riley clenched his jaw so, so hard so he didn't go crying accidentally.

He didn't want them to regret adopting him. He didn't want to be left all by himself in this house in the woods.

It didn't matter that he didn't really know these two ladies—Riley wanted them to stay with him. To live in this new house together, at least until Riley grew up, or went crazy from being so hungry, or was killed for being a monster.

He really hoped he didn't get killed for being a monster.

There was a flash of movement from the window, and Riley whipped his head to the side. He caught sight of a squirrel climbing up one of those green, green trees.

Riley had been so full just a minute ago from all those blood bags, but now his stomach cramped. That stupid voice stirred, rustling around inside him.

Bite it. Drain it. Feed.

It wasn't normal for vampires to eat animals that weren't humans, but apparently Riley was an exception. A freak among freaks.

Riley's new moms shared a glance, and then Daphne gave him

a small smile. "It's okay, Riley. You can hunt if you need to. That's why we're here."

She'd barely finished speaking before Riley was scrambling out of the car, his body moving before his brain could stop it.

He needed to eat something.

He *always* needed to eat something. He was a growing boy, with a growing monster inside him.

But it wasn't time to think about that. The squirrel was running back down the tree. Riley crouched next to the car, waiting for the little warm-blooded thing to hit the ground.

It was time to chase his dinner.

1

SETH

Seth had no idea why he'd moved to Washington. Like, what the hell had he been thinking?

Okay, maybe he had *some* idea. He'd wanted—drumroll, please—a change. (God, could he get any more basic?)

To be fair, he'd also wanted to finally open his own bakery, and his tiny town in Maine hadn't had any opportunities in that regard. So that had led to—of course—impulsively moving all the way across the country, where Seth knew nothing and no one, to a *different* tiny town, and then opening his beloved new bakery for the first time on a cold, rainy weekday, where he'd had his doors unlocked for two hours and had served approximately zero customers.

Seth straightened his little plate of samples for the fifth time in a minute.

This was a disaster.

He'd known this was a small community—in taking this

rental, he'd been replacing the only other bakery in town—but didn't anyone here eat pastries?

They were damned good pastries too. Seth had made sure of that. His new place might have only been big enough for three tables and a pastry case, but the case was full, the walls were now painted a cheerful yellow, he had hot coffees and teas and—

Was that a customer? Seth craned his neck to peer out the front window.

But no, it was only a bird flying by. Seth had just been catfished by an avian shadow.

Oh God, he was screwed. So screwed.

So, really, what the hell had he been thinking? Back at home he would have served all his regulars by now. Townspeople Seth knew not only by name but by pastry preference and morning constitution. He'd known who to flirt with, who to sympathize with, and who preferred Seth be a wordless automaton exchanging silence for Danishes and coffee (not Seth's forte—silence—but he'd done his best). He would have been complimented on his headband by now too, an adorable cloth number he'd made himself out of a bright sunflower pattern, to offset the gloominess of the weather.

But there were no compliments to be found here. No regulars. No nothing.

The front door opened, Seth's cheery little bell ringing, and Seth tried very, very hard not to look off-putting in his intense, ecstatic enthusiasm over his first customer.

"Welcome to Coastal Crumbs!"

Oh, he'd said that too loud. Way too loud.

The tall, scruffy man with a wiggling bundle in his arms gave Seth a nod, then set down his load. The bundle turned out to be a little human, somewhere in the toddler years, with round cheeks and damp curls, his tiny body all wrapped up in a puffy rainproof jacket.

As soon as the toddler spotted the pastry case, he started chanting, "Doh-nuh! Doh-nuh!"

The scruffy man, who might have been this toddler's father, gave Seth a look somewhere between a wince and a smile. He was kind of cute, if one liked older, wholesome types. Which Seth sometimes did, depending on his mood. But his mood right now was life regrets and panic, so he wasn't focused too much on the rest.

"Hey, you got any donuts?"

Seth's overly enthusiastic smile fell. No, of course not. Of course he hadn't baked one of the most classic bakery fares in existence. He had croissants, and scones, and a really amazing kouign-amann he'd had to beat into submission with layers and layers of rolling and folding and so much butter he should have had a share in the nation's dairy business. But no donuts.

Seth had gotten out of the habit back home, where one of the local cafés was known for their maple donuts, and Seth hadn't wanted to step on any toes and...

"Um..." Seth cast his gaze around, as if a wild donut might appear from nowhere.

The man's face fell, although he quickly turned it into a smile when the little toddler looked back at him, asking again, "Doh-nuh?"

The presumed dad cleared his throat. "I made the mistake of giving him a bite of mine the other day, and ever since—"

Struck by sudden genius, Seth leaned forward, whispering, "If I cut a hole in the center of a brioche bun, would he know the difference?"

The dad's look of relief was almost painful to witness. "No, no, he really wouldn't. I tried not to give him the bits with icing anyway."

Seth leaned back, raising his voice loud enough for the kiddo to hear. "One donut, coming up!"

The toddler started clapping his chubby hands, chanting again, "Doh-nuh! Doh-nuh!"

Seth got to work, taking a brioche roll off its stand and cutting it surreptitiously into something resembling a donut. The dad busied himself perusing the case, then added, "And a coffee and one of those pecan scones, please."

"Sure thing." Seth couldn't stop grinning, although he was doing his best to keep it a trifle less manic. A real customer and a real order, even if Seth was busting out a fake donut to make it happen.

"Slow day, huh?"

"I might be a pariah already."

Seth said it cheerfully enough—his mood was picking up with this bit of human interaction—but he wasn't exactly joking either. Had he offended the townspeople here without knowing it? Because as much as he didn't mind a solitary kitchen when he was working, Seth needed balance. He simply wasn't made to waste away in silence with only his own thoughts for company.

"Oh, no." The dad rocked back on his heels. "They're just waiting on the verdict."

Seth paused in the act of placing the fake donut in a white paper bag. "Verdict from who, exactly?"

"I guess me, if I'm the first." The dad rubbed a hand over his scruffy facial hair, ignoring the little creature tugging on his pant legs, clearly getting impatient with Seth's slow pace.

"Let me just..." Seth snagged a croissant and a lemon bar, adding them to the bag. "On the house."

The dad laughed, flashing white teeth. "You don't need to bribe me. Even if I say it's awful, they'll start trickling in over the next few days. And on the weekends you'll get traffic from the highway, folks on their way up to the islands. People like to stop here for coffee and a bite."

"Really?" Seth sagged against the counter as he handed his

goods over, relief making his bones weak. "You're making me feel so much better."

"I mean, be warned: it *is* a small community." The dad broke off a piece of fake donut and placed it in his son's grabby hands before reaching for his wallet.

"I like small communities," Seth told him.

The small size of the town had been part of the appeal when Seth had chosen Pine Bluff for his big move. But he'd been operating on such a whim—and moving in such a hurry—that he hadn't made as big a deal of his grand opening as might have been good for business. Seth had thought, since he'd been replacing another bakery, that he'd have a built-in customer base.

Apparently he should have won the locals over first.

"Moh!" the toddler cried, having consumed his bite in record time. Although, it appeared he had more crumbs around his mouth than whatever had actually made it inside. "Moh!"

The dad looked down at his son as Seth ran his payment. "What do you say?"

The toddler grinned, displaying four tiny front teeth. "Peez?"

Oh, lordy. Seth didn't want any little chaos gremlins of his own right now, but he still melted, just a little. He was tempted to rush to the back and make a baker's dozen of donuts right that second.

The dad gave his son another bite, tossing Seth a smile. "You have your first rave review, I think." He held out a hand. "I'm Luke, and this is my son, Colby."

Seth shook hands. "Nice to meet you." So nice. The nicest.

Luke picked Colby up, juggling his coffee and bag of pastries in the other hand. Before they turned away, Colby reached out a small, pudgy hand, pointing to the cloth headband holding back Seth's curls. "Piddy."

Luke grinned. "It is pretty, isn't it?" He shot Seth a friendly wink, and they walked out the door.

A rave review *and* a compliment, albeit from a small human with a filthy face.

Seth would take it. He'd take all of it.

It wasn't like he had much choice.

But now Seth was left alone again, with only his soothing rainy-day playlist to keep him company. He resisted the urge to bang his head down on the counter, as that would be unprofessional and thus beneath him.

Really. What the hell had he been thinking?

By the time Seth closed up for the day, he'd had a few more customers, to his immense relief. There'd been an older couple who'd stopped bickering only long enough to order two croissants and two hot chocolates, a young woman who'd chosen a large selection of pastries and politely ignored the fact that Seth had almost wept from gratitude, and a teenage girl Seth was clocking for future makeup tips before his next big night out.

It was better than nothing, surely, but it still wasn't exactly the warm welcome of Seth's dreams.

It was his own fault though. He should have put more effort into integrating into the community in the weeks leading up to his opening. Sure, he'd made social media accounts for the bakery and posted a few times, passed some flyers to local businesses, but he hadn't done much schmoozing on his own.

But he'd had his whole life to unpack, and the weather had been so daunting, and it had been easier to focus on prepping recipes and redecorating the small space, keeping himself in his own little bubble.

He needed to get over all that, though, if he wanted to make this work. And he *did* want to make it work, even if he wouldn't exactly be homeless and destitute if he failed. He'd been pretty frugal and had a decent nest egg for padding, and he was only twenty-six, which was probably the perfect age for a life failure or two.

Who are you trying to convince? a little voice asked him as he packed away far too many leftover pastries.

Himself, obviously. He was trying to convince *himself.*

Methinks the Seth doth protest too much.

See? Seth needed more customers. Too much time on his own was never good. His inner monologue got far too bitchy and pretentious.

What he also needed was to binge something cozy on his laptop, snag a phone call with his favorite cousin, and get a good night's sleep. He would recalibrate, and tomorrow would be a fresh start.

Seth had meant what he'd told Luke—he didn't mind a small community, as long as he was a part of it. In the morning he'd put up a little bulletin board for people to post local events, and maybe come up with something of his own to add. A board game night at the bakery? Except no, he didn't have enough room for that. Cookie decorating? Possibly, if everyone agreed to do it without chairs.

He'd figure it out. And he'd make some damned donuts too while he was at it.

Seth grabbed the bags of leftover pastries, leaving one for the day-old basket tomorrow. That was another item on his to-do list as he figured out how much to stock each day: make connections in town who might want in on the leftover pastry hustle. Sometimes food banks would accept limited amounts, and he'd had a deal with the local elementary school in Seacliff where Seth had provided free day-olds for the Wednesday teachers' meetings. Whatever helped prevent food waste.

For now, maybe Seth would meet someone in need of a sweet treat pick-me-up on the way home.

It should have still been light out—until Seth managed to hire help, he was closing at 1:00 p.m. every day—but it was pouring again, not a bit of sun to be seen through the rain. Seth tossed the hood of his rain jacket up over his hair and bolted to his car, where he quickly tossed the bags of pastries into the trunk. There was no one out to hand the leftovers to, and Seth headed straight home, driving way too slowly for fear of losing control on the slick roads.

It took less than ten minutes to reach the one-bedroom house he was renting. It might even be a walkable commute when the weather was nicer. Seth had wanted somewhere closer to the beach—he loved the sound of the waves at night—but the town wasn't really set up that way. The coast and its two beaches were on one side of the highway, while the small downtown and residences were on the other side. So Seth had ended up on the edge of the coastal forest instead.

It was peaceful, at least.

Seth parked in the driveway and threw his hood back up. He ran back around to his trunk, popping it and bending forward to snag the pastries that had rolled to the back.

And then Seth was hit by a ten-ton truck.

At least, that was what it felt like. One second he was reaching for a Danish, and the next, Seth was flat on his back on his gravel drive with a hooded figure looming over him, pinning him to the ground.

What the hell had just happened?

The guy was young, Seth thought, but it was a little hard to tell. The stranger's face was blocking the worst of the rain, but there was still water dripping into Seth's eyes and making it hard to see. Seth had a vague impression of dark hair and male features though.

But also he was still trying to get air into his battered lungs after getting knocked on his ass, and it was hard to focus on anything else.

There was a low rumbling, just barely audible over the rain. Almost like an animal was growling nearby.

Seth blinked water out of his eyes, finally sucking in a harsh breath. "Is there—is there a bear or something?" he managed to ask.

That maybe would explain the tackling. Seth was pretty sure they should be running, though, if there was really a bear involved. Or maybe playing dead was the right move? Seth couldn't remember right now in all the confusion.

He was almost positive he wasn't being mugged. The guy peering down at him wasn't asking for anything, or trying to hurt Seth beyond that initial tackle. He was just...staring, silent and still and with a predator's focused intensity.

He had dark eyes, this stranger. Seth could kind of see them now. Or were those...black eyes?

Seth blinked some more. But no, they were brown, although the pupils were kind of blown. Maybe the guy was on something, lost in a bad trip. Maybe he thought *Seth* was the bear.

He didn't smell like a vagrant, although that was judgmental of Seth to think, and he needed to remember to chastise himself later. The guy smelled like the forest, kind of like cedar and damp earth. Seth had the strange urge to lean in closer and huff a deeper breath.

Except the guy was still pinning Seth to the ground, vibrating with some strange, feral energy, so maybe Seth should focus on that and not on the way the guy *smelled.*

Before Seth could ask him what he might have taken, and if maybe he needed to head to the hospital, the stranger finally spoke.

"I want to eat you," he said, so low and soft the words were almost lost to the rain. His voice was oddly pleasant. "I want to eat you so bad."

And then the weight suddenly lifted off Seth, the figure looming over him gone in the next instant.

By the time Seth scrambled up off the driveway, his pants soaked through and stuck to his thighs and bits of gravel trapped in his hair, there was no one there. Just the rain, and Seth's open trunk, and the now-soggy bags of leftover pastries.

What in the actual fuck?

2

SETH

An hour later and Seth had mostly recovered from the bizarre encounter in his driveway.

He still didn't exactly love that he'd been thrown to the ground with zero explanation (and no, "I want to eat you" did *not* count), but he'd come away unscathed, and twenty minutes under a hot spray had soothed the indignity of cold, wet gravel in his hair.

Now he was fresh and clean and cozy in his sweats, a hydrating face mask in place as he happily housed down some microwaved ramen on his couch, his phone tucked between his cheek and his shoulder.

It wasn't the most comfortable couch in the whole world—the rental house had come mostly furnished, and the furniture it had included was relatively outdated. Like, a chintz sofa with a hard back wouldn't have been Seth's first choice, but whatever. The vibe was kind of retro, even, if he sort of squinted in dim lighting. Seth had decided to invest in some vintage accent pieces to set it all off. Maybe he'd go thrifting for some lamps on his next Monday off.

For now, he was overcompensating for the discomfort with an abundance of fleece blankets. And, of course, recounting the whole ordeal of this terrible day to his cousin, Benny.

Seth had started the phone call off with the appropriate bitching and moaning over the slow start to Coastal Crumbs, and he'd just finished with the tale of the stranger in his driveway.

There was a beat of silence as Benny processed. It didn't last long.

"Maybe he meant it sexually," Benny mused in his deep baritone, calm and cool as ever. "Like he wants to eat your ass. Kind of a compliment, really, if he wants to eat it more than anything."

Jesus.

This was exactly why Seth had called his cousin though. No one else would've taken the wind out of Seth's sails in quite the same way. He swallowed his latest bite of ramen in a hurried gulp. "You know, I love the way your brain works, but no, I'm almost positive he didn't tackle me in the rain to whisper that he wants to eat my ass."

Benny hummed doubtfully. "You haven't been doing your squats, then?"

Seth hadn't been doing his squats for the past twenty-six years, so he changed the subject. "I'm pretty sure he stole some of my leftover pastries too. The count is off."

"Don't you give those away?"

"Yes, but he didn't *ask*."

"You would have said yes, though, right?"

Seth let out a huff as he set his mostly empty ramen cup on the coffee table. "Obviously. He seemed like he was in a rough way."

"Then he just, like, cut out the middleman."

The statement was so wrong and yet so right at the same time. Benny was a sweetheart gym rat who might have aptly been called a himbo, and he loved to assume the best in people. So did Seth on his better days, but sometimes it was nice to play the grump for once, especially after putting up with this disappointing day.

Seth considered arguing a little more, just for the fun of it, but then he paused, holding his phone to his chest.

Had he heard something? Over by his window maybe?

When he'd chosen this house to rent, Seth had liked that he was out on the edge of the woods without too many people around, but he suddenly wished he had neighbors on all sides, instead of the one old lady next to him who Seth was pretty sure was half-deaf, based on their few interactions.

Would she even hear Seth if he screamed bloody murder? Or if he was murdered bloodily, for that matter?

Seth crawled off the couch and tiptoed to the window, peering out. The rain had stopped, although water was still dripping slowly off the roof. He didn't see anyone lurking nearby, no hooded figures with ice picks in hand waiting to off him in the dark.

"What if he comes back?" Seth whispered into the phone. "The tackler."

"Call the cops?"

Seth frowned out the window. He didn't love the idea of calling the so-called authorities on someone who was maybe just going through a tough time. "Seems mean."

"Then keep your doors locked and call me. Helio can get us there, like, really fast."

Seth couldn't help a small eye roll, even as he murmured some vague sound of acknowledgment. Benny's husband, Helio, was super odd and super rich, but even private jets could only go so fast. Seth didn't think they'd be able to rescue him from a murderer, unless the murderer was moving at the speed of frozen molasses, or setting up some elaborate *Saw*-esque torture game.

Benny cleared his throat. "Hey, Seth, are you really okay?"

Oh, *that* dreaded question. But Seth loved his cousin enough to give it a good think before answering, "Yeah, I'm good. Just a hard day. But, you know, change."

"You can come back if you want. Everyone would be stoked to have you."

"I know." And he did. But Seth didn't really want to go back to Maine. Not yet, at least. He'd been in a rut back home, living in the same tiny tourist town where he'd been born and raised. And that might have been okay if he'd been *happy*—Seth didn't mind having a quiet sort of life—but he hadn't been. Not for a while. Something had been...off. Missing, maybe. Old friends moving on or settling down and Seth just always *there*, kind of stagnant and ornamental, just another part of the charming scenery.

So, no, Seth wasn't going to go running back after one slow day and a little light battery.

He'd just made it back to the couch when he heard a noise again. A scrape against his wall? A subdued cough? An ice pick sliding through gravel, perhaps?

Seth suppressed his shiver mercilessly. He wasn't going back to the window. He was being paranoid, and it wouldn't help to indulge the madness.

Although, to be fair, his pastries *were* delicious. Maybe his sort-of attacker had tasted them and come running back for more.

Seth deliberately settled into the ugly couch, tucking the blanket around himself like a straitjacket so he wouldn't be tempted to get up and scout the perimeter again.

"Have you gotten a good running route yet?" Benny asked.

Seth made a vague noise that could have been interpreted as a yes or no. "I'm working on it."

Seth wasn't a hardcore fitness maniac like his cousin, but he liked the endorphins of a good run now and again. Trudging along in the rain and the mud was another matter entirely, and he was giving himself time to adjust to the change in conditions. Maybe he'd treat himself to some fancy, waterproof running gear.

Not tonight though. Tonight he was going to chat mindlessly with his cousin, then watch TV mindlessly by himself, and then conk out mindlessly by dinnertime.

The catch about baking for a living was the part where Seth had to arrive at work by four a.m. When he'd been younger, Seth might have partied all night and just pushed through until the next day, but he wasn't up for that kind of life anymore. He was usually in bed by nine p.m. at the latest, and even that could be a stretch. When he'd worked for Marjorie back in Seacliff, he'd at least had a few days off a week, but until he decided he could pay someone to help out, Mondays would be his only free morning here.

Seth resisted the urge to chew on his nails as he considered sleeping in his new house after being tackled in the driveway. He'd painted them bright orange—another sartorial attempt to fight off the gloominess of the weather—which meant he had to wear gloves when baking but also meant he was less likely to engage in old stress habits.

No nibbling, he reminded himself.

"Hey, Benny...I can do this, right?"

Benny didn't hesitate. "Hell yeah, you can."

Seth grinned down at his blanket, immediately bolstered by the vote of confidence.

Hell yeah, he could.

SETH KNEW there were those who would consider the early call time a real downside to his profession. Most people—especially young people—didn't want to wake up at three thirty in the morning to start their day.

But Seth didn't actually mind it. It was kind of soothing, to be going out into the world while everyone else was still asleep. He still loved chatting with people—loved sharing food and gossip—but he also loved this fresh start to each day all on his own.

He didn't know if that made him an introverted extrovert or an extroverted introvert or just a person like any other, with different wants and different moods depending on the time of day.

But he did love it, getting into his car at quarter to four, with everything quiet and still around him. Today it was gray but not rainy, and the air smelled like forest and damp earth.

Seth's gloomy mood from the day before was gone, washed away during the night. He was ready to start anew, ready to bear the slow and bumpy grind to starting his own business.

Everything stayed that way—quiet and still and peaceful—until Seth arrived at the back entrance of his bakery, the one that led into his kitchen.

There was a young man standing there, right in front of the door, in a collared shearling-lined jacket and faded jeans. His dark hair was parted more or less in the center and was long enough to tuck behind his ears, and he had dark brows to match his dark eyes, and a startlingly pretty face.

Seth stopped where he was, about three feet from the door. He was 90 percent sure this was the guy who'd knocked him over in the rain. Even though Seth hadn't gotten a detailed picture of his features, the impression was somehow the same.

Which maybe should have been freaking Seth out more than it was, but the guy looked so...normal. Younger and hotter than a random assailant had any right to be, but...yeah, more or less normal.

"Hello," Seth said calmly, clutching the keys to the bakery in his fist. "We're not open yet."

Dark eyes watched him closely, but the kid didn't say anything. He seemed to be studying Seth, clocking every inch of him. Seth was suddenly overly conscious of his own appearance. Of his untamed hair and the soft pants he was wearing—the ones that were comfortable to work and stand in for hours—his ugly waterproof coat, the headband hanging around his neck, and the apron slung over the crook of his arm.

Seth would have guessed the stranger to be somewhere in his late teens or early twenties, but it was hard to say. His face was pretty in an almost boyish way, but his eyes...

Those eyes were deep and soulful and older than any easily estimated years.

Plus, Seth knew a thing or two about being baby-faced. People always thought he was younger than he was. It was the round cheeks paired with the slender build—it threw people off.

Was this kid living on the streets? Was that why he kept showing up at odd hours? His clothes looked clean, but that didn't necessarily indicate anything. Plenty of people kept themselves neat and tidy while they struggled with housing. The kid actually had a bit of dirt smudged on one cheekbone, but somehow it only looked charming.

"Are you hungry?" Seth asked. Maybe that was why this stranger was standing outside the bakery. Maybe he was hoping Seth would toss out some more day-olds.

After a moment, the kid gave a small, jerky nod.

"If you come back at six, I'll have fresh pastries, hot from the oven and everything." Seth cocked his head. "Did you like what you tried last night?"

Another pause. Another jerky nod.

Maybe he didn't speak? But no, he'd spoken last night, unless Seth had been imagining it.

I want to eat you. I want to eat you more than anything.

Seth couldn't square those words with what he was seeing now in front of him, this seemingly shy kid who wasn't speaking a word. Still, just remembering it sent a little shiver through him.

The kid cocked his head, his gaze darting over Seth like he'd noticed the tremble. He stepped to the side, away from the door.

Seth took advantage and walked confidently forward—*fake it till you make it*—managing to get the keys into the lock after only one misguided attempt. The movement put the quiet stranger a little behind him, and the hairs on the back of Seth's neck stood at attention, as if in warning. *Do not turn your back on this one.*

There was a stir of air, and the light, breathy sound of an inhale.

Had Seth just been sniffed?

He glanced over his shoulder, but the kid was right where Seth had left him, his hands tucked in his pockets now, his gaze unerringly focused on Seth. There was a stillness to him that was unnerving, and yet Seth still couldn't summon any real fear.

He opened the door quickly but paused there, one foot inside. "Come back at six, okay?" something had Seth saying. "I'll give you something to eat."

There was no response, not even a nod. Only that same rapt attention. Seth considered asking, *Why did you knock me over last night?* But decided against it. The kid seemed skittish, and maybe mostly nonverbal. And he wasn't knocking Seth over *now*, so why not let bygones be bygones?

"Are you going to be okay out here?" he asked instead.

He received another nod this time.

Not sure what else to do or say, Seth went inside, closing and locking the door behind him. He felt oddly cruel in doing so. But that was ridiculous. It would have been insane to ask the stranger inside. The bakery wasn't open, and Seth still had pastries to make. What was he going to do—work with the kid lurking behind him, watching Seth's every move with those ancient dark eyes?

Another strange, internal shudder ran through him. Seth wasn't sure if it was the good kind or bad kind, but he wasn't going to overanalyze it. The gray weather was doing weird things to him, like it was giving a spooky edge to everything. Next thing Seth knew, he'd be wearing all black and trying to commune with ghosts or cast spells with his cinnamon sticks.

Seth got some coffee started and his music going, selecting one of his favorite morning playlists, all low and moody and lyrical. He pulled his headband up to push his hair back and washed his hands thoroughly in the sink, donning his gloves afterward.

He was making a smaller selection of pastries today, keeping his supply low until business picked up. It was easy to get lost in the act of creating food, even the basic scones and muffins he'd made a million times over, with different flavors and twists based on Seth's mood that day.

So Seth was focused. It was only every now and then his mind drifted back to a certain pretty face and probing dark eyes.

And when six o'clock rolled around, Seth went to the front with his heart lodged strangely in his throat. He unlocked the front door and turned his sign over to "Open" with hands that weren't quite steady.

He wasn't sure why he was so nervous, but it turned out it didn't matter either way. The kid didn't show up at six. He didn't show up that day at all.

Or the next. Or the next one after that.

For all Seth knew, he was gone for good.

3

RILEY

Riley ran through the forest as fast as his feet could carry him.

Which was, to be honest, very, very fast. It was a good thing too, since his house in the woods was a twenty-minute drive from the little coastal town on a good day. And it seemed really important, in this moment, to get to that house. To get very far away from...other places.

Because the sights and sounds and smells of the forest were surrounding Riley on every side, but all he could see were messy brown curls, and soft cheeks, and strong-looking hands with delicate fingers. All he could hear was a bright, warm voice asking if Riley would be okay. All he could smell was tart orange, and sugar, and a hint of what he thought might be vanilla. Like a cake. A bright sunshine cake with sticky-sweet icing.

Riley had eaten a lot of human food over the years—any intake helped with the hunger pains—but it had always been about quantity, not quality. Nothing made in an oven or on a stove had ever compared to the hot, rich burst of blood on his tongue, so what had been the difference?

But now—*now* Riley could see the appeal. A big slice of cake, placed oh so carefully on a beautiful, breakable plate. Just for him. Just for Riley.

Mine. Mine, mine, mine, MINE. Turn back. Turn BACK.

Okay, not *just* for him. Because Riley still had his stupid fucking voice to think about, because he was still a stupid fucking vampire.

The thing inside him was mad as hell that Riley had made them leave. It was throwing a tantrum, furious enough that it hurt to think, its yelling and snarling creating a pounding rhythm behind Riley's eyes.

Riley hadn't been able to say anything to the beautiful baker with the voice raging inside him like that. He'd barely been able to nod. And now the voice was yelling about mates, and biting, and... other stuff.

But that was fine. Riley was used to ignoring its tantrums. He'd had years of practice.

Fuck off, fuck off, fuck off! he yelled inside his own head, a childish counter to its enraged growls.

It didn't like that, but whatever. Sometimes it was nice to yell back, even if it was a useless exercise.

When Riley finally made it home, he didn't pause on the porch or stop in the entryway to toe off his muddy shoes. He ran straight to the dining room, where his moms were playing cards on their oversize, ornately engraved, admittedly ostentatious dining room table.

His moms were used to him running—in the forest, in the house, to and from town—and barely blinked at the speed of his entrance. "Oh, but the mud, darling," Mama Daphne only scolded softly, as Mama Sybil cursed under her breath at whatever strategic move Mama Daphne had just pulled.

"How was town?" Mama Sybil asked without looking away from the cards arranged on the table.

They hadn't used to be so casual about Riley returning from town. It had once been a whole event, every time he'd managed to surround himself with humans without trying to tear into someone's throat.

But things had changed over the past year, as Riley's growth had leveled out and his hunger had eased. His moms were trying their best to treat him like the adult he'd grown to be and not the child they'd worked so tirelessly to protect.

Riley stood there for a few moments, working to catch breath he didn't technically need.

His moms were beautiful women on their own terms, and as a pair they were pretty damn striking. Mama Sybil, all tall and pale and curvaceous, with bountiful chestnut waves and a preference for formfitting dresses. And Mama Daphne, petite and slim, with rich brown skin and sleek black curls, who matched Mama Sybil in ferocity but tricked people into thinking otherwise with sweet smiles and a cottagecore aesthetic.

They were mates—bonded by fate and by blood—and they loved each other so deeply it was a mystery that they had room to love Riley at all. But they did, with a devotion he wasn't sure he deserved. And they were clever and cautious, and they would know what to do here.

Oh fuck, Riley hoped they knew what to do.

Every vampire was supposed to have a fated mate, a matching soul that would tether them to their humanity and keep them from going feral. A bond that would keep them from giving in fully to that whispering, growling entity inside them that demanded blood and violence and the thrill of a hunt.

But Riley had been half-feral since the day he'd turned, and since vampire children didn't usually survive until adulthood, he and his moms didn't have any prior cases to help guide them. Those turned young were too driven by hunger, too much of a risk of discovery, and they were often put down by others of their kind to keep their species's secret safe.

Riley knew, without a shadow of a doubt, that the only reason he'd escaped that fate himself was because of his mothers' care. Their constant efforts to remind him who he was, the person inside him that was separate from the hunger and bloodlust. Their care in keeping him fed and keeping him full.

Still, none of them had been sure if Riley would have a mate like the rest of his kind. He was an anomaly, and he hadn't... meshed with his inner vampire like he was supposed to.

They hadn't known if fate would give him a match.

But the baker smelled like his, and he made that voice inside Riley rage in a different, new way. A confusing way.

Like...Riley wanted to sink his teeth into the pretty man—that wasn't exactly a foreign desire—but he also wanted to hold him so close that their skin merged together. He wanted that orange cake scent covering him from head to toe.

He wasn't sure what that was about.

His moms seemed to finally notice Riley hadn't answered their question. They turned in unison to look at him fully. At whatever they saw on his face, they each placed their cards face down on the table.

Mama Sybil cocked her head, red lips pursed. "Did you eat something before going into town, Riley?"

Riley couldn't help clenching his hands into fists. Some inner part of him rebelled at being treated like a child again—he was nineteen, not a little boy anymore. But he'd only been going into town for the past year. His appetite as an adolescent had been too voracious to allow it. And it had only been the past six months that he'd been able to go alone, without his moms to chaperone.

That kind of timeline was a blink of an eye to vampires like his moms.

It would be a blink of an eye to *him* one day too, although it was hard to believe it. Not when every day since he'd been turned had felt like its own eternity.

"I ate," Riley said, unable to go into further detail with so many thoughts in his head.

"A human?" Mama Daphne asked. Even with all their efforts to keep Riley from harming anyone, there was no judgment in the question—most vampires had taken a life or twelve in the early days of their new lives, when they were still learning how to manage their hunger—but Riley could hear the calculation behind it. The steps that would need to be taken if he'd snapped and drained someone dry.

He shook his head.

Mama Daphne studied his face. "Was it a hard visit?" she asked eventually. "Someone had an accident, maybe? Fresh blood?"

Riley took a deep breath and let it out deliberately. With the familiarity of home and the reassurance of his mothers' light, floral scents, both with their hint of copper, the voice inside him had quieted a bit. "There's a new bakery," he managed to say.

"Oh, yes. Coastal something or other, wasn't it?" Mama Sybil drawled. "We wanted to try it. I've been dying for a decent croissant." She pronounced the word with a perfect French accent.

"And—and a new baker. The owner."

There was an almost imperceptible shift in the air. Riley could sense it, even as Mama Sybil kept her voice carefully neutral as she asked, "Is there? And what are they like, this baker?"

"Soft cheeks," Riley said instantly. "Delicate hands, but they're strong. Smells good."

Riley watched as Mama Daphne grabbed for Mama Sybil's

hand, her voice not quite as calm as her mate's as she asked, "Smelled good like blood or good like…?"

"Like cake. Orange cake with vanilla icing."

"I see."

"I want to eat him," Riley said in a rush, unable to stop himself. "I want to eat him more than I've ever wanted to eat anything."

He could picture it now. Pulling the baker close and tucking his head into that sweet-smelling neck, right where the blood pounded so fiercely. Opening his mouth to breathe in the warmth of his skin.

The voice inside him agreed, bringing to Riley's mind visions of the bits he'd missed. The curve of the baker's throat, the pounding of his jumpy pulse when Riley had tackled him, a stray freckle under his left eye.

Riley hadn't meant to jump on him the other night. He really hadn't. He'd been walking in the woods, wanting to be close to town but not around any people yet, and he'd smelled something so delicious he hadn't been able to stop himself. He'd lost control, leaping onto the stranger before he'd even known he was moving, only coming back to himself when he'd been met by a pair of frightened eyes, their color not quite green, not quite brown, but something dancing in between.

Riley had meant to run home, to tell his moms that very night about what had happened, but he hadn't. Instead, he'd lurked outside the stranger's home, listening while he tried to catch glimpses through the window. The baker had a friend he'd been telling about his day. He'd been sad about his bakery, the new one in town that didn't have enough customers.

When the baker had finally gone to sleep, tucked away where Riley couldn't see him, Riley had wandered the forest, draining small animals to fill him up. He'd crossed the highway and sat on the sandy beach, and then, while it was still dark, he'd headed back into town. Straight to the bakery.

Riley had thought he'd have a handle on things, now that he'd known what the baker smelled like. He'd thought he wouldn't be caught by surprise this time, and he could have a conversation with him, maybe ask him if all bakers smelled like walking, talking cake.

But Riley had been just as overwhelmed the second time, unable to say a word, and now the baker probably thought he was a creep.

Riley's moms exchanged a glance and then immediately began murmuring between themselves. "We'll need blood," Mama Sybil said. "Lots of it. We need to keep him full."

"Is it wise?" Mama Daphne asked. "Perhaps if he remained—"

"He won't be able to resist. Not for long. Caution is better than avoidance."

Riley's stomach sank at their whispered plans. He'd been in better control for the last year, and he'd forgotten this feeling of panic, this sense of being some rabid creature in need of shackling. It was depressing to be back in it so quickly, after just one mistaken encounter.

But also...soft cheeks. Strong hands. Warm voice.

Riley wanted to see him again. Maybe even more than the monster inside him did. He wanted to see if he'd misjudged how good the baker smelled. Wanted to see if the human would speak so warmly to him again, even though Riley had disappeared without a word.

Maybe the discomfort would be worth it, for that. To see his baker again without worrying about draining him.

"What does it mean—" Riley started to ask, then stopped.

His moms turned to face him again. "What does what mean, darling?" Mama Daphne asked.

"What does it mean that I want to bite him but also want to...I don't know...lick him?" Riley frowned, trying to parse through it even as he spoke the words. "Touch him, maybe. I think I want to wrap my fingers around his throat and see if it feels just as delicate as it looks."

"Well." Mama Sybil cleared her throat, sharing a look with Mama Daphne. "That sounds like it might be attraction, darling."

Oh. Right, that could be it. Riley wouldn't really know. He'd never had so much as a kiss, and he'd never really wanted one. His moms had asked him a few times over the past year, if anyone in town had caught his eye, now that he was interacting with humans. But even though Riley could see on the surface if someone was good-looking or not, he hadn't ever wanted to press them back against the door of their bakery and...Riley didn't know exactly what.

But the baker's lips had looked soft. And Riley sort of wanted to see if they tasted like cake.

So maybe he *did* know. Maybe, now that he thought about it, he had a really good idea of exactly what he'd like to do with the sweet-smelling human.

And then maybe it was okay if his moms fussed over him again. Riley's entire life until now had been a study in hunger, a fight for control. This was only more of the same, but also...different. Better.

Because the prize at the end of this, if Riley could manage it, wasn't just survival. The prize was a kind of hope, wasn't it? For something more. For some*one* who wasn't a parent, or some older vampire friend of the family being nice to Riley because he was a lonely anomaly.

Riley could have something like what his moms shared, couldn't he, if he could only be...good. Normal. Normal enough to hold a conversation, at least, because judging from that phone call, it seemed like the baker liked to talk. So Riley should try to manage a few words in a row, and maybe practice smiling at his pretty human instead of just growling.

Because now that Riley had seen him, smelled him, pressed

him against the dirt—he was almost certain he wanted to keep this mate he'd been given. The voice inside him agreed.

But Riley had to acknowledge—looking down at his mud-splattered jeans, his long fingers trembling from the need to chase something down and drain it of its blood—that his mate might not want him back.

4

SETH

It wasn't until Friday that Seth was able to ask someone about his odd visitor.

Business had picked up over the week, the townspeople either warming up to Seth or craving carbs enough to override their hesitancy. But there'd been no one Seth felt comfortable with interrogating about one of their own.

And then late Friday morning, Luke and Colby appeared again, little Colby chanting a familiar refrain.

Seth grinned at them. "Guess what I haaaave," he sang, making showcase display hands at the small selection of glazed and chocolate donuts in the corner of his case.

Colby shrieked with delight, earning an eye roll from the teenage goth girl who'd ordered a black coffee and a plain brioche bun at opening, had parked at one of Seth's tables, and had been typing furiously at her laptop for the past few hours.

Seth served Luke and his son, and Luke gestured to a table.

"Mind if we sit and hang for a while? He's really into chairs right now."

Sure enough, Colby was already clambering up one of the chairs, stubby legs flailing for a minute before he got his grip. He barely reached the top of the table when seated, but he was undeterred, holding out his hands for more bites of donut, minus the icing.

"Not at all," Seth said. Then, because he wasn't one to waste a golden opportunity, "Hey, do you know a kid in town? Doesn't talk much, maybe nineteen or twenty? Dark hair and brown eyes. Really, um...good-looking?"

Seth felt like a creep as soon as he'd finished speaking—had he really had to mention the good-looking part?—but Luke was already nodding. "Riley? Yeah, he's a local, more or less. Lives deeper in the woods with his moms. Think he was homeschooled; we never saw much of them until this past year."

Seth nodded back at him in a way that was maybe bobble-headed, but he couldn't seem to stop. "Cool, cool. And is he in the habit of, perhaps, accosting people?"

"What?" Luke looked genuinely shocked by the question, which was mildly reassuring. "No. If anything, the kid's overly cautious. Shy. Keeps his distance. You're lucky to get two words out of him most of the time."

The teenage goth suddenly spoke up. "I think they're serial killers."

Luke turned in his seat to stare at her while Colby muttered under his breath, "See-wull kehs." Luke gave him another bite of donut without looking.

"Who is?" Luke finally asked, when the goth girl didn't seem inclined to elaborate.

"The whole family."

"Violet," Luke chastised with a frown. "That's unkind."

Of course they already knew each other. The familiarity made Seth smile. The joy of a small town.

Violet swept black bangs out of her eyes, finally glancing up to give Luke a look of deep disdain. "I mean it as a compliment."

"I'm not sure anyone would consider it a compliment," Seth called cheerfully from behind the counter.

The look of disdain was immediately turned his way. "Washington has one of the highest serial killer rates per capita, you know. Statistics are in my favor."

"Why do you think they keep to themselves so much?" Seth asked. He directed the question to Luke because Violet definitely already had her theories.

Luke rubbed a hand over his scruff, considering. "Rumor is they adopted him from a rough situation. Needed time to acclimate."

"Oh." So this Riley was, like, some traumatized kid looking for a little kindness. Damn, Seth really should have let him in the other day. What was a little intense staring to start the morning, anyway?

"They say you're a spy," Violet said, completely monotone, her focus back on her laptop.

Since Luke didn't respond except with an aggrieved sigh, and little Colby seemed a bit young for espionage, she could only be talking to one person.

"Little old me?" Seth straightened in surprise, more or less delighted by the accusation. He'd been called a few things—a flirt, a die-hard optimist, a person with an unhealthy amount of energy in the early hours—but never something as exciting as a spy. "For whomst?"

"That creepy research institute."

"I have no idea what you're talking about."

Luke winced, like Seth might be offended by what he was about to say. "There's some scientific research station opened up this week," he explained. "I think they study marine life? Or maybe forest growth? People were hoping they'd be bringing jobs with them, but they seem to have brought their own people. Nobody likes that much."

"And you think they have an undercover baker on their roster?" Seth asked Violet, fighting to bite back his grin.

Violet looked up again, narrowing her black-lined eyes at him. "Timing's suspicious."

Seth leaned over his counter, placing his chin on his fist, entertained as all get-out. He might have a new favorite customer, sincerest apologies to the adorable Colby. "Are you here to keep an eye on me, then?"

Violet waved a hand, then returned to furious typing. "I've got better things to do."

"I've noticed." Seth gestured to her laptop. "What are you working on over there?"

The teenager gave him her haughtiest look yet. "I'm writing erotic fanfiction about Hannibal Lecter."

Seth could only nod. That sounded exactly right.

SETH WASN'T SURPRISED to find Riley hovering outside his bakery door at quarter to six the next day.

He felt almost like he'd summoned his quiet stalker by asking questions. And maybe summoned him for a second chance to be a little kinder. Seth felt oddly responsible for him. Like they were connected somehow.

Which he wasn't. And they weren't.

But Seth knew what it felt like to be on the outside, still trying to find his people. He'd been lucky enough to figure it out early—who he was and what he wanted to surround himself with—but that wasn't always the case for young men who didn't fit into any easy mold.

Maybe this Riley was looking for his people too. Or maybe he just wanted some pastries. Whatever his reason for showing up, Seth wasn't going to turn a hungry kid away.

He was stocking the display case when he saw the shadow at the front window. Seth returned the tray to the rack stand before heading over to unlock the front door, holding it open just wide enough to poke his head out.

Riley was wearing the same collared jacket and another pair of worn jeans, his hair slightly messy in that careless, heartthrob way that could have been genuine or could have required a fistful of mousse and a diffuser.

"It's freezing out here," Seth said by way of greeting. "Why don't you come inside?"

Riley's dark eyes were just as intense as Seth remembered, boring into him without mercy. He didn't say anything to Seth's offer, but when Seth turned around, Riley was right behind him, following him inside.

Seth couldn't hear Riley's steps—the kid was light on his feet, that was for sure—but he could feel the heat against his back and smell the scent of forest invading his bakery.

"Take a seat," Seth said without looking, heading back behind the counter, where his coffeepot was already up and running. "I'm having coffee. You want some?"

When he turned to catch the answer, Riley was already sitting obediently at one of Seth's two-seater tables. He shook his head.

"Hot cocoa?" Seth offered.

Another head shake.

"Tea?"

A pause, and then Riley nodded.

Seth grabbed an English breakfast tea bag and, after a moment of deliberation, selected one of his ceramic mugs rather than a to-go cup. He filled the mug with hot water, then grabbed a plate, tossing a broken maple-pecan scone on it.

He set both in front of his guest. "This broke coming off the pan," he said, pushing the plate a little closer. "It's yours if you want it."

"Thank you."

Riley's voice was just as pleasant as Seth remembered, still low and soft, even when he wasn't murmuring vague threats about eating innocent bakers.

"You're Riley."

Riley didn't seem surprised that Seth knew his name. He only nodded.

That odd dichotomy was still there—the face of a lost, pretty kid, the eyes of someone who'd seen more than their fair share. Seth fought not to stare, although he only would have been matching his guest vibe for vibe if he did.

"I'm Seth."

"Seth," Riley repeated. And then he smiled, full and wide.

And yeah, the dark and brooding look really worked for this kid, but that smile? Devastating. *He* was sort of devastating. Seth needed to watch himself. He couldn't go getting smitten with a guy barely out of his teens. It screamed creepy old man vibes, and he wasn't having it.

He cleared his throat, turning away again. "There's milk and sugar on the counter. Stay as long as you like."

He went back to stocking the case. They didn't speak for a few minutes, although Seth's music filled the silence and kept everything from feeling too awkward. Seth was usually better at mindless small talk than this, but his guest's presence had him strangely off-kilter.

"Pretty."

Seth looked up from his task to find Riley watching him again. He felt his cheeks go hot against his will. "Um. What is?"

Riley pointed upward, and it took Seth a second to realize he was pointing to one of the speakers in the corner of the ceiling.

Seth relaxed, pressing a hand to his cheek and willing the warmth to go down. "Oh, the music? Thanks. I can share the playlist with you." He grabbed his cash drawer and started setting up the register. "I like a mellow mix in the morning, you know? Unless I'm extra tired, and then we're going pop divas all the way. Get the blood flowing." He did a little shimmy in demonstration, stopping when he only received a blank stare. "What are you into?"

It took a moment for Riley to answer. "Everything. Nothing. I'm in the forest a lot. Have to be quiet. No music."

The words were a little disjointed, but they were more than Seth had been expecting. He paused in the act of loading the till to look fully at his guest again, who was already watching Seth closely.

Always watching, this one.

"You like to...run in the forest?" Seth asked, trying to parse through Riley's meaning.

After a moment of hesitation, Riley nodded. "Running."

Seth grinned. "I run too. Sporadically," he amended.

"I'm faster," Riley said immediately.

That surprised a laugh out of Seth. "I've no doubt. I prefer more of a slow trudge. It's the arm swinging that gives the illusion of a run." He gave a little demo, laughing again at how dorky he knew he must look.

Riley didn't laugh with him. He was staring so intently that Seth suddenly wondered if he had flour on his face. He touched a hand to his forehead to check. Sometimes he smeared it there when he wasn't paying attention.

"I like your headband," Riley said after another moment, a roughened edge to his voice.

Seth tried to remember what he was wearing today. A tangerine print, he was pretty sure. "Thank you."

"And your hands."

"My hands?" Seth looked down. "Oh, my nails, you mean! You can borrow some polish, if you like. Next time you come in."

Seth had a bad habit of giving makeup away to customers after compliments. But he'd made genuine friends that way—his gorgeous pal Sascha came to mind, the little minx—so maybe it was actually a *good* habit.

And it seemed like maybe Seth had a friend in the making here, albeit an unconventional one. It was nice to have company as he opened. Even with his intensity, Riley had Seth weirdly at ease. He didn't seem to expect to be entertained or catered to. He didn't seem to expect anything at all, except to be in Seth's presence.

Seth's alarm went off, and he hurried to turn his sign over. He had customers almost immediately, which was a relief.

First there was Violet, an alarmingly early riser for her age. She gave him and Riley both long, appraising looks, then ordered a black coffee and a glazed donut, immediately claiming one of the other tables with her laptop.

Next was an older man who ordered a bacon roll and a cherry turnover to eat in. Seth served him up, turning around to hide his gleeful smile that all three of his tables were seated after only ten minutes. He didn't do a victory dance, exactly, but it was a close freaking call.

If he rearranged that plant in the corner, he could probably fit another two-seater in here. Maybe it would be worth doing. His business was mostly intended for takeaway, but it was cozy having a little crew here with him.

Seth turned back around to find Riley at the counter, leaning in over the till.

Jesus.

Seth kept himself from yelping in surprise, but only barely. He somehow hadn't noticed the inches Riley had on him before, but the kid was really quite tall. He should have been gangly, even, but the breadth of his shoulders matched his height. They were really quite...impressive, those shoulders. Seth hadn't been filled out like that at nineteen; that was for sure.

Stop. Perving.

"Thank you, Seth," Riley said quietly, his dark eyes as intent as ever. He'd set his empty plate and cup down neatly on the counter. Seth hadn't even seen him eat the scone.

Riley's gaze darted to Seth's lips, then back to his eyes, quick as a blink. He seemed to be searching for something in Seth's face, maybe, but hell if Seth knew what it was.

And then Riley turned away, heading out into the gloom without another word.

Seth hadn't even realized he was holding his breath until the bell chimed over the door. His cheeks were hot again, flushed like he'd been standing too close to his ovens.

In the corner, Violet cleared her throat, giving Seth a pointed look, as if to say, *See?*

Yeah, Seth was going to have to be very, very careful there.

5

SETH

Seth didn't see Riley the next day, but the intense, quiet young man was there bright and early Tuesday morning, fifteen minutes before Seth opened.

Seth got him settled with a tea and a broken Danish (it was possible Seth had put aside one wrecked pastry each morning, just in case), and went about his business. Riley stayed at Coastal Crumbs longer that time—almost an hour—and then left just as abruptly as his other visits.

Wednesday and Thursday were each another no-show, and then on Friday, Riley was at the door by five thirty. He brought a book that time, which he started doing regularly as the days went by, reading for hours at one of Seth's little tables. He had a taste for the classics, it seemed—*Frankenstein*, *Rebecca*, plus more than a few titles Seth had needed to look up later—which Seth might have written off as performative if Riley didn't get so engrossed in them.

Not so engrossed that he still didn't clock each of Seth's movements with the precision of a bloodhound, but whenever there was a lull in customers, Seth had started slyly asking him what was going on in his book, and Riley always had a ready answer.

("She's just been shown the west wing of the house, and it's basically a shrine to the old wife." Or, "They're plotting to switch the two ladies' identities and stick one of them in the asylum after the other one dies.")

Riley's willingness to let Seth know exactly what was happening in his books changed Seth's questions from a teasing joke to a new routine of Riley telling him bits of stories while Seth neatened his display cases.

It was silly and entertaining, and Seth was kind of growing to love it. He wasn't much of a reader and never had been, not even when he'd been required to read for school assignments, and he'd missed out on a lot of the classics. He hadn't realized how batshit some of the plots actually were. And Riley's voice, when he used it, was so soothing that it always mellowed Seth out just to hear it.

Riley had his off days too, when he'd come into the bakery and just sit, staring, no book and no conversation to be found. He usually left quickly those mornings, and though Seth was always sad to see him go, he didn't really mind the quiet version of his wayward guest either. There was something about Riley's unwavering attention that added a little vibrancy to Seth's day that was missing otherwise. Some increased awareness of himself and everything around him that was quickly becoming addictive. It was easy to forget how they'd first met—the oddity of that night in Seth's driveway.

Seth had acquired a steady stream of customers now, and most of them greeted Riley by name on the days he was there, never seeming offended when he only nodded in reply. He didn't talk much to anyone other than Seth, even on his good days.

Seth didn't actually know why he was so fascinated with Riley, or what exactly pulled him to this relative stranger. It wasn't like

Riley was his only new regular, even if he was the only one coming in before opening hours.

Violet and Luke were still showing up multiple times a week, and they were a treasure trove when it came to town gossip. Both had gotten over the shock of one of the town's recluses sitting in their midst pretty quickly, and only greeted Riley absently the mornings he was there.

There were other regulars too. The older bickering couple came in most every day, and there was a quiet guy somewhere in his late twenties with a rotation of anime-themed shirts who apparently lived on his own out in the woods, as well as a gruff lumberjack type who never smiled but always tipped substantially, even though he only ever took pastries to-go.

So Coastal Crumbs was getting into a rhythm, basically, as was Seth himself, but something about Riley...

Seth kept having to fight the urge to touch him, to push back a lock of hair or give his shoulder a squeeze in passing. It wasn't completely out of character for him—Seth was a tactile guy—but he'd never had so much trouble around someone who kept his walls up so clearly.

But the way Riley *watched* him.

The thing was, Seth didn't exactly think Riley would be opposed to Seth touching him. He might even welcome it, if that hot and focused gaze of his was any indication. But that was just as much of a problem. Even if Riley had some sort of crush on him, Seth couldn't *act* on it, right? Besides the fact of Riley being so young, there were too many unknowns.

Like, sometimes Seth caught Riley looking at the toddler Colby with this...sorrow. Seth couldn't tell if Riley wanted kids of his own or if seeing a young, carefree kiddo opened up bad memories. Given the rumors Seth had heard about a traumatic incident in his childhood, it was probably the latter, wasn't it?

And Seth had been worried, at first, that maybe Riley didn't have a safe place to be, and that was why he was gravitating toward the bakery. But with the way Riley talked about his home and his moms, the few times he'd mentioned them both, that didn't seem to be the case.

It was all...odd. Confusing.

But it was ten minutes to closing time now, and Seth still hadn't seen him. And the bakery was closed tomorrow, so there wouldn't be another sighting until Tuesday.

And that was fine. Totally normal for two acquaintances who hadn't so much as exchanged phone numbers. Seth wasn't disappointed or holding his breath or whatever.

He *wasn't.*

Jesus. Maybe Seth needed a night out, if he was this desperate for company.

He could go to the local bar and...well, probably not pick someone up—pickings were slim here—but socialize in a non-business-proprietor way. Get to know the un-pastried crowd a little better.

Seth had gotten a bit of the lay of the land the last few weeks. He knew that tourists passed through but were usually traveling further up the coast. The town's two beaches were walkable but not quite swimmable—the currents too rough, the coastline too unforgiving—and people tended to choose more hospitable shores for their weekend stays. It made the place more isolated in its population than it should be, considering the natural beauty all around them.

Seth didn't mind it, even if it was different from his home of Seacliff, which had been filled top to toe with tourists in the warmer months, transforming the place from a sleepy winter beach town to a bustling summer getaway spot.

Now, with not a customer in sight, Seth went to lock the door and turn his sign to "Closed."

And there was Riley, standing on the other side of it, dark and towering and silent as a ghost.

Seth *didn't* scream. At worst, he yelped. Just a little.

When his heart had stopped threatening to leap straight out of his chest, Seth opened the door, propping it against his back. "Oh, hello," he greeted mildly.

Riley stood there, hands in his pockets, like he hadn't just scared Seth half to death. "Hi, Seth."

"I'm closing up."

Riley only nodded.

Seth let out a sigh, like he was egregiously inconvenienced and not pleased as punch to see his friend, then stepped back and gestured into the bakery. "Come on in, then."

Riley gave him a happy grin, and Seth couldn't help smiling back at him.

"Hungry?" he asked.

"I ate already. A lot."

"Ugh, I'm jealous," Seth groaned, pressing his hands into his belly. "I'm *starving*."

Riley directed a pointed look to the leftover pastries—not many at all now, Seth was proud to say—and Seth made a face. "No, no. I need something not made of sugar, butter, and flour. Like, a big bowl of pasta with veggies. Or, um, I don't know, pea soup."

"Pea soup," Riley repeated dryly.

"Yeah." Seth nodded with enthusiasm, ignoring the obvious skepticism. Now that he'd said it, he was really warming up to the idea. "Doesn't that sound good? Pea soup and crusty bread with the really good butter."

Riley stood at Seth's counter, hands still in his pockets, watching him get back to his closing tasks. "You're going home to eat, then. To have your lunch."

"Yeah. Just wiping things down."

Since Seth hadn't made the jump to hire anyone yet, and didn't have any employees to break him for lunch, he tended to eat a second breakfast right before he opened, and then rely on power bars to get him through until closing. Usually he brought something from home and scarfed it down on the premises as he shut things down, but he hadn't bothered today.

"Mm." Riley turned without another word and started stacking Seth's chairs, as if he'd done it a million times—or seen Seth do it a million times—never mind that he'd never been around during closing hours before.

Seth caught himself staring at Riley's easy, graceful movements. He turned with a start and began wiping down his pastry case. "And what are you up to, mystery man?"

"Dunno." Riley met Seth's gaze from across the bakery as he stacked another chair. "Pea soup sounds good."

Seth immediately narrowed his eyes. "I thought you just said you were full."

"I get hungry fast," Riley told him, his gaze so guileless Seth almost felt guilty questioning him.

Seth wanted to say something about growing boys needing to eat, but even in his head, it sounded too pervy, so he kept it to himself.

Riley's eyes were still on him. Seth shifted in place. "It's the kind that comes in a can." He set a hand on his hip, defensive for no reason. "I bake for a living, and I can't be bothered cooking most of the time."

Riley shrugged. "I'm not picky."

Seth huffed. He set his other hand on his hip and met Riley stare for stare. But Riley's gaze didn't falter.

Shameless.

Seth huffed again, if only because he wanted to tell himself he was being steamrolled. "Riley," he said with exaggerated politeness. "Would you like to come over for lunch?"

Riley immediately beamed at him, and Seth told himself his heart was *not* in his throat. He was probably just getting a cold from working too hard in this dreary weather.

"Yes, Seth," Riley said smoothly, matching Seth's exaggerated courtesy perfectly. "I would."

LEADING Riley into the rental house, Seth couldn't help but be hyperaware of how his guest immediately began studying the place with the same intensity he always studied everything pertaining to Seth.

Seth shifted in place in the living room, which was separated from the kitchen by a little half-wall counter, weirdly self-conscious in a way he hadn't been since he was young. "It came furnished," he offered in explanation.

Riley nodded. He had his hands tucked in the pockets of his loose-fitting jeans again, and it seemed today was one of those good days, where he was maybe more comfortable in his own skin. Able to chat and joke with only a few of his deep silences.

"I thought so," Riley said after a moment, and it took Seth a second to remember they were talking about his home decor. "Doesn't seem like you."

"You can tell?" Seth asked, his lips twitching into a small smile. He supposed he *was* the kind of guy who wore his heart on his sleeve, more or less. Maybe Riley had expected that to be reflected in his home.

Riley nodded again, so incredibly solemn. "I can tell."

"You want the whole tour?"

Seth regretted the question as soon as he'd asked it. The only other rooms here were the bathroom and his bedroom, and neither of them needed to be on display. But Riley was already moving in the direction of Seth's room without waiting for Seth to show him the way.

Seth followed him, fiddling with his headband. This room felt a little more personal, and not just because it was where Seth slept. There was more of himself here, he supposed. It had come with a bed, end table, dresser, and vanity, but Seth had added his own touches. He'd made the bed a cozy nest, with a warm russet-orange comforter and lemon-yellow sheets. There was art on the walls that talented friends had made—bright, colorful pieces that reminded him of home.

And the vanity Seth actually adored. It was small and still in its original dark, unpainted wood, with an upholstered stool and a little oval mirror. He'd decorated it with pictures of home, and the little cheesy Maine tourist knickknacks friends had given him as going-away gifts. He had his headbands hanging on a thrifted jewelry stand, and his makeup selection was on display in a repurposed jewelry box and a few scattered baskets.

Riley took it all in, in his quiet, thoughtful way. "This is you," he eventually said. "This room."

Seth let out a breath. "Yeah," he agreed. "This is me."

Riley took his time studying the vanity especially. He reached out and shook the makeup box oh so gently. "You said I could borrow nail polish."

"I did."

He turned to face Seth, holding up his hands. "Will you do them for me?"

So, after a hasty lunch of stovetop canned soup and toasted bread, they were both on Seth's couch, wearing face masks—because if they were going to do self-care, they were going to go all out—and Seth had his box of polish in his lap. They were sitting cross-legged, facing each other, and Seth had placed a towel in the space between them so he didn't mess up his hideous, uncomfortable sofa with nail polish.

As Seth adjusted the towel, Riley touched tentative fingers to his mask. "What does this do?" he asked. Which was kind of funny, since he hadn't said a word when Seth had handed it to him and shown him how to place it on his face. He'd borrowed one of Seth's headbands to keep his dark hair from sticking to it, and he looked so adorable that Seth had the odd urge to pinch his cheeks.

"It nourishes, hydrates, and plumps," Seth told him dutifully, rifling through his polishes. There were a few key ones missing—Sascha had definitely been hoarding what he borrowed; Seth was sure of it. "Not that you need it," he added. "Youthful skin and all."

Riley cocked his head, his gaze once again fixed intently on Seth's face. It should have looked ridiculous, with the white mask covering his features, but the intensity of his dark eyes shone through like always. "How old are *you*?"

"Twenty-six," Seth told him.

"Young too."

Seth arched his brows. "Older than you."

Riley scoffed. "Young."

Seth straightened, weirdly affronted. "Excuse me," he said haughtily. "I've lived a life."

"So have I."

Riley said the words with such calm, quiet certainty that Seth immediately felt like a complete dick. Seth was older than Riley, yes, but he'd always had a comfortable life, with supportive friends and family and a place in his small community. Even without the town's rumor mill, he'd have known the same didn't apply to Riley. There had been struggle there, either in his past or in his present, and it was plain to see, even if it did nothing to dampen his appeal.

And lord, that appeal.

Riley was young, and a little odd, but he was also absurdly beautiful, and intriguing in the way only a man of few words could be. Seth had seen how some of the town's young women looked at him. And a few of the men, for that matter. If they'd entered a time vortex and Seth could have met Riley when they were both the same age, he was sure *he* would have been the one following Riley around like a lost puppy and not the other way around. He had the vibe of someone who was destined to be a first crush.

Seth shook the unwelcome thoughts out of his head, tilting the box toward Riley. "What color do you want?"

"Black."

Seth tsked teasingly. "Of course. You and Violet, my goodness." But he fished out the black polish, shaking the bottle heartily as he took Riley's left hand in his.

Riley had big hands to match his height. For such a creature of the forest, Seth might have expected them to be rough and calloused, but they were surprisingly soft. Warm too.

Seth cleared his throat and got to painting with small, deft strokes.

"Me and Violet?" Riley asked, once Seth had gotten to his middle finger.

"My local goths," Seth explained with a fond smile, thinking of his brusque, aspiring writer. He wondered if she had a favorite pastry. He should ask.

"I'm not goth."

Seth glanced up to find Riley frowning at him. He shrugged. "Maybe not, at least aesthetically. But you do like your gothic lit."

Riley's frown only deepened. "I'm different from Violet though."

"How?"

"Older."

"Not by much."

They were left in silence again, and even though Seth was focusing on his work, he could feel the weight of Riley's gaze.

"You like me better," Riley said eventually, his voice low and soft. He shifted closer on the couch, his knees brushing against Seth's.

Seth gave him a stern look, holding Riley's hand steady in a pointed way. "Presumptuous."

Riley wasn't the least bit chagrined. He lowered his head, dark eyes boring into Seth's. "You do though."

"I can't choose a favorite regular," Seth said lightly, not sure why his voice came out a little huskier than usual. "It's like choosing a favorite child."

"I'm not your regular. I'm your—" Riley broke off, his lips tightening as he seemed to be warring with himself. Seth could have sworn his eyes flashed black for a moment, but then they were normal again, and it must have been a trick of the light.

"Friend," Riley said eventually, although it didn't seem like he was quite satisfied with the choice of word. "I'm your friend."

"Why do you want to be my friend?" Seth asked, unable to stop himself from taking advantage of this chatty version of Riley.

"I like you," Riley told him immediately, as if he didn't have a coy bone in his body.

Seth grinned, charmed in spite of himself. "Is it that simple?"

Riley gave a single solemn nod. "It is to me."

"Why did you knock me over, then, that first night?"

Riley didn't answer. Seth waited him out patiently, but Riley stayed silent, his gaze locked on Seth's. Guileless yet again.

Seth narrowed his eyes. "You're slyer than you look, aren't you?"

In answer, Riley wiggled the little finger of the hand still in Seth's hold. "You have to do my pinkie."

So that was it for today's chattiness. Seth blew out a breath, hunching back over Riley's nails. "Yeah, yeah."

It wouldn't be the first friendship of Seth's with an undercurrent of mutual attraction. He'd maintained plenty of those over the years, actually. Some of them he'd acted on, some he hadn't. It hadn't ruined things either way. Seth wasn't the kind of guy people pined over when the deed was done.

This one, though, he wouldn't act on. He couldn't. Absolutely not.

Right?

Right.

Seth finished Riley's pinkie with a nod of satisfaction, grabbing Riley's other hand to give it the same treatment. He let go of the tangle of his thoughts and settled in to do his *friend's* manicure.

6

RILEY

Riley was doing so, so well.

He'd been taking it slow and steady, building a rapport with regular visits to the bakery. Nothing out of the ordinary, nothing that screamed, *Creature of the night come to mate you for eternity*.

Sitting in a warm bakery for hours on end while reading a good book? Totally normal. Not visiting too often, keeping it to every few days? Super casual and completely human.

And yes, maybe showing up before official opening hours like a stray cat was a *little* unusual, but Riley couldn't help it—he liked the quiet time before the other humans arrived. He liked to breathe Seth in and catch his little furrows of concentration as he set up his cash register for the day.

It kept the voice calmer too. It was a covetous fucking maniac when it came to their mate, and it would prefer Seth only ever looked at them. It helped to feed it with some moments of alone time before they were surrounded with human customers.

The voice didn't like it—the customers in their space, the shift in Seth's attention when serving someone else—but it wasn't stupid either. It had learned, over the last few weeks, that the more it behaved, the more the two of them got to see their mate. Because for every day at the bakery that it ranted and raved and tried to push Riley into sinking his teeth into Seth's perfect neck, Riley sequestered them one day longer in the forest.

And oooohhh, it fucking *hated* that.

But too bad. Slow. Steady. That was Riley's mantra. There would be no exchange of blood, no bite marks that bonded them forever—not until Seth chose it himself. Eyes open, heart full. Hopefully. Maybe. Pretty fucking please.

Stuck in the woods to protect himself and those around him, Riley hadn't ever had a boyfriend, or even a real friend beyond the den of vampires in Colorado he only knew because of his moms. And now that he'd found someone he wanted, he wasn't going to let the voice fuck it up and ruin it like it had ruined everything else in Riley's life.

It had stolen his childhood, it had stolen his birth mother. It was *not* going to steal his chance to date Seth for real.

And yeah, maybe Riley's "slow and steady" approach wouldn't have worked if Seth wasn't the type of warm, kindhearted person who couldn't seem to turn a lost soul away. And of course, Riley basically inviting himself over to Seth's house for lunch today was probably *two* steps forward instead of just the one.

But holy shit. So worth it. Because getting into Seth's home was like the secret key, and Riley hadn't even known it. There was something to the fact that it was Seth's safe space, to the way he was so attached to the little things he'd surrounded himself with. He kept showing them to Riley—his photos, his self-care tools, the personal touches he'd added to his home. It was like he couldn't quite help himself, even if Riley coming over hadn't been his idea.

First Seth had done Riley's nails, and then he'd taken off their face masks, and they'd both put some weird serums on. And then Seth had wanted to show Riley his favorite ASMR videos. He claimed Riley would have a good voice for it, if he ever wanted a side hustle.

Riley didn't have a *main* hustle, even, but he didn't know a chill way to say that, thanks to his undead adoptive mothers, he was independently wealthy and never had to work a day in his long life if he didn't want to.

That was the least of Riley's secrets, anyway.

And now, after a short tour of Seth's backyard, they were sitting cross-legged together on the couch again, watching video after video. Riley's inner voice was surprisingly calm and complacent, although he could feel it coiled within him, vibrating with the thrill of being so close to their mate.

Seth leaned forward to click another link on the laptop, which he'd placed in front of them on the coffee table. The videos were odd—a young creator who talked in a whisper voice while pretending to do their makeup, or acting as if they were performing a doctor's check-up on the audience, only dressed as a mer-person for some reason. Still, Riley had to admit they were soothing.

And yet Seth's pulse was jumping, and Riley couldn't stop staring at it, that hint of movement under Seth's soft skin.

Riley liked that Seth—who was so self-assured with every other human—got a little nervous around him. He didn't know what that said about Riley, how much he liked it, but he did.

Riley liked the way that pretty pulse sped up when he was around. And he liked the little hitches in Seth's breath he didn't seem to be aware he was making when Riley moved closer to him.

Riley wanted more of it—that nervousness, that heightened awareness. He wanted to see what other sounds he could get out of sweet Seth if he tried. He wanted to know just how fast he could get that tender heart to beat for him.

Maybe that was what attraction was like for everyone, or maybe it was the predator's instinct inside him acting out, wanting to startle their perfect prey. Riley didn't know.

There was so much he didn't know.

Seth leaned back again, letting the video he'd chosen play. He folded his hands in his lap, giving Riley a small, bright grin.

Riley wanted to take those hands and hold them in his again, like when Seth had been painting his nails. He wanted to study them closely. They were fascinating to him, the way they were small but strong, with all these little nicks and burns. Seth had told him the burns were from the ovens, and they ran along his forearms too. They were pretty, in their way, but Riley still felt protective over them.

Vampires had healing properties in their saliva. It was convenient for closing bites, a way to keep their victims from bleeding out after a feed. Riley had never had a chance to use it that way, since he'd never fed from a live human deliberately. But if Seth burned one of his fingers in the oven when Riley was there, Riley could put that finger in his mouth, couldn't he? He could suck so gently. No teeth. Just lips and tongue and—

"I'm gay," Seth said out of nowhere, giving Riley a sidelong look. His pulse was still jumping, so maybe it was something he was nervous to admit. "Not sure if that's something I need to say, but—" He shrugged.

"I know," Riley told him. He'd already overheard Seth talking to Violet about the queer scene in Seacliff.

"Okay," Seth said easily, his gaze drifting back to his video.

He didn't ask. Didn't push Riley to divulge his own interests.

But Riley wanted to.

He just didn't know what to say. Riley didn't know if he was gay or bi or what. There hadn't been anyone before Seth, and there wouldn't be anyone after, so what did it matter?

"It...depends for me," Riley said eventually, his voice barely louder than the whispers coming from Seth's computer screen.

Seth turned to him, giving him his complete attention. "Depends on what?"

On if it's you.

"On the person."

Seth nodded. "Ah, gotcha." He placed a hand on Riley's knee, a friendly squeeze, there and gone again. "Thank you for sharing, Riley."

Seth had that way about him, Riley had noticed. He could be flirty and silly but also very sincere. Riley liked that.

He was pretty sure he liked everything about Seth.

Seth let out a happy sigh. "I really love this creator, you know. They do the prettiest makeup. Like, it's the usual audio component, but also it's so visually soothing."

Riley had the sudden, overwhelming urge to shut the laptop. Or at least cover it up with something. They only needed to *hear* the video, right? They didn't need to see the pretty creator with the glittery eye makeup that Seth *loved.*

But then Seth turned to him again. "Have you ever had your makeup done?"

Riley lived alone in the woods with two extremely fashionable mothers. He'd had his makeup done hundreds of times, at the very least.

But Riley thought of Seth touching his face, sitting close, breathing his air. He tried to look guileless and was pretty sure he succeeded. "Will you do mine for me?"

In answer, Seth scrambled off the couch, running into his bedroom with a laugh. Riley almost regretted asking—he wanted Seth back on the couch with him—but it was barely a minute before Seth returned with another little basket that held eye pencils and little pots of eye shadow and other makeup supplies.

Seth settled next to Riley, cross-legged but facing him this time. Riley faced him in turn. Seth's eyes were bright, his cheeks flushed happily.

He was the prettiest, cutest thing Riley had ever seen.

"Okay, so," Seth began, "just a little something on the eyes, I think. Purple hues can look really cool with a dark brown like yours." He cocked his head, studying Riley's face, and it was a struggle not to preen under the attention. "And a little shimmer on the cheeks," Seth mused. "We can wipe it all off afterward, if you want. I know wearing makeup isn't for everyone."

"I don't mind." Riley would wear whatever the fuck Seth wanted to paint him with. He'd wear it proudly.

Seth grinned at him, sorting through his basket. "I'm too lazy to rock a full beat all the time, but it's just fun, you know? To play. Or to have a little something extra on a good night out." He set his selections on the same towel he'd used when painting Riley's nails. "You go out a lot? Is there a fake ID somewhere in your wallet or is that too hard with a town this small?"

"I'm—" *Trapped in the woods so I don't eat the locals.* "More of a homebody," Riley hedged.

Seth nodded, then held out a cupped hand in front of Riley's face. "Lean forward, please. Eyes closed."

Riley leaned forward, barely daring to breathe. He was already getting high off Seth's sweet, buttery orange scent. Getting this close, it was hard to resist doing something stupid, like licking Seth's face to see if his skin tasted as sweet as he smelled.

Fingers settled on Riley's chin. They were rougher than they looked, but Riley liked the texture. He wanted to feel it everywhere, that soft scratch of hard-earned calluses.

The voice inside him stirred, restless with the increased proximity.

Everything smelled like cake.

Chill out, Riley told it. *Chill out or we're leaving.*

It let out an angry growl, loud enough that Riley had to fight off a wince at the echo in his skull. Then it settled again, petulant and pissed off.

"How about friends?" Seth asked, oblivious to Riley's inner struggle. He dusted something along Riley's eyelid, his one hand still cupping Riley's chin. "Do you have a good group here?"

"I'm—" *—too afraid I'm going to rip someone's throat out.* "Kind of a loner."

"No wonder you've latched onto me," Seth said, and there was a teasing lilt in his voice. He was using some sort of pencil now, drawing it along Riley's lash line.

"Do you mind?" Riley didn't know why he asked. What was he going to do if Seth said yes—stay away? It was unlikely. Maybe impossible.

There was a moment of silence as Seth moved along to Riley's other eyelid. "No," he finally said. "I'm kind of a loner now too, moving to a new place and everything. It's good to make a friend."

Riley felt the voice twist inside him again, huffing in annoyance. *Mate*, it corrected.

Friends first, Riley told it.

And then the sneaky little shit flooded Riley's mind. With impulses. Visions. Riley pushing Seth bodily back on the couch and covering him completely. Riley mouthing at that butter-orange throat. Riley sinking his fangs in and swallowing a hot rush of blood. Seth would like it—humans always enjoyed a vampire's bite. He'd whimper and harden against them, and Riley's voice would drink more, drink deeper. They'd bite open their own wrist and—

Riley's breath caught. He jerked back before he could stop himself.

Seth's pretty eyes widened in concern. He settled his fingers with their light-as-a-feather touch on Riley's face again. "Are you all right?" he asked. "Did I press too hard?"

Slow and steady. That was the plan. But Seth's lips looked so inviting. Reddened and full, like he'd put color on *them* instead of Riley's lids. Maybe he'd been nibbling on them while he did Riley's makeup.

But that was Riley's job. *He* should be the one nibbling. Licking.

Kissing.

"Hey, Seth?" Riley asked softly. They were so close still, their knees just touching. And Seth was already gazing up at him, so focused on Riley's face. That was nice, that focus. At the bakery, Seth's attention was always split. "Do you ever make orange cake?"

"Um..." Seth swallowed hard, then shook his head like he was clearing it. "Sometimes," he said, his voice rougher than before. "It's a less common flavor. But I've done a few. There's this spiced olive oil version that's nice around the holidays and—"

"Hey, Seth?" Riley interrupted.

Seth swallowed again, and if Riley wasn't so focused on those pretty lips, he'd be following the tantalizing motion of his throat. "Yes, Riley?"

"Can I kiss you? I'd really like to."

"Oh." Seth blinked at him. "I don't think—"

Riley shuffled a little closer, until Seth's knees brushed against his thighs. "I've never kissed anyone before."

Seth's fingers trembled against Riley's skin. "Well, you're young," he said in a voice that didn't sound any steadier than his touch.

Riley frowned down at him. He was really looking forward to the day people stopped reminding him of that. "I'm not a child," he argued.

It sounded exactly like something a child would say.

Seth let out a harsh breath. "Oh, I'm aware. But there's a gap in experience here."

"I think about you," Riley pressed. He didn't know anything about seduction, an unfortunate deficit here. But he knew about want. Hunger. And it seemed like honesty might be his best advantage. "At night. In my bed. I think about you, and I *want*. I get —I never used to do it much, and now I do it all the time. I think about your skin and your smell, and I get so hard it aches, and I have to do something about it." Riley cocked his head. "Do you know what that's like? That aching?"

It was fascinating, watching Seth's pupils grow so large, the darkness blotting out the green-brown color. His breaths were coming faster, and his cheeks had flushed the prettiest pink.

He was so handsome when he was flustered.

"Um..."

Riley blinked down at him. "I think you should kiss me," he said again. "If you want to," he amended. "It's okay if you don't want to."

Seth's gaze darted away and back again. "It's not that I don't *want* to, per se."

Per se. That was cute. He was so cute, even when caught off guard. Maybe especially so.

Riley waited him out. His whole life up until now, appeasing hunger had been about the chase. Overtaking his prey with his speed and his strength. But this was different, wasn't it? Riley wasn't hunting; he was....luring. Lying in wait, timing the pounce just right.

Seth licked his lips.

Riley sat perfectly still.

"Oh, fuck it," Seth sighed, after another long moment. "Just once, okay? Because I want your first kiss to be nice." He used his hold on Riley's chin to shake Riley's head a little, as if admonishing him. "Just this once."

And then he was leaning forward, pressing his lips to Riley's.

Oh fuck. Finally.

Unlike his hands, Seth's mouth was just as soft as it looked. Soft and sweet. Delicious.

Riley pressed forward with a hungry groan, swiping with his tongue before he could stop himself. Diving in. Trying to get more. To taste *more.*

Seth leaned back, cupping Riley's face with both hands now. "Slow," he soothed when Riley made as if to lunge forward again. "Okay, baby? Slow. Hold still and part your lips for me."

Restraint had always been a battle, but it was easier with Seth's warm voice telling Riley what to do. Calling him "baby." Riley wouldn't like that with anyone else—he wasn't a goddamn baby—but it was nice coming from Seth.

Riley parted his lips obediently, and Seth leaned in again. He kissed Riley's top lip, then the bottom. He did it once more, sucking a little on Riley's bottom lip as he leaned back, sending a flash of heat swirling in Riley's belly. Then he came in again, his tongue darting out in the lightest tease.

God, that felt nice. Riley sighed into it, and Seth made the sweetest sound of encouragement. "There you go," he murmured against Riley's mouth. "Now you try."

Slowed down like this, it was a sort of dance, one that made Riley's lips tingle and his cock hard. Soft breaths and teasing tongues. Devouring but also getting devoured in turn.

Not prey after all. A partner.

Riley must have been doing better too, because Seth started letting out little moans of his own, his heart rate speeding up more the longer they kissed. His muscles relaxed, enough that he fell back into the couch cushions when Riley pressed forward.

Riley followed him down eagerly. He was hard. So hard. Everything was moist orange cake and hot, pumping blood. Riley ground down, finding Seth equally hard beneath him. That felt good. That felt *so* good.

Riley clasped Seth's hands in his, pressing them into the couch over Seth's head and deepening the kiss, licking into Seth's mouth in a way Seth seemed to really like now, because he moaned loudly, wrapping his legs around Riley's waist.

Riley broke the kiss but only so he could taste the skin on Seth's neck. It was perfect. Delicious. Tender. He felt the voice inside him pushing at its limits, wanting to come out. Wanting a taste of its own.

"Wait," Seth gasped.

Bite him. Drain him. Turn him. Make him ours.

"Wait."

Riley stopped.

Seth was panting underneath him now, his chest heaving as he gulped in air. His lips were red and almost bruised, his eyes heavy-lidded. "That's—that's enough," he said between breaths. "That's plenty."

Riley frowned, pressing in with his hips, just a touch. "You're hard though."

"Oh, I'm very aware," Seth told him, unwrapping his legs from Riley's waist. "But we're not—we're not doing anything about that. That's way past kissing."

"I don't mind," Riley said magnanimously.

Seth narrowed his eyes. "Up," he ordered.

Riley released Seth's hands and climbed off him, sitting in the far corner of the couch so he wouldn't be tempted to sneak in more touches. He didn't try to hide his erection. He didn't know what the point of that would be.

Seth sat up slowly, taking a minute to catch his breath. He ran a hand down his face, then gave Riley a searching look. "Still friends, right?" he said after a moment.

"Friends," Riley agreed.

He meant it too. He wanted to be Seth's friend. He wanted to be Seth's *everything.*

But he also ached to press Seth down on the couch again. Not to bite, no matter what the stupid voice said. Not to drain. Just to... grind. And maybe undress. Maybe press more bare skin against bare skin. Maybe see where Seth liked to be kissed, beyond just his mouth.

Riley let out a long breath, trying not to pout in his corner.

Maybe there were a few drawbacks to slow and steady after all.

7

RILEY

Riley found his moms on the covered porch at the back of the house, curled up together on the couch, looking at something on one of their phones.

"He thinks I'm too young!" Riley called out as soon as he'd burst through the door.

He knew that, once again, he sounded like nothing more than a frustrated child, but he couldn't help himself. He needed to vent, and there was no one else to vent to.

His moms had already been supporting him in his quest for Seth's...friendship. Mostly they'd taken over the practical matters, which all centered around not letting Riley get too hungry.

They'd stocked up on blood bags from neighboring cities—Pine Bluff's urgent care was too small to pilfer from too often, and the town didn't have a hospital of its own—and they'd been reminding Riley to go hunting more often than usual.

Most vampires, once they'd adjusted to the change, needed to feed only about once a week. They didn't need to take all that much blood either—their kind didn't have to kill to feed. But even though Riley was more or less fully grown now, he still usually had to feed two or three times a week. It was a vast improvement from when he'd been a growing kid and had needed to feed every day, sometimes more than once a day. The only thing that had stopped Riley from creating a national blood supply shortage during his childhood was that he, unlike most vampires, could feed from animals. And elk were plentiful in these parts.

But now Riley's moms had been stuffing him full of blood in the hopes that it would help him remain calm around his future mate.

After the events of today, Riley couldn't say for sure if they'd been successful.

He could still feel the press of Seth's soft lips against his own like a phantom touch. Could still hear the echo of Seth's quiet, gasping moan when Riley had ground down against him. Could still smell the scent of orange cake growing sweeter and richer around him until Riley could practically taste it on his tongue.

"He likes me," Riley said in a much calmer voice as he approached the couch, speaking to himself more than his moms now. "I know he does. But he thinks I'm too young to act on it."

And maybe immediately running to his moms about it was proving the point, but Riley didn't exactly have anyone else to talk to.

Mama Daphne clapped her hands, like Riley had said something wonderful. "Oh, he's a gentleman! Well, that's lovely."

"It's *frustrating*," Riley countered, rubbing a hand over his mouth in an effort to wipe away the phantom touch and stop dwelling on that perfect fucking kiss.

Instead of offering reassurance, Mama Sybil gave Riley a devious sort of smile, holding up her phone. "Cheer up, sweetheart. We have a surprise for you."

Riley reached for the phone without looking. "Is it Jay?" he asked hopefully.

Jay was the nicest of his mothers' vampire associates and the most likely to listen willingly to Riley wax poetic about beautiful bakers and their delicious scents. Plus, Jay had always claimed his stoic, mobster mate smelled like vanilla cupcakes, so...common ground.

Mama Sybil cocked a brow. "Even better."

Riley looked down at the phone and scowled at what he found. "Hello, Wolfe," he greeted grudgingly.

The face staring back at him remained impassive, with its thin lips and perfectly coiffed hair. Riley could only see from the neck up, but he already knew its owner was wearing a ridiculously garish suit to top it all off.

"If it isn't young Riley," Wolfe drawled, amusement lacing his tone. "Covered in dirt. And...is that purple eye shadow?"

Riley was only covered in dirt because the voice inside him had been furious they'd left their mate back at his home instead of throwing him over their shoulder and retreating to their lair with him forevermore. Hunting little innocent woodland creatures had helped calm the asshole down.

Riley made a face at his moms—*Really, you're going to make me talk to* him?—but they only smiled beatifically back at him.

Ugh. Wolfgang.

He was a vampire Riley's moms had turned years and years ago, at the psychopath's own request. He was a cold, unfeeling asshole except when it came to his human mate, Eric, who was actually pretty decent as far as middle-aged dudes went. Eric was also the one who'd caught Riley when he'd been a scared child running from his vampire maker, terrified of getting captured again and equally afraid to get close to any humans. And then it had been Wolfe who'd brought Riley's moms in to adopt him, and together they'd all given Riley a fighting chance at survival.

So Riley should probably be grateful to Wolfe for saving his life or whatever, but it was hard to overcome the instinctual annoyance, especially since Riley's moms liked to tease that they were brothers.

They were *not* brothers.

"Your mothers have been apprising me of the situation," Wolfe told him.

Riley's scowl only deepened. If his moms were contacting Wolfe for backup, that meant they were worried Riley was going to lose control.

"If you do drain him dry," Wolfe continued, his tone almost conversational now, "make sure you're somewhere private. Secure."

Riley flung himself onto the couch on the opposite corner from his moms, giving Wolfe his harshest glare. "I'm not going to drain him. Just because *you* lost control when you found your mate doesn't mean I'm going to do the same."

"I didn't lose control," Wolfe countered coolly. "Eric simply happens to be immensely irresistible."

Um, no, he wasn't. Eric was just a normal, decent-looking dude. Plus, he was like, forty or something.

"Where is Eric?" Riley asked, narrowing his eyes. "I'd rather be talking to him."

Wolfe pursed his lips. "Otherwise occupied." He cocked his head, his gaze darting every which way like he was trying to read something on Riley's face.

Riley went carefully blank, refusing to give anything away. Wolfe would have to make do with admiring Riley's awesome makeover.

"You've been given a gift from fate," Wolfe said after a long moment. "A person of your own, someone to covet and care for. Is your human correct in his assessment? Are you too young to manage it?"

Riley resisted the urge to crack the phone in his hands, but it was a close call. "I'm *not*."

"We'll see, won't we?"

Riley had reached his limit. He hung up the call, tossing the phone onto the couch cushion. If his moms really wanted to talk to this jerk, they could call him back after Riley left.

When he looked over to the women in question, both their faces were the picture of concerned sympathy. Riley let out a sigh and closed his eyes before thunking his head against the back of the couch. "He wants to be *friends*. Seth does."

"Well, those are great strides," Mama Daphne said, and Riley could picture her encouraging smile. "Only a few weeks ago, you were strangers."

Riley wrinkled his nose. It didn't feel like *great strides*. It felt like a roadblock.

"How old *is* he, anyway?" Mama Sybil asked.

"Twenty-six."

"Psh," she scoffed. "A pittance of an age difference. He'll be over it in no time."

"I thought he was younger, anyway," Mama Daphne said brightly. "He doesn't look a day over twenty-two."

Riley whipped his head off the couch in an instant, leaning forward and narrowing his eyes in accusation. "When did you see him?"

"Hm?" Mama Daphne gave him her most innocent look, waving a hand in the air. "Oh, just driving through town, I believe. In passing. So brief."

She and Mama Sybil exchanged a look. Mama Sybil patted Riley's hand. "All will be well, darling. We'll make sure of it, won't we?"

Riley only wished he felt more encouraged. But the phone call with Wolfe was more revealing than any empty words his mothers could give him.

No one had any faith in Riley, did they? And Riley couldn't even say he blamed them.

He didn't have much faith in himself these days.

RILEY CLIMBED the pull-down steps to the attic, eager to take refuge in his hideout that wasn't really a hideout at all.

He had his own bedroom, of course—the house was big enough for him to have two, if he really wanted—but this was where he went when he needed his moms to know he preferred to be alone.

He and Mama Daphne had cleaned and decorated the space not long after they'd first arrived, when his moms had realized Riley had a tendency to run and hide when he was feeling overwhelmed. He'd been going through a growth spurt at the time, and he'd eaten all the blood bags in the house, as well as all the members of the local rat community. He'd been ashamed, and he'd hidden alone in the bare, filthy attic until Mama Daphne had come for him.

It wasn't filthy or bare anymore, not after Mama Daphne had finished with it. There were strings of fairy lights hanging from the angled ceiling, which was just tall enough to walk underneath without hunching. And by the little square window that looked out onto the forest below, there was a cozy armchair, a basket of blankets, and two small bookcases full of favorite books.

Riley didn't feel quite the same shame that had once driven him here either. He was old enough now to know it had all been beyond his control, even if sometimes that was hard to remember. He'd been young and hungry—so, so hungry—and the fact that he hadn't killed any humans yet was honestly a miracle.

Mostly that miracle had been achieved by avoidance. Riley hadn't been allowed to leave the woods surrounding the property until he'd turned eighteen. The closest he'd come to a mishap was when he'd been out hunting elk and stumbled upon a young woman lost in the woods. It had taken everything in him to leave without feeding, even knowing he wouldn't have been able to stop in time to save her from himself.

Would Seth have forgiven Riley if he had slipped? Would he still kiss Riley so willingly if Riley had used that same mouth to drain someone dry?

He might have. He seemed the forgiving sort.

But maybe that was only wishful thinking.

Riley made his way over to the window and sank down into the armchair. It was low to the ground, with soft fleece-like upholstery and a wide seat. Wide enough to fit two people, actually, a fact that Riley had never considered until now. Seth could be sitting here right next to him, warm and soft and smelling like orange cake.

Arousal stirred low in Riley's belly, almost against his will.

God, he wanted him. He wanted Seth so badly.

Riley had wanted him from the first moment he'd seen him, even if he'd confused it for a very different kind of hunger at the time.

It wasn't like Riley was naive. Not exactly. He'd been as curious as anyone else growing up. He'd checked out porn furtively on his laptop late at night. With his enhanced hearing, he'd heard couples in the woods too, teens sneaking out to bump their parts together without parents interfering. Riley always tried to retreat when that happened, but he'd caught enough snatches to have an idea of things. Not that those fumbling teen boys were exactly Casanovas to emulate or anything.

It just hadn't ever...appealed. The porn especially. All those fake moans and the frantic humping. Everything happened so fast, and the close-up shots seemed almost clinical, body parts sticking into other body parts. What was so sexy about someone's dick thrusting in and out of someone else's hole?

It hadn't ever gotten him riled up in any serious way. Even the voice had been bored, and vampires were supposed to be wired for sex as well as violence. Masturbation had always been infrequent and not due to anything specific—just an itch that occasionally needed scratching.

Riley had thought it was another area in which he was an anomaly, another way he was maybe broken, another sign that he probably didn't have a mate waiting in the wings.

But Riley *did* have a mate after all. And he smelled like everything delicious in the world, and his calloused hands were so careful in their touch, and he felt so good under Riley, whether on the pavement or on an ugly couch.

Riley's cock twitched with interest, and he hurried to unbutton his jeans. It hadn't been a lie, what he'd told Seth earlier: Riley touched himself more often now. Usually after visiting the bakery, after having Seth invade his senses for hours and hours.

Riley wished he'd gotten to touch him more today. Wished he'd gotten to taste other parts of Seth besides his soft lips.

Riley grasped his cock, which was filling more rapidly the longer he thought of having Seth underneath him.

He thought back to that first night, when he'd overheard Seth talking on the phone. There'd been a theory as to why Riley had said he wanted to eat him...

Did Riley want to eat Seth's ass? It hadn't been the reason Riley had tackled him, but...probably, right?

It was another thing that didn't sound appealing out of context, but the thought of *Seth* beneath him, his fleshy globes in the air and his face pressed into a mattress while Riley devoured him?

Riley stroked his cock, letting out a harsh breath. Fuck, yes. *That* would be appealing.

True, Riley had no idea what the fuck he was doing, but Seth would tell him, wouldn't he? He'd be good at it too. He was warm and kind and encouraging by nature, and he'd tell Riley exactly what came next, just like he'd shown Riley how to kiss him.

Riley's fangs dropped as his cock throbbed in his hold.

And maybe, just maybe, Riley could sink his teeth into Seth's soft skin. Vampire bites felt good to humans. Arousing, even. So even if Riley was inept and clumsy, a bite would help smooth things over. He could close his mouth around Seth's throat, or maybe his inner thigh, and taste what flowed through those veins. Riley could be careful, couldn't he?

The voice inside him stirred, intrigued by the direction of his thoughts. Riley's hand went faster. He hadn't bothered with lotion, and his touch was dry and bordering on painful, but he couldn't bring himself to reach for anything to ease the glide. He just needed to take the edge off this want. This yearning. So that next time Riley saw Seth, he could be good for him again.

Fuck. Riley wished Seth were here now. Wished he was breathing Seth in. Wished Seth had those perfect calloused fingers all over Riley's cock.

Maybe he'd use more than his fingers. Maybe he'd use that perfect, smiling mouth.

Hold still and part your lips for me.

Riley's back arched, his balls drawing up tight, and then he was coming into his fist with a ragged groan.

He sat there silent for a few long moments, then grabbed a tissue from the closest bookshelf and cleaned himself up, making a face at the sticky mess.

It wasn't very satisfying, was it? All this pathetic masturbation. Would it be more satisfying if it was Seth's hand Riley had finished in? Or maybe that mouth he'd been picturing? Or that hole Riley was supposedly so hungry to devour?

Riley's spent cock twitched again, and he frowned down at it, buttoning his jeans back up before he could be tempted to touch it. He tossed his head back with an aggrieved groan.

Maybe Riley should be grateful attraction hadn't been a big part of his life before now. He really didn't seem to have much patience for it at all.

8

SETH

Seth spent his day off in a horny, shameful daze.

What. The hell. Had he. Been. *Thinking*?

Well, he knew what he'd been thinking. He'd been thinking that an earnest, gorgeous boy had been asking Seth to be his first kiss and that it would have taken buckets more self-control than Seth had ever possessed in his life to say no.

But he'd meant it to be...quick. Simple. A generous peck, perhaps. Soft lips and no tongue. Definitely not making out and grinding on the couch like Seth had reverted back to teendom himself.

But then Riley had pounced. Again. Only this time he hadn't been attacking Seth in his driveway with his freaky panther ways. He'd been attacking Seth's mouth with his freaking panther *tongue*. And it had been sloppy and a little clumsy and still hotter than it should have been, and Seth had just wanted to *show* him how it was done.

He hadn't realized how quickly Riley would learn, was all.

Seth should have. He really should have. Riley was too damned observant, and Seth knew that very, very well. He should have realized Riley would take to kissing like a duck to lascivious waters.

Riley had copied Seth's demonstration perfectly, and then he'd seemed to make it a personal mission to find out every single move that might make Seth whimper and moan.

Seth paused on the trail he'd been trudging along, pressing his hands to his overheated cheeks as he leaned against a tree. He was out of breath far beyond what he should have been for the turtle-slow jog he'd been running. All it ever took was a week off from putting his paces in to feel like he'd never run a mile in his life.

There were birds twittering around him, apparently as grateful as Seth was for a break in the rain. Although, overall, there was less wildlife than Seth might have expected. He could have sworn there had been more squirrels running around here when he'd first moved here. Maybe they migrated in the winter.

Yes, dummy, that's what your main concern should be right now: the local squirrel population.

Seth scowled down at his feet. It was better to think about long-tailed rodents than about that kiss. About the way Seth had let Riley press him down to the couch and cover Seth with his body. The way Seth had been *this* close to letting Riley do whatever else he'd wanted.

How many more of his firsts would Riley have wanted Seth to take?

Seth already knew the answer, somewhere deep in his bones.

All of them.

Because underneath his loner status, Riley was...sensual. That was the only word for it. Seth could see it in the way he ate and drank, and in the way he carefully ran his fingers along the books he brought into Seth's bakery. And definitely in the way he watched Seth with not-so-secret, feral intensity.

He was a young man with big appetites, and for some reason all his hunger was focused on Seth.

It was disorienting, to say the least. Seth was cute. He knew that much. Men had never kicked him out of bed or anything, especially when he was being a little flirt. But they didn't, like, *yearn* for him either.

He'd had two serious relationships, one monogamous and one less so. They'd been sweet and tender and had ended easily, without anyone's heart breaking too badly. And Seth had entertained other, less serious dalliances with equally cute friends that had never turned into anything more.

So Seth wasn't some great catch, some once-in-a-lifetime hunk. He'd never turned someone's life upside down just by existing. Riley just...didn't know any better.

That was the thought that had stopped Seth when he'd been lying there on the couch, his legs wrapped around Riley's hips, his hands trapped above his head in Riley's hold. When Seth had been so close to letting Riley undress him and suck more hungry kisses into whatever bit of skin he wanted. The thought had run through Seth's head that if Riley hadn't grown up so isolated, he'd have realized from the get-go that Seth wasn't anything special, and he'd regret giving Seth so much undivided attention.

So Seth had stopped him.

Seth kicked at the dirt on the trail, annoyed with himself. It wasn't like him to be cock-blocked by low self-esteem. He *liked* himself. He liked the way he looked, even. But he was just being a realist. Wasn't that supposed to be a good thing? Both feet firmly planted on the ground and all that.

Being a scaredy-cat, some inner voice taunted.

But that wasn't true at all. There was a difference. This was a small town—no doubt Riley hadn't been exposed to too many men he was attracted to, especially if he was...particular. Possibly demi, from what he'd told Seth. His pool had been too small for him to really get a sense for what his options were.

Well, whatever. It wasn't like Seth had heard from Riley today, anyway. They didn't have each other's numbers yet, and it wasn't realistic to expect Riley to just show up at Seth's doorstep out of the blue, even if that *did* seem to be a very Riley thing to do.

Riley would probably appear at the bakery sometime later this week, and they would resume their weird, sexually charged friendship, and the kiss would be forgotten, and that would be that.

Seth picked up his trudging again, unwilling and unable to wipe the scowl from his face..

If he was going to be miserable anyway, he might as well get some cardio done while he was at it.

SETH LET himself into the bakery Tuesday morning determined *not* to dwell on who may or may not be visiting that day. He put on bright, bubbly, early 2000s pop, donned his apron and his headband, and got to work.

By the time he made it to the front of the shop to start setting up for the day, he'd almost succeeded in keeping his mind focused solely on work. Almost.

Still, Seth wasn't surprised to see a shadow lurking on the other side of his bakery door.

Although, if it wasn't shock, Seth really didn't want to speculate on why else his heart sped up like that at the sight.

What *was* a little shocking was that it wasn't Riley waiting outside but two immaculately dressed, unbelievably beautiful women. One was pale, tall, and statuesque, with a waterfall of dark hair and a velvet wrap dress clinging to her frame. The other was dark-skinned and petite, wearing a puff-sleeved gingham number that Seth would have loved to repurpose into an apron and headband for himself. They were holding hands, and neither was wearing a coat, despite the chill in the air and the promise of rain.

"Um, hello," Seth said after he'd unlocked the door and peered outside, biting back his disappointment that Riley wasn't lurking somewhere behind them. It hadn't seemed right to leave them standing there without a word, though, not when neither of them was wearing appropriate outerwear. "I'm so sorry, but I open at six."

The taller beauty made an exaggerated face of dismay, red lips pursing. "Oh, but don't tell me we got the time wrong! I could swear Riley told us you opened at five thirty."

"Riley?" Seth gave the duo a startled second glance, putting two and two together. "You're...Riley's moms?"

They barely looked old enough for the title, although if Riley was adopted, Seth supposed it didn't much matter. And Riley *had* told Seth once that his moms were the two most beautiful women in the world. Seth had thought at the time that it had been the exaggeration of a devoted son. But now that he'd seen them...

Seth realized both women were gazing at him with matching expressions of wry amusement. He stopped his gawking and stepped back from the door. "Come in!" he said hurriedly. "If you don't mind me finishing up while you sit."

"Oh, not at all," said the pretty gingham-clad one with a blinding smile. Seth had learned their names from Riley, but he wasn't sure who was Sybil and who was Daphne. "You really must forgive us for showing up early. I woke up with a hankering for pastry and decided we had to indulge straightaway."

Seth nodded absently, taking down the chairs from one of the tables and gesturing for them to have a seat. They must have been early risers, considering they were both decked out with flawless faces of tasteful makeup and hair that could have been in shampoo commercials. Now Seth kind of wished he'd thrown on some bronzer, or at least a swipe of mascara. He wasn't exactly presenting himself at his best.

"Can I get you something hot to drink?" he asked, surprised that neither one was shivering after standing out in the cold. "Coffee or tea?"

"Aren't you a dear?" the tall brunette cooed. "I'll have a coffee, and my darling Daphne will take a tea, thank you."

That confirmed who was who, at least. The taller woman was Sybil; the petite one was Daphne. Seth hustled to get them their drinks.

When he returned to their table, mugs in hand, Daphne was gazing around with open admiration. "My, it looks wonderful in here! So bright and yet...cozy. Warm, I'd say. I'm very impressed."

"Oh, um, thank you," Seth murmured, more awkward than he should have been with the praise. Normally he took it in stride—he was proud of his little bakery and wasn't the type to wave aside compliments with false modesty—but his customers weren't usually this...gorgeous and sophisticated.

Meanwhile, Seth was fighting the urge to ask after Riley's whereabouts. Something about these two made him think the question wouldn't be mistaken for casual.

As he began stocking his display cases, Seth realized his fingers were trembling. It wasn't just the surprise of meeting the parents unexpectedly—not that he and Riley were *dating* or anything, only—

Well, whatever.

It wasn't just that though. It was also a certain...tension in the air. Seth tried to untangle its source as he got things settled and the two women murmured between themselves.

He'd felt it before, Seth realized. This tension. This...awareness, like a prickling at the back of the neck. He'd felt it in Seacliff, actually, first with his friend Sascha's husband, Kai, back when he'd first arrived in town, and then with Matty's husband, Night. Benny's grumpy-ass husband, Helio, had it too. Some air about them all that made them seem…*more* than other people.

And, of course, Seth had felt it with Riley. But with the undercurrent of reluctant attraction between them, Seth hadn't really dwelled too much on the rest of it. Not for a while, at least.

Was it just the heightened awareness that came from being around extremely beautiful people? Maybe this was what civilians felt like around movie stars or famous models.

Could Seth wrangle up a movie star for a test comparison?

He realized with a start that both Riley's moms were watching him closely as he stared off into the distance. God, he was being both way too quiet and totally rude.

"Sorry," he said sheepishly. "I'm in my head a little this morning."

The two women exchanged an indecipherable glance, and then Daphne smiled kindly at him. "We don't mind," she said as Sybil sipped her coffee. "We know we've barged in."

"Oh, that's fine," Seth hurried to tell her. "I'm, um, very fond of your son, you know. He keeps me company before opening sometimes."

"Yes," Sybil said dryly. "He's mentioned."

Seth came around the counter with two pastries for them, hoping he'd chosen something they'd each like. He'd selected a classic croissant as well as a cherry-almond Danish, each of them perfectly whole. No broken castoffs for the goddesses.

The two women made delighted noises that made Seth's cheeks warm, and Seth returned to the counter, getting his cash register in order. He watched through his eyelashes as Sybil took a dainty bite of croissant, then shut her eyes with a hum. "Divine," she assessed.

Daphne smiled adoringly at her, then took a bite of the Danish. "Why, this is delicious!" she cried, covering her full mouth with one hand. "Who taught you, darling Seth?"

Seth felt his cheeks heat again at the "darling Seth" bit but gamely answered, "My grandmother did."

Daphne sighed happily, like his answer was a good one. "She must have been a treasure."

"She was. I still use her recipes for a lot of my favorites."

"Is that why you have more of a, let's say, classical repertoire?" Sybil asked, her gaze skimming over his filled pastry case. "I don't see any mishmashes of donuts and croissants or bagels crossed with muffins, or what have you."

"Oh yeah, I'm a little old-fashioned that way," Seth told her, slicing into his raspberry pistachio Kringle so he'd have pieces for a sample plate. "I prefer playing around with flavor combinations and leaving the basics—"

Seth broke off with a yelp as the front door swung open. He hadn't even realized he'd left it unlocked.

But there was Riley, completely soaked through—it must have started raining again in the past ten minutes—and looking more ferocious than Seth had ever seen him.

Riley's dark hair was plastered to his face, his hands clenched tightly at his sides. If Seth wasn't mistaken, he was pissed right the hell off.

"What. Are. You. *Doing*. Here?" Riley gritted out, and Seth was so taken aback by the unexpected venom that he thought for a second Riley was questioning his presence in his own damned bakery.

But then Daphne rose swiftly from her chair, Sybil following suit right after. "Now, darling. We only—"

But she didn't complete her sentence. Instead, all three heads turned to Seth in unison, so smoothly and in such perfect sync that he could only gape.

Their gazes shifted downward, and Seth found himself glancing down as well.

Oh. He'd sliced his finger.

His knife must have slipped when the door had banged open. Seth had been so shocked by Riley's sudden arrival he hadn't even noticed the sting.

"Whoops," he said, trying to sound light and flippant and probably falling short. There was just so much tension in the air, and Seth had no fucking clue why. "Haven't done that in a while."

The next few moments were pure, terrifying confusion.

One moment, Seth was looking at Riley, trying to figure out why his friend was so angry at his moms' visit, and why his nostrils were flaring like that, and then the next moment Riley's face...changed.

His dark eyes went even darker, the whites disappearing completely, and his lips twisted into a snarl, revealing two very pointed canines.

Fangs, Seth thought distantly. But there wasn't time to dwell on it because Riley was lunging toward Seth from across the room, and then Riley's moms were on him, holding Riley back.

Seth didn't understand. For all that Sybil was tall and built, Seth didn't see how the two women *could* hold Riley back, with his youth and his imposing size. Seth had tasted a sample of Riley's strength the night Riley had tackled him, and it wasn't insignificant.

But the women were managing, until suddenly they weren't. And then Riley was leaping toward Seth again. But then Sybil was moving faster than anyone should have been able to, and she was behind Riley with her hands clutching the back of his head.

There was a horrible crunching sound.

Someone was screaming.

It was Seth. *Seth* was screaming.

Because Riley was on the bakery floor now, his body limp and his neck bent at an unnatural angle, and Seth couldn't think. Couldn't breathe. Could only scream and keep screaming.

What had just *happened*?

9

SETH

Someone was still screaming.

It was Seth, of course, since neither of the women were uttering a sound.

The two beautiful, friendly women who had just...killed their son?

Or—or maybe Riley was okay, somehow. It didn't look like he was breathing, and his neck was at the wrong angle, but also, how could he not be okay? He'd been standing at Seth's front door only a minute ago.

He couldn't be dead. Of course he couldn't be.

Seth tried to steer away from the gaping chasm of despair that was opening up inside his chest, afraid to let himself drop in. His cheeks were wet. Screaming *and* crying, then. He was fucking useless in a crisis, wasn't he?

The police. Seth needed to call the police. Or—or an ambulance. He was out of his depth here. He still didn't understand what had happened, but he knew it was bad. He knew *something* had gone terribly, terribly wrong.

Before he could even think of where his phone might be, two hands were on either side of his face, holding him in place.

Seth hadn't even seen Sybil move. How had she gotten to him so fast? Was she about to twist his head off its axis too? Was it going to hurt?

Dark eyes bore into his. Black eyes. Like, completely black, without any white around the edges at all. They hadn't been that color when he'd first met her. *No one's* eyes were that color.

No one except Riley just now, when he'd been trying to leap at Seth. And that first night too...hadn't Seth thought Riley's eyes were black? He'd convinced himself it was a trick of the light.

Seth wanted to ask him. He wanted Riley to get off the floor so Seth could ask him what the hell was going on.

Please get up, Riley. Please, please get up.

"You will remain calm," Sybil told Seth sternly, her palms warm against his skin. "And you will listen."

It was nonsense, what she was saying. Nothing on earth was going to quell Seth's panic, his impending grief. And he sure as fuck wasn't going to listen to the woman who'd just snapped Riley's neck.

But it was like Seth's body and mind were reacting without his permission. His mouth slackened, all his screaming suddenly done with. The horrible, constricting feeling in his chest loosened, his muscles unknotting without his say-so.

And then he was just...staring back at Sybil and her freaky eyes, suddenly able to breathe again, even though in the back of his mind, Seth knew he should be rioting.

He'd calmed down. And he hadn't wanted to.

"Very good," Sybil said.

"Should we take it all?" Daphne asked. Seth was able to dart his gaze her way for only a second before he was pulled back into the abyss of Sybil's black eyes. Daphne was cradling Riley in her arms on the floor, and Seth had to blink back tears at the sight. "Pretend this morning never happened?"

She looked so sad, so devoted.

It was confusing. Everything was confusing.

"No," Sybil told her, not taking her eyes off Seth. "It would only leave room for another disaster. But we don't have a lot of time. People will be here soon." She stroked her thumb over Seth's cheekbones in a way that was maybe meant to be soothing. "Seth. You cut yourself, and it woke Riley's hunger. We were worried he would drink too much. We did what we thought was needed. He'll wake in a few hours, good as new. I promise."

More nonsense. Why was everyone only speaking nonsense riddles today?

Seth shook his head, focusing on the last part of what she'd said. The promise that Riley would wake up. "I don't believe you," he said dully.

Sybil gave him a hard look, and then she was...biting into her wrist? Savaging it with her teeth. She seemed to have her own pair of fangs, which somehow Seth hadn't noticed until now.

Seth would have let out a horrified gasp, if he'd been able to gather the emotion out of whatever complacent fog she'd summoned within him. Instead, he could only watch.

"Sybil," Daphne scolded. "We don't have *time*."

"Showing is always easier than telling," Sybil told her. Her mouth was bloody. So was the wrist she held up for Seth's perusal. Bloody and torn.

But then it began...knitting itself back together. Damaged flesh filled itself in, and the sight was so beyond Seth's comprehension that everything took on a surreal cast, like he was watching CGI. Soon the wrist was whole again, the skin bloodstained but unbroken.

"He will be good as new," Sybil repeated, one hand still cupping Seth's cheek. "I really do promise."

"Seth," Daphne called from the floor. "Do you have a friend you can phone to be with you? You're in shock, you poor dear."

Seth shook his head. All he could think was, *I had a friend, but he's on the floor, and he doesn't look like he's breathing. How can he be good as new if he's not breathing?*

Sybil's grip tightened on his face, although her touch was still anything but rough. She cocked her head, her gaze growing distant, like she was listening to something. "Time to go," she announced after a moment. "Seth. Do you understand what Riley is?"

Seth shook his head again. That seemed to be all he was capable of doing. Staring and shaking. At least he wasn't screaming, although he didn't think that was due to his own self-control but whatever spell Sybil had put on him.

Sybil tutted. "I think you do. You're a clever boy, aren't you? We'll be seeing you soon." And then she was tucking some sort of business card in Seth's hand. His fist clenched around it almost without his permission.

Sybil released her hold on his face and turned away, leaving Seth on his own behind the counter. Seth watched in a daze as, despite her tiny size, Daphne picked Riley up in her arms like he weighed nothing at all. She carried him out the door, Sybil right behind her.

They were gone.

Seth didn't know how long he stood there, his body frozen and his mind whirring. Riley's face had changed, when this had all started. He'd had black eyes and sharp fangs, just like Sybil had when she'd bitten into her wrist.

Sybil had said Seth's blood made Riley hungry.

Sybil could heal her wounds in mere moments, and Riley could apparently do the same.

If Seth believed them. If Riley woke up at all.

Seth didn't stir until Violet showed up however many minutes later. Seth's door was still unlocked, even if he hadn't turned his sign. She waltzed right in.

Violet stopped. Stared. Seth stared back.

And then Violet was walking over with a determined stride, looking for all the world like she was going to join Seth behind the counter.

Seth turned in place to follow her movements as she slid around the counter's edge. "What are you doing?"

"You're bleeding," she told him matter-of-factly.

Seth looked down. Right. He'd cut his finger. Funny how he'd forgotten about that, even though his slip with the knife was exactly what had started this whole mess in the first place.

"So you're robbing me while I'm weakened?"

Violet gave him the kind of eye roll only a true teenager was capable of. "I'm covering for you. Go in the back and make yourself a tea or something. You look kinda insane." She cocked her head. "Unless you want to close for the day instead?"

No, Seth didn't want that, actually. If he went home alone after what he'd just seen, with only his own thoughts to accompany him...

Yeah, then he probably *would* go insane.

"My mom owns that woo-woo crystal shop a few blocks down," Violet told him, tucking her black hair behind her ears. "I know how to work a register."

It wasn't her aptitude with a register Seth questioned so much as her ability to be civil with the general public. But then again, Seth was pretty sure his whole world had just been turned upside down in one horrifying instant, so what did it matter if some goth teen was rude to a customer or two?

He wordlessly handed Violet his apron, then made his way to the back kitchen. He untied his headband and wrapped it tightly around his bleeding finger, unwilling to expend the energy searching for the first aid kit right now. He slid down to the kitchen floor, his arms around his knees.

Seth added together what he'd seen this morning, again and again. He calculated and recalculated. And eventually he couldn't stop the refrain from repeating in his head:

I think my friend Riley's a vampire. I think his moms are too.

Seth thought again of their first meeting. He thought of what Riley had told him, crouched over Seth in the rain.

Seth amended his refrain.

I think my friend Riley's a vampire, and I think he wants to eat me.

SETH DIDN'T KNOW how long he sat there.

Long enough for his ass to go numb against the linoleum but not long enough for him to make any sense of what had happened this morning.

He could hear muffled voices every now and then, so customers must have been coming through the bakery. The voices were never raised in anger as far as he could tell, so theoretically Violet was handling things. Seth wasn't sure he would have had the energy to care even if she hadn't been.

Eventually, Violet came back into the kitchen, holding a mug of steaming coffee out to him with one hand and his phone with the other. "Here. I've noticed you like yours with a gross amount of cream and sugar. And you left your phone on the counter."

Seth took the mug and the phone. Violet eyed his headband bandage with raised brows but didn't say anything about his half-assed attempt at first aid.

"Thank you, Violet."

Violet nodded, but she didn't head back to the front right away. She leaned against the counter instead, one combat-booted foot resting on the cabinet behind her. "Did someone die?" she asked. Not sarcastically either, but like she was genuinely wondering if Seth was bereaved.

"I don't think so," was all Seth could manage in response.

Violet nodded, like that was a reasonable answer. "Stay back here a little longer. You still look like hell. But I'm taking a free donut after."

"For life," Seth amended weakly. "Free donuts for life."

She gave him a small smirk and turned as if to leave. Seth stopped her with an outstretched hand. "Hey. What-What made you think they were serial killers?"

"Riley and his family?" Violet shrugged. "Just a vibe, you know. They're hot and they're friendly enough, but when you get close, something has the hairs on the back of your neck standing up."

It was such a perfect mirror of what Seth had been thinking that morning that he couldn't come up with a response. Violet didn't seem to need one anyway. She walked through the door to the front without another word.

Seth took a sip of his milky coffee, then set it down on the floor next to him when his gut roiled in protest. Jumpy nerves, he guessed. He didn't usually have a sensitive stomach, but then he didn't usually witness a nonmurder murder and self-healing mutilation all in one morning.

He stared down at the phone in his hand. Riley hadn't texted.

How long did it take a supernatural creature to heal from a snapped neck?

Seth might never find out. Riley couldn't text him anyway, a fact that Seth had once again conveniently forgotten. Somehow they still didn't have each other's numbers. Seth didn't even know for sure if Riley had a phone.

Did vampires use cell phones? Maybe they communicated via trained bats instead. Had Seth been seeing more bats than usual lately? Maybe that was why there were fewer squirrels. Maybe there was some inverse bat-to-squirrel ratio.

He wasn't making sense, was he? Was this what shock felt like?

Anyway, no text, but Seth did have a missed video call from Benny. He must have forgotten which day Seth closed up shop.

After a moment of deliberation, Seth called him back.

It didn't take long for Benny to pick up, his handsome, tanned face beaming at Seth through the phone screen. He'd buzzed his dark hair short again.

Seth caught a brief glimpse of Helio scowling behind Benny's shoulder before he scuttled out of view.

"Seth!" Benny's smile tipped down into a frown. "Are you sick or something? You look rough, dude."

Seth didn't have it in him to pretend to be hale and hearty, so he ignored the question, cutting right to the chase. "Hey, Benny, do you believe in the otherworldly?"

"Like outer space?" Benny scratched at his chin, his dark brow furrowing. "Would be hard not to. Pretty sure we've been up there already."

Seth cleared his throat. "I mean, like, the paranormal. Ghosts. Magic." Seth swallowed hard. "Maybe...vampires?"

Benny's face brightened. "Oh yeah. For sure. Well, you know, Helio's fae. And then there's the devils in town. It'd be weird if there was nothing else out here. Plus, I think Sascha said his brother-in-law is a vampire."

Fae. Devils. Brothers-in-law.

Seth's head spun. He let if fall back against the counter.

"*Nix*?" he finally squeaked, thinking of the gorgeous redheaded flirt who came into town a few times a year. He was married to Sascha's oldest brother, Ivan. "Nix is a vampire?"

Benny shook his head, raising his voice to be heard over the loud protestations of Helio, who seemed to be objecting heartily to

Benny's honesty. "No, Nix is a sex devil, pretty sure. The other brother-in-law. The one married to Alexei."

Seth was having an out-of-body experience. He could see himself on the floor, chatting to Benny about sex devils and vampires, as if he was looking down from above. Maybe he'd passed out when Riley had jumped him. Maybe he was dreaming.

He cleared his throat. One insane statement at a time, right? "When you say Helio's *fae*..."

"Well, he doesn't like the word 'fairy.'"

There was more grumbling, and Benny turned away from the phone, presumably to face Helio. "He asked though. I'm not going to lie to Seth."

"And the devils?" Seth asked before things could devolve into a full-blown couple's argument.

Benny turned back around. "Oh. You know, Kai and the others. Thought you knew about them. Actually, I think they prefer to be called demons, so maybe use that word instead."

"Demons," Seth repeated.

"I really thought you knew." Benny scratched at his chin again. "It's been, like, six years."

"*How*?"

"They leave their blinds open more than they think."

"No, I mean, how—" *How does all this exist? How did you get wrapped up in it? How could I not know after all this time?* Seth pressed a hand to his forehead. "You know what, never mind. I need to go."

"Wait, buddy—"

Seth hung up. He had more questions than he'd started with, but the nausea that had been simmering under the surface was letting itself be known in full force. Seth wrapped an arm around his stomach, trying to keep himself from hurling.

Seth had just found out that the town he'd loved so much, the one he'd left reluctantly to pull himself out of his supposed rut, was crawling with nonhuman entities. People he'd fed pastries and danced with and grown very, very fond of over the past years.

Well, not Helio, but that guy was kind of an ass. That *fae.*

But Kai? Night? Nix?

Actually, come to think of it....all three of those men were the kind that raised hairs on the back of the neck, just like Violet had been saying. Seth had just chalked it up to them being too hot to function or something. They were all inhumanly beautiful in their own way, like Riley's moms. Like Riley.

Jesus, was Seth an idiot? Had everyone been laughing at him this whole time, the dumb human who couldn't figure it all out even when it was right in front of his face?

But then again, if it was true...

That meant Riley really would wake up. Seth would see him again. He could ask him all the questions crowding his brain.

So many damn questions.

Assuming Riley didn't eat him first...

Seth picked up the card he'd dropped on the floor when he'd collapsed.

Sybil Beauchamp. With an address. Did she want Seth to come find them? To make his way to their isolated house in the woods?

Seth didn't know what to do with it. With any of it.

For now, he rose from the floor, removing his headband bandage. First thing first: he needed to wash his hands and put on a glove. Then he was going to go out and serve pastries. When the mind was running wild, it was best to keep the body busy.

Seth would do what he needed to do to get through the day.

The rest he'd figure out later.

10

RILEY

Riley screamed.

He screamed at the trees. He screamed at the birds. He screamed at all the stupid mud on the stupid fucking ground.

He'd been doing so *well.* He'd been cautious, and he'd moved slow. He'd mostly kept his hands to himself. He'd stopped kissing Seth when Seth had asked. Riley had been like a person. Not an animal or a monster but a *person.*

And then he'd completely, 100 percent, fucked it all up.

"It's your! Fucking! Fault!" he yelled up at the sky. It had stopped raining, and the clouds were beginning to disperse for once, like they were mocking Riley's bad mood by letting the sunshine through.

Riley wasn't talking to God, obviously. He was talking to that stupid fucking voice. The one that wasn't a voice at all but part of him. The vicious monster part. The *bad* part.

It didn't answer him, that stupid voice. It was hiding. Sulking.

Ashamed or maybe just biding its time. Riley didn't know, and he didn't fucking care.

He'd woken up in the back of Mama Sybil's car. He hadn't known how much time had passed at first. Riley's healing was always erratic, sometimes much faster and sometimes much slower than that of his moms. So he'd had one horrifying, soul-destroying moment of thinking they were driving him away. Out of town. Out of Washington. Away from Seth. They could have been driving for hours and hours already, and he wouldn't have known it.

Riley had panicked, his limbs flailing as he'd tried to open the door without unlocking it first.

Mama Sybil had turned around, looking at him with one raised brow. "If you kick a hole in my vehicle, we will be having *words*, Riley."

And Riley had stopped. Not so much from the threat but from the knowledge that she wouldn't have been nearly so calm and matter-of-fact if she'd been forcing him to leave his mate.

"Did—did I hurt him?" he'd asked.

Mama Sybil had turned back to face the road, sniffing at the question. "Of course not. We'd never let that happen."

"And you made him forget?" Riley had asked, more to get it straight in his head than as a real question. Because of *course* they'd made Seth forget. Of course they'd compelled him—they wouldn't leave him with the memory of Riley leaping at him like a deranged beast.

But his moms hadn't answered.

"And you made him *forget*?" Riley had asked again.

Mama Daphne had cleared her throat from the passenger seat. "No. We thought it best to let things lie."

Then Riley *had* gotten out of the car, unlocking the door and rolling out of the moving vehicle without another word. He'd ignored the scrapes and bruises from the road—they'd heal quickly or they wouldn't, and what did a few more rips in his jeans matter? He'd decided it was best to run home, before he stayed and said something horrible to his moms, the women who'd loved him and protected him—and protected Seth *from* him—and to whom he owed everything.

But letting Seth remember like that?

It was too soon. Riley and Seth were only starting to get to know each other. What chance did Riley have if Seth already knew he was a monster, bloodthirsty and uncontrolled and so very hungry?

The worst part was that Riley didn't even know what he'd been trying to do back in the bakery. He'd smelled the rich, decadent scent of orange and copper, had realized Seth was bleeding, and then he'd been...moving. Fangs already out, that voice in control and Riley relegated to the back of his own mind. Had the voice been trying to protect Seth? To lick at that cut until the skin healed and Seth was no longer hurt? Or to bite in, to create another, worse wound by tearing into his throat and draining him dry?

Riley wasn't sure, and the voice wasn't talking.

Well, Riley was done talking too. Or yelling, if he wanted to be specific. Screaming out in the woods by himself like a lunatic wasn't doing any good, other than sending all the birds flying. He'd go home, go up to the attic, and try to figure out his next move.

It wouldn't be sulking. It would be *planning*.

Did flowers and chocolate work in a situation like this? Maybe a card that said, *I'm sorry I tried to maul you a second time. Third time's the charm, I promise.*

Maybe Seth wouldn't open any card Riley sent him, anyway. Maybe Seth hated him. Or maybe he'd convinced himself it wasn't real—he wouldn't be the first human to engage in denial when faced with the supernatural.

As Riley came through the trees surrounding the house, he saw there was a car parked by the porch, next to Mama Daphne's —a car he didn't recognize. And a man standing there by the front door, waiting for someone.

Riley had one gut-wrenching moment where he thought it might be Seth come to see him, but the details were all wrong. That wasn't Seth's car, that black, nondescript thing. And the man standing there was taller, with short dark hair and a suit that made him look like he'd come straight from FBI headquarters.

It was all...unusual. Super weird, actually. No one ever came to the house. Even delivery vans stopped at the mail drop much further down the drive.

Riley made his steps deliberately loud as he approached, and the man turned to face him. He was wearing glasses, and they glinted in the ray of sunlight peeking from behind the clouds. "Ah. Hello," the man said, his voice smooth and mild. "Are you Mr. Beauchamp?"

He pronounced it the French way, just like Riley's moms did. Riley gave him a nod, halting at the bottom of the porch.

"I heard some yelling," the man pointed out. "Is everything all right?"

Riley said nothing.

"You encountered...a wild animal, perhaps?"

Riley shook his head. "Scream therapy."

The man blinked at him. "Oh. Right." He seemed to shake off Riley's rudeness in an instant, giving him a bland smile. "I'm Tim Perkins, a lawyer from the Northwest Institute of Wildlife Research, or NIWR, if you don't want to say the whole mouthful. We're neighbors. Not *close* neighbors, of course." That bland smile sharpened. "Your family has an extensive property here."

Mr. Perkins paused then, his head cocked expectantly, like Riley was supposed to say something, or maybe invite him in.

But Riley didn't want this stranger in his house, and he wasn't the type to be cowed by uncomfortable silences. So he stood there at the bottom of the porch, staring without speaking.

After a few long moments, Mr. Perkins cleared his throat. "Tell me, Mr. Beauchamp, have you encountered any unusual activity in the area?"

Riley tucked his hands into his pockets, rocking onto his heels. "Like UFOs?"

Mr. Perkins narrowed his eyes, apparently not amused. No sense of humor with this one. *Seth* would have thought it was funny. "Like predators."

"What kind of predators?" Riley asked. "I thought you all studied marine life."

He'd heard the rumors in town, sitting for hours in Seth's bakery like he did. The creepy institute about which no one knew the exact details, but plenty wanted to speculate.

Of course, Riley had also heard his own family was made up of undiscovered serial killers, so he took the rumors with a grain of salt.

The light hit Mr. Perkins's glasses again, hiding his expression as he drawled, "Oh, we study strange fauna of all kinds."

The hairs on the back of Riley's neck stood up.

Careful, the voice warned, speaking up for the first time since they'd woken up in Mama Sybil's car. It was probably the first bit of useful advice it had ever given Riley. Not that he needed it.

Riley was just debating whether to attempt compulsion to get the man to leave their property when Mama Sybil's car pulled up. She and Mama Daphne were out in an instant, though they managed to make it look like neither one of them was rushing.

"This is private property," Mama Sybil announced before Mr. Perkins could even say a word. She sounded haughty as hell, and no matter how angry Riley was with her, he could appreciate the way she could make any man feel like a bug under her shoe.

Mr. Perkins was all genial smiles now. "Hello," he said. "I'm aware, actually. I'm Tim Perkins from the Northwest Institute of Wildlife Research. I've been sent to request permission for access to your land."

"For what purpose?" Mama Daphne asked.

"As our name suggests, we study wildlife in the area," Mr. Perkins said, not mentioning anything about *strange fauna*, Riley noticed. "You own quite a bit of forest property. The larger the field we can cover, the more data we can collect."

But Mama Sybil was waving a dismissive hand. "I'm afraid that won't be possible."

Mr. Perkins coughed gently into his fist. "We'll stick to the outskirts, of course. You won't even notice we're there."

"You'd be surprised," Riley muttered.

When he glanced back up, Mama Daphne was subtly shaking her head at him. Before Riley could question the warning, she smiled brightly, holding out her hand to him. "Riley, darling, why don't you come inside? I think we're done here."

Mr. Perkins didn't make a move to come off the porch. Instead, he held out a card. "In case you change your mind."

Mama Sybil swept up the stairs and past him, grabbing the card as she went. She shot him a brief smile over her shoulder that didn't reach her eyes. "We won't."

Mr. Perkins maintained his own bland smile as he finally walked off the porch, nodding politely as he passed Riley and Mama Daphne to get to his car. Riley inhaled as he passed—no scent of copper. Not a vampire, then. Just a kinda creepy lawyer.

Back inside the house, Riley watched his moms hang their purses on the hooks in the vestibule. They weren't indulging in their usual easy chatter, and Riley couldn't tell if that was because of their most recent visitor or the events of the morning.

If nothing else, Mr. Perkins had served as a distraction from Riley's self-recrimination.

His moms led him toward the kitchen, and Riley finally broke the silence. "Weird guy."

Mama Sybil's brow furrowed as she grabbed three mugs from the cabinet. "If you see him or anyone else from his so-called institute, tell us immediately."

Riley was already supposed to tell his moms if he encountered any strangers on the property. The fact that she was specifying now was telling. He took a seat at the table. "You think there's something wrong."

"I think it's wise to be alert." Mama Sybil tossed Mr. Perkins's card into the garbage. Riley had a feeling she would have preferred to set the thing on fire.

Mama Daphne stopped by his chair to press a kiss to Riley's cheek, then sashayed over to the stove to start the kettle. "You should be sure to stay presentable, darling. Seth could be here at any moment."

Riley's stomach swooped. So much for a distraction. "What do you mean?"

"I gave him our address," Mama Sybil said lightly, like that was a totally normal thing to do after their son had tried to eat a man.

"So he could run as far from it as possible?"

Mama Daphne grinned brightly as she spooned tea leaves into her favorite teapot. "I think he'll surprise you."

Riley dropped his head in his hands, tugging at his hair. He loved these women, but— "Why were you even *there*?" he gritted out.

"We wanted to meet him," Mama Daphne said, the absolute picture of innocence.

"You couldn't wait?"

"Not when he holds your fate in his hands." Mama Sybil covered Riley's shoulder with a warm hand. "We told you that everything would be well. We told you we'd make sure of it."

"I'm surprised you didn't just attack and form the bond by force, then," he said bitterly.

His moms exchanged a glance. "We'd like to give you a chance to do it your way first," Mama Daphne told him.

"And if I don't succeed?"

Mama Sybil gave his shoulder a tight squeeze. "Then, darling, we'll do it for you."

It was as much of a threat as it was a promise.

Sometimes it really sucked having vampires for parents.

11

SETH

Seth hung up the phone and folded his hands on the table in front of him, covering the card he hadn't yet let out of his sight.

That had been an illuminating conversation, to say the least.

It wasn't that Seth hadn't *believed* Benny. He'd believed him with an immediacy that was almost absurd, actually. But he'd had more questions than answers in the end, and Seth's cousin wasn't the most straightforward source of information, even on a good day.

So after somehow getting through the rest of the workday—thanks in large part to Violet, to whom Seth owed approximately one thousand favors—Seth had called his friend Sascha.

It had been the right move to make. Several hours later, Seth no longer felt like a joke. And he wasn't worried anymore that everyone back at Seacliff had been laughing at his ignorance all along. It seemed instead to be a very tangled web of paranormal lives they were navigating, and as Sascha had told him, "It wasn't my secret alone to tell."

On top of that, apparently there *had* been discussion about letting Seth in on things further down the line, before the group of demons and their mates had to leave Seacliff due to a lack of obvious aging. (Benny had conveniently forgotten to tell Seth about the whole prolonged lifespan thing, but then again, Seth had hung up on him pretty quickly.) But then Seth had decided to move away, and they hadn't wanted to blindside him right before he made such a major life change.

Had Seth noticed his friends failing to grow noticeably older over the last six or so years? Not really. They were all young enough that it would be hard to tell for a while. And in this day and age, who knew what kind of cosmetic work people were getting done in secret?

But maybe Seth had noticed *something*, at least subconsciously. Maybe that explained some things, actually.

Because Seth had always thought he'd stay in Seacliff all his life. And then suddenly he'd decided otherwise.

Was it because he'd gotten some strange, unknown feeling, surrounded by all these otherworldly men, that he'd decided there was more out there for him? A sense of being a perpetual side character to people who were living lives more magical than he could imagine?

And then somehow, in the midst of his quarter-life crisis, Seth had landed himself smack in the middle of a vampire den.

Out of the frying pan and into the fang, as no one had said ever.

That was what it was called when multiple vampires lived together in one community, Seth had learned: a den. Sascha's brother-in-law was part of one in Colorado.

Seth wasn't sure if a den of three counted, actually, but maybe there were more vampires than Riley and his moms living on that property. Maybe there was an entire horde of them, lying in wait.

Seth could feel the sharp edges of the card under his palm. The address Sybil had given him. Seth had looked it up on his phone—it was about a twenty-minute drive from town, straight into the woods. From what he'd been able to tell via map sleuthing, there weren't any other houses nearby.

So there would be no one to hear Seth if things went very, very wrong.

He wouldn't exactly be going in blind though. Sascha had told Seth as much as he could about vampires. As much as Sascha *knew*, at least.

Like, for example, how newly turned vamps were volatile and dangerous until they settled into their new being, unless they already had a mate to ground them.

Because oh yes, vampires had fated mates—kindred souls that would tether them to their humanity and keep them from going feral and getting lost to bloodlust.

So maybe Riley was newly turned, and that was why he kept jumping on Seth at every opportunity. Or maybe he was very, very old, and had gone too long without a mate, and *that* was why he couldn't seem to keep his fangs to himself.

Wouldn't that be funny, if Seth had been worried about being too old for his new friend, and Riley was secretly a thousand-year-old geezer?

Seth grimaced down at his folded hands. *Funny* wasn't exactly the right word.

Either way, it seemed like Riley was definitely less stable than the other vampires of Sascha's acquaintance, who were all happily living in a small town without murdering any of its local small-business owners.

So Seth should probably stay away, was what Sascha had warned him. Far, far away from Riley and his very sharp teeth.

Seth wasn't going to do that, of course.

Because now that Seth had realigned his worldview to include paranormal creatures, he had to face facts. And the fact was, if Seth wanted to stay true to his own moral compass, then it didn't matter *what* Riley was. It mattered *who* Riley was.

And the person Seth had gotten to know over these past weeks was intense and a little sad and surprisingly funny. And achingly, desperately in need of a friend.

And friends didn't abandon friends because of a few struggles with uncontrolled bloodlust.

Besides, Riley had been in Seth's home. He'd been on top of Seth, kissing him like he was dying for it, and he hadn't hurt Seth at all. He hadn't sliced him with a fang, hadn't ignored Seth's request to stop.

Riley didn't *want* to hurt him; Seth knew that much.

Which meant he was probably beating himself up for his lapse in control this morning. Riley was probably hurting out there in the woods, lonely and full of regret. It hurt Seth's heart to think about it, to a degree he was almost reluctant to admit to.

So Seth was going to ignore good advice and sound warnings.

He was going in.

But he wasn't going empty-handed.

Seth's breath caught as the winding dirt road he'd been driving on finally led to a break in the trees, revealing the woodland mansion that had been hidden up to this point.

He'd made it just moments before nightfall, the sun already well on its way to setting. Not that it mattered, right? Seth already knew these three weren't hampered by pesky little things like sunlight. The daytime wouldn't have afforded him any sort of protection, even if he'd thought he needed it.

Seth *had* thought—what with the talk of serial killers and Riley's tendency to dress like he'd just rolled out of bed—that he'd be looking for a simple log cabin. But then again, he'd seen Sybil and Daphne's flair for style, so maybe he should have known to expect a secret mansion in the woods.

It looked to be at least three stories, with a beautiful front porch with steps leading to a path that wound around to the back of the house. It had a steepled roof and didn't show any of the wear Seth might expect of a property in such a wet, coastal climate.

Seth sidled in next to the two other cars already parked on the gravel drive. The vehicles weren't flashy, but they *were* expensive; Seth didn't know enough to name the make and models off the top of his head, but he knew that much from a quick glance.

He put his car in park and grabbed his tote bag from the passenger seat before getting out. No doubt they'd already heard him coming, so there was no use delaying. He steeled his spine and squared his shoulders as he trotted up the short set of stairs to the porch.

Seth knocked three times on the door and waited.

Hardly a moment later, Daphne opened the door, Sybil looming right behind her. Sybil's smile was almost mocking—or maybe that was just her resting snob face—but Daphne's was pure warmth. "Seth!" she greeted brightly. "How brave you are!"

Seth couldn't help smiling back at her, biting back a nervous giggle while he was at it. He slid one handle of the tote down his arm and began rummaging inside. "I brought something."

"Holy water?" Sybil drawled, arching a brow. "A hastily carved wooden stake, perhaps?"

Seth presented his Tupperware. "Cookies, actually." He lowered his voice into a conspiratorial whisper, even as he ignored the rampant pounding of his own heart. "I have it on good authority stakes and holy water wouldn't be much help."

"Do you now?" Sybil's mocking smile turned wryly amused, and Seth had a hard time not considering that a win.

Without a word between them, Daphne and Sybil stepped back from the door, and Daphne ushered Seth inside with a friendly but firm hand on his arm. Neither of them took his offering, although Seth knew they could eat human food if they wanted.

The inside of the house was just as impressive as the outside, as Seth had known it would be. They were in an open foyer, with a living room off to their left and a stairway directly in front of them. Behind the stairs was a hallway that no doubt led to a kitchen, and who knew what else beyond. The ceilings were high, the floors were real hardwood, and the walls Seth could see from here were painted in deep, vibrant colors, rendering the space rich and sumptuous.

It had less the appearance of a vampire's lair and more the home of timelessly stylish women who appreciated old-fashioned elegance.

Seth stopped his gawking and faced Riley's moms again. "Your home is lovely, but I came to check on Riley." The words sounded stilted to his own ears. "I should have said. Is he...awake?"

Seth didn't know what he'd do if Riley wasn't. Probably turn right back around and drive home. He was trying to be brave, but he didn't think he could bear looking at Riley's bent neck and limp form again. That horrifying vision was already going to haunt Seth for the rest of his days.

Plus, he'd most likely burst into tears in front of the goddesses, and wouldn't that be mortifying?

Except he already had, Seth remembered abruptly. And screamed himself silly while he was at it.

In his embarrassment, Seth jerkily raised his cookie offering into the air once more. "Baked goods, anyone?"

Sybil waved a hand. "Save them for Riley. Though, they do

smell delicious." Her eyes gleamed with some secret humor. "Is that orange I detect?"

Seth nodded. "Orange meltaway cookies."

Riley had asked Seth about orange cake, and Seth hadn't forgotten it. But he hadn't had the steady hands necessary for cake baking today, and he definitely hadn't had the patience to run out for extra ingredients. He'd gone for something simpler, with items he'd already had on hand.

"He'll be delighted," Daphne told him. She tilted her chin toward the stairs. "He's up in the attic."

Seth hesitated. "The...attic?"

"It's not as gothic as it sounds. He'll be so happy to see you." Daphne was already urging him up the steps with that firm hand on his arm, leaving Sybil behind in the foyer.

Seth and Daphne hit a landing that split into two directions. To the right, a short hallway led to what looked to be a bedroom, and straight ahead was a much longer hallway, with doors on either side, in the middle of which a ladder hung from the ceiling.

Seth stopped in place, and Daphne gave him a not-so-subtle push. Seth turned, raising his brows. "Just so you know, I *do* have people who'll miss me if I disappear."

Daphne broke into a peal of delighted laughter, like he'd just told a wonderful joke. "Of course you do! You're too lovely not to. Go on."

Seth secured his tote bag on his shoulder and climbed the ladder, trying not to feel like he was offering himself up as some sort of human sacrifice.

But his anxiety melted away as soon as he crested the top of the ladder, climbing less gracefully than he'd like onto his feet on the attic floor.

Because *Riley* was there, waiting for him. And he wasn't limp and broken on the floor but standing tall and upright.

Upright and whole and breathing.

He'd changed out of the wet clothes Seth had last seen him in, and he was wearing ripped jeans and a faded tee. He looked so young and handsome and *alive.*

Riley stared back at Seth with a heartbreaking expression on his face, somehow stubborn and expectant and hopeless all at once.

He was clearly bracing himself to be met with anger or derision or fear, and that was just—just *wrong*.

Before Seth knew it, he was across the attic, flinging himself into Riley's arms, wrapping his arms around him and not caring one bit that Riley didn't hold him back yet.

"You scared me," Seth said, the words muffled as he mumbled them into Riley's neck. "God, Riley, you scared me so bad."

12

RILEY

Riley didn't know what to do with his hands.

Seth was holding him. Holding Riley. And not just holding him but holding him *tightly*, squeezing him with all his meager human strength while he pressed his warm face into Riley's neck, his breath hot against Riley's skin.

Riley was so surrounded by the scent of buttery orange perfection he barely dared to breathe.

He'd scared Seth. Scared him badly.

Riley had known that already, of course, but the way Seth was saying it, it didn't sound like he'd been scared *of* Riley. It sounded like he'd been scared *for* Riley. Like maybe Seth had been worried for him. Like he was worried for him even *now*, and maybe that was why he was holding Riley so perfectly tightly.

Slowly—so slowly and oh so carefully—Riley lifted his arms and wrapped them around Seth's back. He held them there as loosely as he could bring himself to, so that Seth could still get away if he wanted.

Seth didn't seem to want to get away though. If anything, he held Riley even tighter, his arms constricting around Riley's neck. Then, with a deep sigh, he lifted his head from Riley's shoulder and grabbed Riley's face with both hands, his gaze searing into Riley like fire.

"You should have *told* me."

And then he was kissing Riley.

It wasn't like before, when Seth had given in and taught Riley how to kiss someone properly. Because back then, even when Seth had been moaning, letting Riley crawl over him on the couch and grind against him with shared enthusiasm, there had been a barrier between them. Seth had been holding part of himself back, and Riley had known it, even if he hadn't wanted to.

But here and now, Seth wasn't kissing Riley like he was instructing someone. He was kissing Riley like he needed to. Like maybe the want in him burned almost as brightly as the fierce desire Riley had been living with these past weeks.

Wouldn't that be something? To be wanted with even a fraction of the intensity Riley felt for his mate? He couldn't think of anything better.

Riley accepted Seth's kiss eagerly, even if he didn't know exactly what Seth had meant. Riley wasn't sure what it was he should have told Seth. That he was a vampire? That Seth was his mate? That he craved the taste of Seth's blood like an ordinary human craved water in the desert?

He didn't know how much Seth knew, and—as Riley opened his mouth, crushing Seth tightly against him, their tongues battling for dominance—it didn't much matter.

Not when Seth was here, in Riley's arms, kissing Riley like he was trying to steal Riley's very breath out of his lungs.

Seth wasn't scared of Riley. He wasn't even angry with him. Or if he *was* angry, he was taking it out on Riley's mouth, chastising him with tongue and teeth and bruising lips.

That was fine. Riley took his punishment willingly. He welcomed it even, hardening instantly, the blood rushing to his dick so fast it made him dizzy.

Seth was wearing another pair of those soft pants he liked, and Riley could feel that he was hard too, his cock pressing urgently against Riley's hip.

And that was the last straw, wasn't it? Riley had been restrained for too long, and he was being offered everything he wanted, and he couldn't pretend not to want it anymore.

"Can—" Riley asked when Seth paused to take a gasping breath. "Can I touch you, Seth? Please?"

"Yes," Seth answered into Riley's mouth, frantically shuffling off a tote bag Riley hadn't realized he'd been carrying and dropping it on the ground. "Yes. Fuck, yes. Touch me."

Seth grabbed Riley's hand from around his back and guided it beneath his waistband. It made Riley's lower belly clench hotly, the way Seth showed him exactly what he wanted.

Seth didn't stop until Riley's hand was around his cock.

It was burning hot to the touch, already leaking precum from the tip, the skin so silky smooth Riley ached to lave it with his tongue.

Seth gasped as Riley wrapped his fingers around it. Then he gripped Riley's wrist, urging him to move. He was still kissing Riley, still pressed so close to him that Riley could barely get enough space between them to stroke him off.

Riley had thought there was nothing better than kissing Seth, but kissing Seth while gripping his cock, stroking it roughly, finding out exactly what angle and pressure made him whimper into Riley's mouth? That was a level of heat and desire beyond Riley's previous comprehension. And it was still only hands and clumsy fumbling.

If Seth ever let Riley fuck him, Riley would probably burst into flames on the spot.

As Riley jerked Seth off with full enthusiasm and zero skill, Seth still had one hand on Riley's wrist, no longer guiding but gripping. The other hand was fisted in Riley's shirt, Seth's fingers pressed hard against Riley's chest. He kept breaking the kiss to pant and moan against Riley's lips, and he was so perfect and so beautiful that Riley wanted to drop to his knees and worship him.

So he did.

"Oh! Oh fuck," Seth gasped.

Riley tugged at Seth's waistband as he went, drawing those soft pants and underwear down to the tops of Seth's thighs. What followed couldn't be called a blow job by any means—Riley was too scattered and hungry and clumsy for that. Instead, he stroked Seth while mouthing and tonguing at whatever skin he could get to. Licking around his own fingers, nuzzling into Seth's groin, planting openmouthed kisses to the soft skin at Seth's hips.

But whatever it was Riley was doing, Seth seemed to like it. His buttery orange scent grew so sweet and heavy Riley could taste it on the air. His cock pressed painfully against his zipper. He wanted to free it. He couldn't let go long enough to do so.

Seth now had one hand on Riley's shoulder and one in Riley's hair, and he was gazing down at Riley with heavy-lidded eyes. "Oh my God," he moaned when Riley stared back up at him, his fist squeezing the length of Seth's cock while he mouthed hungrily at the base.

Seth's hips bucked, and he bit into his lower lip so deeply it looked painful. "Oh *fuckkk.*"

Riley moved his hand faster, in the way he liked when he was close to coming. He widened his legs, trying to relieve some of that aching pressure. He knew his touch was rough, the precum only easing the glide so much, but Seth didn't seem to mind.

He especially didn't seem to mind when Riley let his thumb pass over the head of his cock, teasing it with every pass of his fist.

Riley could hear the way Seth's heart was racing wildly, could practically taste the blood rushing through the pretty blue veins just under his skin.

And right at the crest—when Seth's dick grew impossibly harder, twitching and pulsing in a way that let Riley know Seth was going to lose it soon—Riley's fangs dropped.

It happened naturally, easily, and he barely noticed the change, too focused on the feel of Seth in his hand, the smell of his mate invading his senses.

It was as easy as pressing a kiss to Seth's skin, the way Riley's teeth sank into Seth's upper thigh. Coppery, orange-tinged blood filled Riley's mouth, and he groaned around the flesh between his teeth.

Seth's cry of pleasure was a far-off sound, secondary to the blood rushing in Riley's ears, the feeling of falling away somewhere deep inside himself.

Riley felt the wet heat of Seth's cum spurting over his hand, and then he was gone.

Copper. Orange.

Sweet. Salty. Rich.

Delicious.

This was what they'd waited for. *This* was what they'd been denied over and over again.

For too long they'd been subjected to puny woodland creatures and plastic bags of stale, refrigerated garbage. But no more.

There were hands in their hair, tugging and lifting. They allowed it, their tongue drifting over their lips to catch stray drops of liquid perfection.

They met his stare. Light brown. Flecks of green. Or was it vice versa?

"Oh." Their mate's eyes widened, his reddened lips parting in surprise. His grip on their hair loosened. "*Oh*. Riley?"

Yes. No. All of the above.

They said nothing. They made no gesture.

Their mate tried again. "Riley? Can you, um, hear me in there?"

They fought against that gentle hold then, long enough to dive back down and tongue at broken, bleeding skin, growling at the flavor as their saliva healed their bite marks.

They were left with a patch of perfect, unblemished skin. A shame. But there would be more bites. More marks. More opportunities to claim.

They wouldn't be denied any longer. They'd had enough of so-called higher human reason.

The fingers in their hair tightened again, and they let themselves be tugged back. On their knees, gazing upward.

Their mate's eyes were no longer wide but narrowed. At them. "I'm not so sure I should let you do that."

Ridiculous words. *Let. Should.* They were beyond such meaningless tripe. Their lips curled into a sneer.

Need. Must. That would have been more like it.

They had more of their mate's essence—of a different variety—covering their fingers. They busied themselves lapping it up. Salty and bitter and perfect.

The tugging in their hair increased in strength. "Up," their mate commanded.

They stood, and while they were up there, they captured that pretty red mouth again, because it was bruised and inviting, and they wanted to share the taste they'd stolen with their beautiful mate.

He should know just how delicious he was.

Their mate sighed into the kiss. Then he stiffened, pulling

back and ignoring their warning growl. He glanced down, frowning. "You're still hard."

Of course they were, with their mate so close, smelling of musk and salt and coppery orange. They growled again, pressing in closer, rubbing against his slender form.

They needed to merge with him, body and soul. They needed to drain him into ecstasy, and then offer their own lifeblood in return. They needed to stretch him around their cock again and again, until he knew the perfect, hedonistic joy of being worshipped by one of their kind.

They needed to bind him. Mate him. Claim him.

"I think you should give Riley back to me now."

They frowned. Let another warning rumble leave their throat. This body was *theirs*. Too long it had been ill-fitting and unnatural and starved. No one had let them fix it. No one had let them give it what it needed.

Their mate stroked down their arms with steady hands, soothing the savage beast as he gentled his tone. "You see, I want to give Riley another first, and I want him to be here for it. Present. Aware."

They cocked their head, considering.

After a moment, their mate's hand drifted down, cupping their cock through the constricting denim.

He squeezed. They groaned.

"I want to touch him now," their mate whispered. "If you give him back to me..." He squeezed again. "Will you be able to feel it?"

They rumbled an affirmative. They would feel it. And they wanted that. A mate's eager hands. Perhaps even a mate's eager mouth.

But first.

They pulled their mate off the ground with one arm, cupping the back of his head with the other hand. They claimed his mouth again, and he opened for them, eager and wet and wanting, accepting their lips and tongue with perfect submission.

Good. *Good.*

They sucked and stroked and nibbled. A reminder as much as a claim. That it was all of them together. Not just Riley but also the yes, no, and all of the above.

When they separated from him, their mate was flushed and panting again, no longer spouting nonsense words of "go away" and "bring him back."

That was better. That was as it should be.

They kissed him again, hard and merciless.

Then they allowed young Riley back to the surface.

13

SETH

Seth couldn't believe it worked.

It was so strange too, watching the all-consuming black receding from Riley's eyes until the deep-brown color returned.

Riley's brow furrowed. He looked shaken and more than a little dazed. "W-What? Did I—?"

"Shhh, baby, it's okay," Seth soothed, stroking back a lock of Riley's dark hair. "Come here."

Seth kissed him, for lack of any better ideas. And because he wanted to, and today seemed to be a day for giving in to the things he wanted.

Riley no longer tasted like blood and cum. His vampire self had kissed Seth too thoroughly for anything to remain but Riley's natural taste, something sweet and a little spicy.

Riley sucked in a harsh breath as Seth cupped him again through his worn jeans. "I want to make you feel good," Seth murmured, pressing an openmouthed kiss to Riley's chin. "Is that okay?"

It was what Seth had been planning to do before the...interruption.

Seth still didn't know exactly what had happened. In the moment, he'd barely registered the significance of the bite. He'd been too lost in pleasure and the decadent sight of Riley on his knees, acting like he was so desperate for Seth's cock that he could hardly see straight.

Seth had already been on the verge of coming, and then Riley had bitten him. And that bite had been like a shot of electricity straight to Seth's dick. There hadn't been much room for thought or fear or any reasonable reaction. The resulting orgasm had been too overwhelming, something beyond what a fumbled hand job with a little tongue action should have warranted.

By the time Seth had come back to himself—shuddering through the aftershocks and trying to catch his breath—Riley had been fully drinking from his thigh, all greedy gulps and deeply satisfied growls.

It hadn't been hard to stop him, was the thing. All it had taken was a gentle tug to his hair, and Riley had come off easily.

But it hadn't been Riley staring back at Seth. And it hadn't been the fangs and the black eyes that had keyed Seth into the change. It had been a...difference in Riley's presence. Like a shift in the air around them, something subtle but distinct.

When Seth and Sascha had talked on the phone, Sascha had been vague about what happened when someone was turned into a vampire. He definitely hadn't said anything about an entirely different entity taking over when they fed. But that was what it had felt like in this moment, so Seth had acted accordingly. He'd asked for Riley to be returned to him like that was a reasonable thing to request, and the creature wearing Riley's face had agreed.

Seth should probably stop and take a breath—he'd just been bitten by a vampire, for fuck's sake, one who seemed to have a split personality—but he couldn't do it. He wanted to give Riley something. Something good. He wanted to make him feel even half the pleasure Seth had felt from Riley's kiss and his touch and yes, even his bite.

Or—fuck it—maybe Seth just wanted to touch Riley's dick. He wasn't above admitting as much.

Riley groaned, dropping his forehead to Seth's shoulder. "Fuck. Yes. Of course it's okay. I want it. I want everything."

Everything was a lot to consider and too much to process with a million different thoughts battling for dominion in Seth's brain. But thinking could wait.

Right now, Seth wanted to feel. He wanted *Riley* to feel.

For one brief, terrifying moment, Seth had thought he'd lost him, this strange, captivating friend of his. A friend who'd gotten under his skin in barely any time at all. A friend who Seth already didn't think he could bear to lose.

And maybe sex wasn't the best way to come to terms with that, but it was the way Seth's body and soul were demanding.

Seth hastily scanned the attic. He hadn't been paying attention when he'd arrived—too distracted by the sight of Riley upright and none the worse for wear—but there was a massive armchair by the window, low to the ground and perfect for Seth's purposes.

He steered Riley backward in that direction with one hand on his broad chest, working to unbutton Riley's jeans at the same time. Seth pushed Riley down into the chair, and he went easily, his gaze locked onto Seth's face, something akin to pure devotion in his dark eyes.

Not for the first time, Riley was looking at Seth like he was something precious. Something...beautiful.

His vampire self had looked at Seth differently. He'd gazed at Seth with an almost haughty sort of possessiveness.

The naked hunger, though, *that* expression both sides of Riley seemed to have in common. And it was fucking heady to see.

Seth knelt in front of Riley, rubbing his hands over Riley's denim-clad knees. "I want to suck you," he told him, his voice hoarse and way too raw. "Does that still sound okay?"

In answer, Riley threw his head back and groaned.

Was that a no? Riley's dick certainly seemed on board, tenting through his open jeans in a decidedly distracting way. But maybe it was too much too soon.

Seth waited him out, and after a moment, Riley tilted his chin down, somehow managing to peer at Seth from under his thick lashes despite their height difference.

"I'm going to embarrass myself."

"How?" Seth asked.

"I'm going to come in, like, two seconds."

"Oh." Seth grinned, giving Riley's knees a squeeze. "That's not embarrassing. That's hot."

Riley gave him a dubious look. Seth beckoned to him. "C'mere."

Riley leaned forward obediently, and Seth kissed him. Thoroughly. Leisurely. A dance of tongues and sighs and the scent of forest all around them.

When some of the tension in Riley's frame finally relaxed, Seth broke the kiss, murmuring, "It's a compliment, that I can turn you on like that. Do you want me to swallow?"

Seth's hands were still on Riley's knees, so he could feel the full-body tremor that ran through him at the question.

God, it really was a sort of compliment. Even more than that. It was like a shot of pure adrenaline, the reactions Seth got from this beautiful man.

He'd told himself he needed to be careful with this one, right? He probably should have heeded his own warning.

Seth tugged at Riley's jeans. "I'm going to take these off now."

Riley nodded, lifting his hips to aid Seth in undressing him. In no time at all, Riley was left in only his T-shirt. He should have looked fucking silly, sitting there naked except for his shirt, but of course he didn't. Not at all. He was still a wet dream come to life, his dark hair in disarray from all Seth's tugging and petting, his full, heavy, uncut cock standing at attention from a thatch of dark curls.

Seth shifted closer, settling in between Riley's spread legs. "Relax and let yourself feel good, okay? It doesn't matter how fast you come. I'm going to enjoy it either way."

Fuck yes, he was.

Seth wrapped his fingers around Riley's length. God, he felt nice in Seth's hand. Thick and hot and gorgeous, just like the rest of him. Seth's mouth was literally watering, every essence of his being craving a taste.

Keenly aware of Riley's gaze searing into him, Seth lowered his head, mouthing at the fat tip. Bitter salt exploded on his tongue as Riley's legs trembled with tension.

Seth ran a soothing hand along Riley's thigh as he sucked in more of the head, swirling his tongue to get at every bit of flavor. He couldn't help his own moan.

"Mmm."

There was a desperate, mumbled, "*Fuck*," from above him. Seth ignored it.

He slid his hand down to the base of Riley's cock. Seth wasn't any sort of deep-throat champion, and Riley was long—some hand action was going to be helpful here. Seth squeezed, stroking his thumb along the underside as he took more of Riley in his mouth.

The stretch of his lips felt good, as did the weight on Seth's tongue. Riley's natural musk mixed with his earthy forest scent, and Seth felt almost dizzy with the heady combination. He sucked, moaning again.

Riley kept cursing. "Oh fuck. Fucking God. *Fuck*, that's—that's—"

Seth smiled around his mouthful. His taciturn friend was a rambler when he was getting his dick sucked. Cute.

But Seth wasn't going to let a little cuteness distract him. He focused on his task, sliding his lips down until they met his fist. He sucked. Moaned. Sucked some more. Saliva was dripping over his fingers, and Riley kept mumbling and ranting and swearing.

Seth didn't know what Riley had been talking about—he was lasting just fine. What would he do if Seth fished out his own cock and tried to come a second time? This was supposed to be about Riley, but it was doing something to Seth, the feel and the taste of Riley's cock in his mouth, his friend's tortured, frantic mumblings. Seth wanted to stroke himself. Or maybe rut against Riley's leg. *Something.*

And then there were hands in Seth's hair, gripping his curls tightly. He raised his gaze. Riley's face was the picture of pleasured agony. His sharp jaw was clenched, his beautiful dark eyes heavy-lidded. And the way he was looking at Seth...

Seth let his mouth go slack, prepared to let Riley slam his cock down his throat. He definitely had that look in his eye. Seth would probably choke and gag, but oh well. That could be hot sometimes.

But Riley didn't try to fuck Seth's face. He only stared, his body visibly trembling now. Slowly, he started tracing the seam of Seth's lips with his thumb.

Seth opened his mouth wider, letting Riley's thumb dip in next to his cock. Seth was drooling everywhere, but it was hard to care. He closed his mouth as best he could and sucked Riley's thumb in. There was barely room with the rest of his mouthful.

Riley stared, breathing heavily. He withdrew his thumb and pressed a hand over his face. "Fuck. I'm gonna—" Seth hollowed his cheeks, sucking harder, and Riley shuddered. "Gonna come."

Yes. *Yes*. Seth wanted that. He wanted hot cum in his mouth, and he wanted to swallow every bit of it.

Seth bobbed over Riley's cock, fisting the base as he went. Riley thickened in his mouth—"*Fucking fuck*!"—and then exploded over Seth's tongue. He made desperate, strangled noises as he pumped down Seth's throat, his hips lifting in the air.

Seth was fully hard again, his dick aching like he hadn't just emptied it into Riley's hand barely ten minutes ago.

He couldn't help it. Riley's reactions were just so raw, so unpracticed and sincere. And he really, *really* seemed to like Seth's mouth. It wasn't like Seth was some blow job master, and the appreciation was flattering as all hell.

Seth swallowed and sucked and finally let Riley slip from his lips when Riley's shuddering curses turned pained.

Seth rested his head on Riley's bare thigh, pressing a hand to his own erection, trying to ease the ache. The world around him took on a dreamy cast. He was lightheaded, even though he'd been careful not to lose his breath. Maybe it was the blood loss.

Riley's other thigh was directly in Seth's line of vision. There was an artery there, Seth was pretty sure. That was where Riley had bitten him, wasn't it?

Would he do it again?

Sascha hadn't warned Seth that a vampire's bite was like a mini orgasm, a shot of pure pleasure that went straight to someone's dick. Maybe he didn't know. Or maybe Seth's reaction was abnormal. Maybe he had a rare "vampire bites make me come" gene. Maybe he should be studied by scientists.

Gentle hands carded through Seth's hair, and he hummed his approval.

"I bit you, didn't I?" Riley asked, soft but clear, as his fingers teased through Seth's strands. "I drank your blood."

There was something in his tone that warned Seth to be

cautious. Some self-recrimination that Seth didn't quite understand.

Wasn't biting people what vampires *did*? And Riley had stopped when Seth had wordlessly asked him to. The experience hadn't been scary. It had been...exhilarating.

But something about how Riley asked the question made Seth think he wouldn't see it that way. And Seth was too cum-drunk to mince words.

He sighed, his breath puffing along the coarse dark hair on Riley's thigh. "I made you cookies."

"Seth..."

Seth raised his head, meeting his friend's concerned gaze. Riley was going to get wrinkles, with the way he kept furrowing that poor brow. Except vampires probably didn't get wrinkles. "Eat some cookies, Riley. Then we'll talk."

14

SETH

Seth somehow found himself curled up in Riley's lap, feeding him cookies by hand.

He hadn't meant to end up sprawled over Riley's thighs. He really hadn't. He'd *meant* to reestablish a bit of distance, but after they'd redressed and straightened themselves up, Riley had tugged on Seth's arm until he'd toppled over on top of him, and that had kind of been that.

And here Seth had been hoping to remind them both that—despite Seth jumping Riley's bones the second he'd walked through the door—they were *friends.*

Friends with an almost absurd degree of sexual attraction, yes, but friends nonetheless.

Because—and Seth was going to remind himself of this every other second if need be—Riley had a mate out there somewhere. And Seth might have had his faults, but he wasn't stupid enough to give his heart away to someone who straight up cosmically did not have a place for it.

That was what he was telling himself, at least, but the strength of his argument might have been sabotaged a little by the way he was cuddled so cozily into Riley's chest on this massive armchair, slipping orange meltaways into Riley's waiting mouth.

Practically all the cookies Seth had made were already devoured, and he'd made a double batch. This vampire could *eat*. It was very satisfying to watch. In a professional baker sense, of course.

After offering Riley the last meltaway—like, really, where did he *put* them?—Seth cleared his throat, dusting his fingers off on his jeans.

For all that he'd pulled Seth onto his lap like someone with a claim on him, Riley had been shooting narrow-eyed, sideways glances Seth's way, even as he chewed. He was basically acting like *Seth* was the shady one in this friendship.

Maybe refusing to let him speak right away had set his hackles up.

Whatever. Seth would begin, to make sure everything started off on the right foot.

He straightened just enough to get a clear look at Riley's face. Seth might even have tried sitting to the side of Riley's lap, but Riley's iron hold on him wouldn't let Seth go any further than the scant inches he'd already claimed.

No matter. Seth started with the obvious. "So you can eat human food."

Riley didn't answer, only finished chewing and swallowing his last cookie in a way that seemed decidedly pointed.

Seth pressed on. "Does it fill you up? Like, you aren't hungry anymore after eating it?"

Riley licked a bit of powdered sugar off his lips. "It can take the edge off, but no. I need blood." His gaze darted to Seth's thigh, then back up again.

Seth took a dry swallow. "Because you're a vampire."

It seemed necessary to say it out loud, at least once. Maybe Riley would laugh and ask Seth what drugs he'd been taking and Seth would realize he'd been wrong about everything.

But Riley didn't laugh.

"My moms told you," Riley said instead, his tone almost petulant.

"They hinted. I figured it out." Seth straightened his spine a little more. "You're not the first supernatural of my acquaintance, you know." Seth didn't mention he hadn't *known* his other acquaintances were supernatural until today. There was no reason to reveal all his cards at once. "And how old are you really?"

Riley frowned at him. "Nineteen."

Seth scoffed. "Riley."

"What?"

"Don't make me say it. It's embarrassing."

Riley's frown deepened. "Say what?"

Oh God. Seth was gonna have to do it. Riley was forcing his hand. Seth steeled himself. "Riley. How long have you *been* nineteen?"

Riley looked no less confused, but he shrugged. "Like a few months? My birthday's the end of October."

Right. Well. Seth ignored the new warmth in his face. So Riley was still too young—that wasn't the point of this conversation. "Were you born a vampire, then?"

"No. That's not a thing."

Seth gazed at him expectantly. Riley sighed, taking the empty Tupperware out of Seth's hand and placing it on the attic floor. He tucked Seth closer to his chest, denying Seth his hard-won view of Riley's face. "It's a whole story. Are you sure you want to hear?"

Seth rolled his eyes. "Oh, well, if it's a whole *story*," he drawled. "Jesus, Riley, of course I want to hear."

Riley ignored his sass. Instead, he tucked his chin over the top of Seth's head, as if maybe he needed the extra comfort. "I was turned when I was a kid."

Seth's breath caught. Riley had been changed into a vampire when he was still a *child*? Seth couldn't imagine. He really couldn't. "Your...moms?" he asked.

"No," Riley told him fiercely. "*No*. They would never. It was some drifter vampire, trying to give his estranged wife the so-called gift of a child. I wasn't the first he took, but I was the most... successful."

"What do you mean?" Seth asked, forcing the words through the new lump in his throat.

"It isn't done, turning kids," Riley explained. "It just doesn't... work well. We get too hungry and rampage, have to be put down to keep the secrecy. Or we won't feed right and starve, which usually also ends in a rampage. And there's, like, a presence, when you're turned. The vampire part waking up or something. And from what I know, you're usually pretty entwined. But me and my voice, we're...separate. We're all wrong. Abnormal."

Seth thought of the presence he'd seen, looking into Riley's black eyes. The Not-Riley of it all. He hadn't been sure if he'd been correct in categorizing it as some separate entity, but apparently he'd been spot-on.

His chest ached. Poor Riley.

"I ran from him, the vampire who turned me," Riley told him. "Twice. The first time... Well, he got me back eventually, and then the second time, other vampires found me. They took me in before I could hurt anyone and fed me blood bags, called two vampire women they knew who wanted kids of their own. My moms adopted me, and we moved here, where there are lots of elk and not too many people. I can feed on animals *and* humans. Most vampires can't. My moms kept me full. Kept me safe."

Riley told Seth more then. About being stuck here in this house, in these woods, for the remainder of his childhood, afraid to so much as spot a human. About growth spurts where he'd felt like a monster, so hungry he was afraid he'd eat the world. About his first trips into town this past year, the thrill and the fear and the hope that he might be able to act somewhat normal.

There was so much to take in, so much to feel. The *life* Riley had lived. Taken from his family. Taken from his humanity.

"So you *actually* wanted to eat me that first night," Seth eventually joked, because everything else felt too big to say out loud. "Like I was some sort of...strawberry tart."

"Orange cake," Riley corrected.

He really seemed to have a thing for orange.

"I met your vampire," Seth told him. "Just now."

"I know." Riley didn't sound happy about it.

"Were you there? Watching from inside?"

"Not really. That's part of what's wrong with me, I guess. When I change...*it* takes over. Sometimes I have flashes of awareness. Sometimes I can't remember at all. It's not supposed to be that way." Riley's voice roughened. "And it's not fair, because I can hear *it* when I'm me. It's always here. I've spent my whole life since the day I turned trying to live with it, its hunger and its rage. It's not the sort of presence that should be in a child's mind. It—it *changed* me. Ruined me. I don't know who I am without it anymore, and sometimes I hate that so much it burns me up from the inside out."

There was so much anger in his words. A deep, unrelenting bitterness. And it broke Seth's heart because he didn't think Riley was a bitter person by nature.

But maybe no one was. Maybe people simply reached the limit of what they could tolerate from what life gave them. Maybe Riley had reached his limit a long time ago.

"I don't know who you are without it either," Seth said softly. Carefully. "But I know who you are now. And I like that person a lot."

The words felt insufficient, but there were...*things* happening inside Seth, and he didn't know how to say anything better. His fondness for Riley and their magnetic attraction and this new way of seeing him were all melting together into something dangerous.

Seth was in awe of Riley's strength. His endurance. No matter what Riley thought about himself being monstrous, the fact that he was still so much a *person* after everything that had happened to him—the kind of person that sat in Seth's bakery and told him bits of stories to make him laugh, who stared like a kid with a crush and flirted terribly and spoke so carefully...

It was a testament to Riley's humanity, to the boy inside him he'd maintained against all odds. Seth wished Riley could see it that way.

Riley held Seth tighter. "God, Seth, I—" He let out a harsh breath. "Thank you for saying that."

Seth had to ask, no matter how painful the answer. "When you find your, um, mate, do you think that would help you and your... voice? Aren't mates supposed to, like, ground you?"

It was strange, the way Riley went so very still beneath Seth. There was a long pause before he spoke. Seth wished he could see his face.

"Someone told you about mates?"

"Yes."

"Did they tell you it's not just finding a mate?" Riley asked, an odd note to his voice. Maybe this was a touchy subject for vampires. Maybe Seth should have kept his mouth shut. "They have to be turned for the bond to take place."

"Oh." Seth let out an awkward laugh. "No, they didn't. Still... shouldn't you be looking for them, maybe?" Oops. So much for keeping his mouth shut. "Or...is that not how it works?"

Riley was silent for a long time, his soft puffs of breath rustling Seth's curls.

"Seth," he said eventually, his tone so even it was unreadable.

"Yes?"

"I've found my mate already."

"Oh." Seth didn't know how to catalog the ache that stabbed in his chest. Maybe it was sympathy heartburn for all the cookies Riley had eaten. "In—in town? Who?"

He waited, but Riley didn't answer except to let out a strange, huffing laugh. Then he released his hold on Seth, his hands drifting to rest gently on Seth's hips. He leaned back, allowing Seth to meet his gaze. And there was a...look there, in those dark eyes. Like Seth was being dense. Like Seth was...

Oh. *Oh.*

Seth fought the strange urge to break into hysterical laughter. He wasn't— No. No, no, no. He swallowed. Coughed. Swallowed again. "But how—how do you know?"

"I know."

The way Riley said it was so definite. Like there was no room for argument or doubt.

But there had to be room for doubt because *Seth* doubted. Seth doubted very, very much.

Jesus. His palms had gone sweaty in an instant. When had the attic gotten so sweltering? They should put a fan in here. Two fans. Twenty fans.

Seth scrambled to his feet, wiping his sweaty palms on his pants as he backed away from the armchair. "Well, I should get going," he said brightly. Possibly too brightly. His tone might have been bordering on unhinged. "I wanted to make sure you're okay. And I have. And that's great. So I'll just—"

"Seth."

Seth grabbed his tote bag off the floor, almost falling on his face before he righted himself. "I go to bed really early every night, you know. And it's already dark out. I'm miserable without sleep. You have no idea. Why would you? We've never slept together."

Riley was starting to rise from the chair, each movement

abnormally slow and exaggerated, like Seth was some wild animal he was trying not to startle. But Seth had already made his way to the ladder, and before Riley could take a step, he was scurrying down it faster than was probably wise.

He knew this wasn't his best moment, even as it was happening. Panicked retreat was never a good look. But Seth's brain was rioting. *Rioting.*

It was just...too much. He'd just found out vampires existed, for fuck's sake. And now he was destined to be one? To be *mated* to one? According to some hot nineteen-year-old semirecluse?

Too much. Too. Much.

Seth needed to be at home, under a pile of blankets, with a hot tea and something terrible on the TV. He needed a moment of normalcy where no one's neck had been recently snapped and no precious childhoods had been stolen by roaming monsters.

Poor Riley. Poor fucking Riley. All that trauma, and the fates had given him *Seth*? It didn't make any sense. Seth wasn't special. He was normal, maybe even on the verge of boring as he got older.

How was *he* supposed to be the consolation prize?

Seth hurried down the hallway, a palpably forlorn Riley following behind him. Down the stairs they went. Somehow, despite how slowly Riley was moving, he was always only a step behind. Those were some horror-movie-level stalking skills he had.

Seth held his breath as he walked through the front door, half-afraid the house might somehow decide to keep him in its clutches. But it didn't. He made it.

He exhaled sharply when he was safely in the fresh air. Riley finally stopped in the doorway.

"Come by the bakery when you're feeling better," Seth found himself saying, as if Riley was recovering from a cold and not having been temporarily murdered. "I'll save you an orange scone."

He was down the porch steps before he could get a chance to see how devastated Riley looked. Or maybe Riley wasn't devastated at all. Maybe Seth was pulling off a very chill and very casual retreat after all, and it only *felt* like he was practically sprinting in the other direction.

Too much, too much, too much.

Seth threw himself into his unlocked car, shoved the key into the ignition, and turned it.

Nothing. Not even a sad engine whine.

Seth tried again. Had he forgotten how car keys worked in his abject panic?

But no. Nothing.

He tried again. And again. When he was still met with nothing, he slapped his palms against the steering wheel, too flustered to even wince with the sting. "Are you fucking *serious* right now?"

He sat there, panting heaving breaths, as two figures approached his dead-as-a-doornail car. One tall, one short. Both beautiful. Neither of them Riley.

The moms.

Seth climbed back out of his car with every scrap of dignity he could muster. Which was, frankly, not very many scraps.

Daphne's face was the perfect picture of sincere sympathy, Sybil's more of a blank mask behind her. Riley was nowhere to be seen.

"Engine troubles, darling Seth?" Daphne asked.

They had to know. About him. About Riley. About...them. Riley and his moms were a close trio, and if Seth had felt capable of reflecting back on things, he was sure he'd find that Riley hadn't been subtle.

Still. The engine not responding could be coincidence. Batteries died all the time. "Could I—" Seth cleared his dry throat. "Could I ask for a jump?"

Now Daphne's face transformed into the perfect picture of

regret, her pretty brow furrowing. "I'm afraid we don't have the proper cables."

Seth narrowed his eyes. "I do."

"Do you?" Sybil asked mildly.

He did. He was sure he did. Seth took jerky steps over to the trunk of his car. He shifted the various bric-a-brac, lifting the floor to where the cables lay beneath.

Except they weren't there. Of course they weren't. Seth wilted, his shoulders sagging.

"No luck?" Sybil called.

Seth took a breath, let it out. He shut his trunk with a grimace. He reminded himself that accidents happened, and that things got lost, and that he needed to be polite to the bloodthirsty beauties. "Could I ask for a ride home?"

"Oh, we never drive at night," Daphne told him.

The statement was so absurd it took several long seconds to penetrate Seth's brain. "I'm sorry?"

She waved a hand toward the trees. "The elk are so unpredictable, you know. We'd hate to hit one by accident."

"You're *vampires*." The words escaped Seth's mouth through clenched teeth.

"But the elk needn't suffer for it."

Seth now had clenched fists to add to his clenched teeth. "Am I — Am I being *kidnapped*?"

Daphne's eyes widened in a very neat approximation of shock. "Why, darling, of course not. But we can't very well let you walk all by your lonesome."

Walking hadn't even occurred to Seth. He looked around at the vast forest surrounding him. It had to be—what—eight miles, at least, if he followed the road? It would be a long walk home, and possibly a wet one, if the clouds did what they seemed to be threatening to do. And it was freezing, and Seth was dressed for car-to-house travel, not a forest hike.

He could call someone to get him—he had Violet's number now—but what kind of friend would he be if he lured a teenage girl out to a vampire den just to save himself some inconvenience? He mostly trusted these people, but Riley's moms were clearly protective of their son, and Seth didn't know how far they'd go with a stranger.

"We'll of course compensate you for any days of business you might lose," Sybil said coolly.

"*Days*?" Seth yelped, any approximation of chill fleeing his body. "Plural?"

"We'll try to get a mechanic out here as soon as possible, but —" Sybil shrugged, a gleam in her eyes Seth didn't care for at all. "We're so very isolated."

Of course, of course. They *were* isolated. Isolated and diabolical. And Seth was stuck here, at the mercy of his supposed mate and his supposed mate's meddling mothers.

Seth tried his best to get his voice back to a normal human register. He knew he'd been bordering on shrill. "Whether my car is working or not," he said slowly, "I would like a ride home first thing in the morning." He'd figure out how to get his car home later, when he wasn't in the midst of an existential crisis. "You know. Once the elk are no longer of such...concern."

He didn't sound like himself, but he didn't feel like himself either. He felt like a character in a play, only he didn't know any of his lines and the director was raging on ketamine.

Daphne clapped her hands in delight. "We have a lovely guest room."

She wrapped her arm around his, and Seth let himself be escorted back up to the beautiful house with a vampire mother on each side of him.

15

RILEY

Riley sat at the kitchen table, listening to the whisper-yells and the thumps of what sounded to be pillows flying.

"I've never heard him swear so much," he murmured.

Riley almost wanted to laugh—the thought of his sunny, cheery Seth driven to such rage that he was cursing like a sailor—but it wasn't funny, was it?

Riley had fucked up. Again.

He hadn't even realized he was doing it at the time. He'd maybe had the vague thought that it was too soon, but also Seth had been handling it all so well—the existence of vampires, Riley's sorry story. Seth had listened, and he'd comforted, and he'd said perfect things.

I don't know who you are without it either. But I know who you are now. And I like that person a lot.

And Riley just...hadn't had it in him to lie. Not after the events of the evening: Seth throwing himself into Riley's arms, letting

Riley touch him, accepting Riley's bite and then turning around and wrapping his perfect lips and hot mouth around Riley's aching cock.

What had Riley been supposed to do in the face of that? Pretend there was someone else out there for him?

He hadn't expected the mate part to be the final straw in breaking his sweet Seth.

Was it really so bad, being stuck with Riley?

A cup of tea appeared in front of Riley's clasped hands. It was one of his favorite cups, even, a delicate china number with pale-blue cornflowers.

"I don't deserve pretty cups," Riley said, scowling down at it.

"Whyever not?" Mama Sybil asked. "It wasn't you who hid the jumper cables."

No, it wasn't. And his moms weren't telling him where they were either. Which was extra thoughtful of them because Riley wasn't certain he would have given them back to Seth if he *did* know, and it was nice not to have to face that side of himself so soon.

Riley could pretend. They could all pretend.

It wasn't like he was falling over himself to give Seth a ride. He wasn't sure if Seth would have accepted one from him, anyway. Because then Seth might have to look at him, and he seemed determined not to do that right now. Even on the way back inside the house, he'd stormed past Riley in the entryway without a glance, silent and fuming as Mama Daphne had led him upstairs to one of their guest rooms.

"I bit him," Riley told his moms. "Did you know that? The stupid voice took over and drank from his thigh while I was... blissed out."

That alone should have been the worst part, Riley losing control like that. But he was a terrible person because what really got to him was the fact that he couldn't remember. He'd finally tasted Seth, and he couldn't *remember* it.

Delicious, the voice taunted.

Get fucked, Riley replied.

"He seems none the worse for wear," Mama Daphne said. She actually sounded sort of proud, which was so incredibly off base Riley couldn't handle it.

There was a crash from above them. Maybe Seth had finally thrown something that wasn't a down pillow.

Riley lowered his head onto his clasped hands. "He's so angry."

"Well, we *are* keeping him against his will," Mama Daphne said cheerfully, placing two more teacups across from him on the table. "I supposed he's allowed his tantrums, isn't he?"

Well, when she put it *that* way.

Riley straightened. "I should take him home."

"I wouldn't advise it," Mama Sybil murmured, taking one of the seats across from him, pushing out the seat next to her for Mama Daphne. She gave Riley one of those *Mother knows best* looks. "Let's get it all out of the way at once."

It was a reasonable suggestion, except for the fact that Seth was angry at him and Riley hated it with every cell of his being. Riley frowned, toying with the handle of his teacup. "Why do you think he doesn't want to be my mate?"

He hated how childish the question sounded, hated the hurt he couldn't keep out of his voice. But really, things had been going so well until the M-bomb. It had to be the thought of being tethered to Riley that was sending Seth into a tailspin. Not the fangs. Not the bloodthirsty presence inside him.

Just...Riley.

Mama Sybil and Mama Daphne exchanged a look. "I think love is very frightening to those who've made comfortable lives in its absence," Mama Sybil finally said.

Riley's frown deepened as he stared at his moms. "Seth *is* loved."

"A different variety, I'm afraid, my darling," Mama Daphne said.

Riley narrowed his eyes as both his moms picked up their teacups in unison. "You two don't deserve pretty cups either," he told them.

Mama Daphne had the gall to look offended. "Riley! Why would you say such a thing?"

Riley pointed up at the ceiling. They could all hear Seth ranting something about elk now. He seemed to be holding a new grudge against the entire species.

The ranting was kind of cute, actually.

No. Riley shouldn't think that. He should be focused on wallowing in shame at his family holding his future mate hostage. Anything else would be glib, and Seth would have to punish him for it later.

Mama Sybil pursed her lips at the ceiling, then met Riley's accusing look. "He wants distance to rationalize and cast doubt. It's very human of him, and we won't hold it against him. But"—she shrugged genteelly—"there's also no need to help him achieve his aims."

Neither of them were the least bit sorry, were they?

Riley cast his own look up at the ceiling. "Should I—should I maybe bring him some tea?"

"That's a wonderful idea," Mama Daphne told him. She sounded proud again. There was another crash from up above, and she seamlessly added, "But perhaps let's wait another quarter hour."

"Cards?" Mama Sybil suggested as the ranting picked up again.

It was a full hour later when Riley finally knocked on the guest bedroom door. He was answered by a muffled, "Come in."

Riley stepped in, making sure to quickly close the door behind him. An open exit would only make it easier for Seth to shoo him out.

Seth was on the bed, lying on his back over the covers. He was holding a pillow over his face. Maybe that was the reason the noise had finally settled down—he was shouting all his viciousness into the down pillow.

"I brought you tea," Riley told him.

Seth lifted the pillow just enough to snipe, "Shouldn't it be water and a crust of stale bread?"

Riley fought a smile. He didn't like that Seth was angry with him, but it was kind of intriguing to be treated to the sharp edge of Seth's tongue. Riley hadn't seen this side of him before, and he had a feeling not many people had. Seth liked to comfort everyone around him—with baked goods, with easy cheer—and Riley was sure he usually kept his bad moods to himself. It was sort of an honor to be bearing the brunt of one now.

Riley peered around the room while he waited for Seth to further acknowledge his existence. He hadn't taken much notice of this current version of the guest room before. It was one of two, and Mama Daphne liked to redecorate them periodically. This rendition could easily be dubbed the Blue Room; there was clearly a theme.

The walls were painted a pale blue, the comforter a deeper, richer shade. The sheets were a blue so light they were almost white, and the paintings on the wall ran the gamut of the blue spectrum.

Riley wouldn't have thought the color suited Seth—Riley always pictured him in bright yellows and oranges—but it kind of worked. Like the sun surrounded by blue ocean.

There was no sign of anything out of place either. Whatever

Seth had thrown around in his anger, he'd put it back almost immediately.

He was so sweet, this human they'd tangled up in their lives. Riley should be drowning in guilt, not trying to weasel his way back into Seth's good graces.

But some things couldn't be helped. There was no world where Riley didn't want to be exactly where Seth was.

Seth lifted his pillow even higher in order to shoot Riley a glare. "I made a joke about being held prisoner."

"I know." Riley gave a helpless shrug, which might or might not have been convincing. "My moms can be…high-handed."

Seth treated him to an unimpressed look. "You don't say." But he lifted himself onto his hands, shuffling back until he was sitting up against the remaining pillows. He placed the pillow he'd been holding over his face onto his lap. "I'll take the tea now, thank you."

That was a quick turnaround. Like Seth's anger had only been a passing storm, and now it was all sunshine again.

Or maybe it was a trick.

Riley decided to risk it. He approached the bed carefully, handing Seth the cup of tea. Riley had added milk and sugar based on how Seth always took his coffee.

Seth stared down at the offering. "This is a really pretty cup."

"It's one of my favorites."

Seth paused in the middle of taking a sip. "Do you have a lot of tea parties out here by yourself in the woods?"

"Yes."

Seth closed his eyes and let out a sigh. He shook his head. "I refuse to be charmed."

That was heartening. Riley walked over to the other side of the bed and climbed on, taking a seat against the headboard next to Seth. He left a few inches of space because he was determined to be considerate of Seth's foul mood.

Apparently not considerate enough. Seth shot him a suspicious scowl. "What are you doing?"

Riley gave him a beseeching look. "There's nowhere else to sit."

"There's a chair right there," Seth countered, pointing to one carved out of dark wood over by the window.

"It's not very comfortable," Riley told him in a half-truth. The other half of it was that the chair didn't smell like Seth, and the bed did, in an intoxicating sort of way. All orange and buttery sweetness. Nothing in Riley's house had ever smelled this good. He wanted to roll around in it. Or roll on top of Seth and get right to the source.

Riley had a feeling the latter wouldn't be allowed just yet.

Seth finally took a sip of his tea, humming a little as he assessed the flavor. "I called you tricky once, didn't I?

"Yes."

"Accurate."

Riley smoothed the wrinkles in the comforter around him. "I wasn't trying to be tricky. I was trying to be...careful."

When Seth didn't start hurling profanities, Riley scooted a few inches closer, biting back a smile when Seth allowed it. Seth took another swallow of tea, and Riley did his best not to think of where those lips had been earlier. He had a feeling if Seth caught sight of the barest hint of an erection, the crazed ranting would begin again.

"You were being careful because I'm your mate," Seth said after a moment, his words clear and concise.

"Yes."

There was more silence as Seth sipped his tea. Eventually he spoke again, with more hesitancy this time. "The thing is, I don't really...*believe* in being destined for someone. I don't think love comes from an outside source like that. It doesn't feel real or—or truthful."

Riley twisted to meet Seth's serious gaze. "You don't have to believe it though."

Seth's green-brown eyes flashed. "Because it'll happen anyway?" he asked, his skepticism clear.

Riley tried to find the right words to express his thoughts. It was a struggle at first because the stupid voice was responding to Seth's skepticism with a determined chant.

Yes, yes, yes. Destined. Meant for. Ours, ours, ours.

Shut. The fuck. Up.

"I was wooing you," Riley finally blurted out.

Seth blinked at him. "Excuse me?"

"Before all this was...revealed...we were getting close." Riley knocked his knee against Seth's, careful not to let it linger. "You liked me. And you were attracted to me. Even though I'm too young. So let's just...keep doing that."

Seth blinked at the far wall now. "Let's keep...wooing me?"

Riley shrugged, trying to seem casual and not completely desperate. "Yeah. It doesn't have to be fate. It can just be...us. We have time for you to—to care about me, maybe."

Seth turned to face Riley, setting his mostly empty teacup on top of the pillow on his lap. "Aren't you annoyed though?" he asked. He looked so sincere, so honestly perplexed, and it tugged at something in Riley's chest. "So much of your life has been out of your control, and this is one more thing. Aren't you *angry*?"

Riley could only shrug again. "It doesn't feel like that."

"What does it feel like?"

Riley hesitated. But he'd already decided on honesty, so he might as well keep going with it. "I smelled you first," he said. "Your scent. Bright and sweet but also...rich. Decadent. I thought it was the most delicious thing I'd ever smelled. And then you spoke to me the next day, and you were wary, but you were also...warm. So warm. And when you smile at me, *I* feel warm." For once, Riley couldn't meet Seth's gaze. He took his turn staring at the far wall.

"I like the way you talk. To me and to—to other people too, even if I get a little jealous sometimes. You give your smiles to everyone, and I hate it, but I also love it. And I think you're beautiful, but maybe that's obvious."

He could feel the weight of Seth's stare. Riley turned to meet it with a rueful smile. "Are you done with your tea?" he asked. "It's late, and you said you get cranky without sleep."

Seth nodded, still staring kind of blankly, and Riley gently took the cup from Seth's pillow, setting it on one of the bedside tables. He settled down on his side, facing Seth.

Seth's dazed expression faded, and he gave Riley an arch look. "What are you doing now?"

"You pointed out that we haven't slept together." Riley gave him a winning smile. "I want to sleep with you."

Seth pointed an accusing finger. "We're not fucking. Just because you said a bunch of...really wonderful things doesn't make this all magically okay."

"No, we're not fucking," Riley agreed, settling even more firmly in place. "We're sleeping. You've had a very long day."

Seth let out a disbelieving laugh. "You and those moms of yours. Jesus. Tricky is the least of it."

But after a moment, Seth lay down on his side facing Riley. They were both over the covers still. At least Seth was wearing his soft pants. Those would be comfortable. Riley would tuck him under the covers later, so he wouldn't get cold. He reached over his shoulder and turned off the lamp.

They lay there together in the dark, breathing each other's air.

"I was trying to get some distance," Seth said eventually.

Riley had excellent night vision, so he could see that Seth had closed his eyes and that his lips were curled into a rueful smile, a little echo of Riley's own expression earlier.

"To rationalize and cast doubt," Riley recited.

Seth hummed. "It seemed like a good idea."

"I don't want you to." Riley scooted closer, until Seth's bare foot was just brushing his ankle. "I want you to keep talking through it with me."

"Do you get everything you want?"

"No. Hardly ever."

Another laugh, soft and sleepy. "Preying on my sympathies."

Riley nodded against his pillow. "If I have to."

"I'm going to sleep now." Seth jabbed a toe into Riley's calf in warning, his eyes still closed. "Save your trickiness for the morning."

"Okay." Riley smiled into the dark. "I will. Good night, Seth."

"Good night."

16

SETH

Seth woke up alone.

He also woke up warm and toasty, wrapped up in the comforter he'd been lying on when he'd fallen asleep. But definitely alone.

It was a surprising turn of events, considering Riley seemed the type to strangle-cuddle a guy all night long.

Maybe he was giving Seth the space Seth had claimed to need. Space Seth *should* take advantage of to make his escape. It was the principle of the thing, really—he couldn't just stay here after they'd stranded him on purpose. If nothing else, they'd think he lacked backbone.

And Seth needed to get out of here before he saw Riley and had to remember all the lovely things his supposed mate had said.

And I think you're beautiful, but maybe that's obvious.

Yeah. Things like that.

It was still dark outside—Seth was an early riser, unasked for day off or no. He tried his best not to think of his bakery staying closed for the day without warning. He hoped his regulars would forgive him the inconsistency.

After poking his head out the door, Seth made his way to the bathroom across the hall Daphne had been so kind as to point out the day before. (Although, after sabotaging his car, providing him with a restroom was really the least she could do.) There was a toothbrush still in its packaging and a tube of toothpaste on the counter. Seth assumed they were meant for him and used them accordingly. There was also a clean hand towel with cheery sunflowers embroidered on the hem, and he splashed water on his face while he was at it, patting his face dry and trying to ignore how soft the fabric was.

Then he grabbed his tote from the guest bedroom and went downstairs.

Seth could hear music in the kitchen—Etta James, if he wasn't mistaken. He found Daphne and Sybil sitting at the table, delicate cups of tea in hand. They were both wearing silk robes. They looked timeless, stylish in that type of way that didn't seem to belong to any particular era.

"Darling Seth!" Daphne greeted with a smile. "Good morning! How did you sleep?"

Kidnapping or no kidnapping, Seth couldn't be anything but polite in the face of a smile like that. "Really well, thank you," he said. "Could I get a ride home now, please?"

He could still open the bakery for a half day, with limited offerings. It would be at least some semblance of normalcy to cling to.

"Oh, I'm so sorry," Daphne told him. She once again looked perfectly regretful. Seth was beginning to wonder if she'd spent some time on the stage. "I'm afraid we've lent our cars to a friend in need."

Seth rubbed a hand over his jaw to stop himself from screaming like a lunatic. He was fine. This was fine. He should have expected it, really.

Still, he couldn't stop himself from pointing out, "It's a little after four in the morning."

"Yes," Daphne said with a nod, bumping Sybil with her shoulder when the other woman started smirking. "They wanted to get an early start."

Seth sighed. "Everyone here acts a lot nicer than they are, don't they?"

But just like that, he was already resigned. He couldn't help it—it wasn't in his nature to stay angry for long, and he'd always been good at going with the flow. He was trapped in this beautiful house. Whatever. At least the towels were nice.

Sybil let out a low, rich laugh. "Now you're getting it, my darling." She waved a hand in the direction of the counter behind her. "Riley told us you prefer coffee in the morning. There's a carafe for you."

There was, and it was still piping hot, with adorable pitchers of cream and sugar next to his waiting teacup. Seth almost hated how perfect it all was, how much he loved this house they were trapping him in.

"Riley's out hunting," Daphne told him, beaming at Seth when he joined them at the table. "He wants to be very full with you staying here."

"I'm going to lose my customers," Seth said without any real bite.

"Our friend promised to put up a sign explaining your absence."

"Closed due to kidnapping?"

Another laugh from Sybil. "Something a little more vague, I believe."

Seth sipped his coffee. He'd fallen into the kind of numb calm that could only follow an episode of pure panic. How he might feel when he saw Riley—Seth's future mate, if no one here was pulling his leg—was anybody's guess.

The three of them sat in a more or less comfortable silence, letting the music take center stage as they drank their beverages. Eventually Daphne slipped out with one more beaming smile, and Seth was left alone with Sybil.

His numb calm left him in an instant. It made him nervous, being alone with this particular mother. She had all the allure and sharp edges of her mate with none of the sweetness.

Riley cleared his throat, no longer satisfied with relative silence. "Is Riley hunting animals or—"

"Animals," Sybil confirmed. She gave Seth a piercing look. "You do realize you're the only human he's ever tasted, aside from blood bags?"

Seth swallowed hard. "I didn't." He should have, probably, based on what Riley had told him. But Seth hadn't exactly been thinking clearly yesterday.

"You've wounded him."

The directness of the statement caught him off guard, and Seth choked on his coffee. "I didn't mean to."

"We know." Sybil folded her manicured hands on the table, cocking her head. "But I'm very protective of my son."

"I've noticed." Seth had the vague suspicion that at any moment a shotgun was going to appear from under the table. But then again, Sybil had no need of one—she only had to use her fangs.

"Is it his youth that has you running scared? I promise he's had his share of life's growing pains."

Seth pushed his coffee away from him. It seemed like a heart-to-heart was on the menu, whether Seth wanted it or not.

High-handed fucking vampires.

"It's not just his age. It's the…intensity." Seth tried to figure out how to word what he meant without saying more than was decent to the mother of his would-be suitor. "I've been wanted before but not…like this." He met Sybil's searching gaze. "I'm just me," he explained. "Normal, average me. I don't know if I'm—if I'm strong enough to handle that kind of devotion."

Because that was what Riley was offering him, wasn't it? Complete and total devotion. Seth had been blind not to see it before.

Sybil was silent for a long moment. "But it's not about strength, is it?" she eventually asked. "It's about generosity. It's about welcoming all that devotion and still finding more within yourself to give in return. It's about resisting the impulse to take it for granted. And I do believe that underneath your fear, you *are* that generous."

"That's...flattering," Seth told her. He'd been dealing in understatements lately, and there was another one for the books. "But don't you think—I mean, he's never even *dated*. He's barely been outside this house since he was a child. Don't you want him to have choices? Other, more impressive options? Wouldn't that be... healthier?"

Seth knew he wasn't a major catch, just like he knew his hair was brown and his baked goods delicious. He'd once had a fun, flirty thing going with a lawyer he'd met at a club. It had seemed like it was going somewhere beyond simple flirting, and then the lawyer had found out Seth worked at the local bakery.

He'd dropped Seth like a hot coal. As if Seth working in the service industry had meant he wasn't worth the time of someone of any caliber. Like the rest of his charms weren't enough to make up for his relatively simple ambitions.

And that had just been an average, decent-looking lawyer, not a beautiful, devastating creature of the night.

Sybil tapped her crimson-painted nails on the table. "Riley may be young, but Daphne and I are anything but. Did you know Daphne was turned first?"

Seth shook his head. Riley hadn't told him anything about how his moms had met.

"Daphne had been turned by someone very old and very cruel, and she was making her way by pretending to fit in. Hiding all that inner sweetness, that softness deep inside her she displays so perfectly now. And she found me on the streets, selling myself to survive."

Sybil waved a hand, like she was dispersing Seth's sympathy before he could give it to her. "Mine was a pathetic, common tale. But Daphne saw something in me, and she made me as she was, and instantly, we were everything to each other. And we still are." Sybil leaned across the table, freezing Seth in her gaze like some vampire Medusa. "I don't care about your modern concerns about what's right or healthy. I want to give our son what he wants. I want him to have what we have."

"Jesus." Seth lowered his head into his hands, peeking out at her from between his fingers. "Each of you is somehow the most intense person I've ever met."

Sybil gave him a slow smile. "And you're fascinated by it. Aren't you?"

Seth let his eyes fall closed, even as he failed to deny it. "Anyone would be."

"But could anyone dance with it the way you do? Draw out the sweetness in Riley, the simple need for joy hiding under all that hunger? Tame the monster within while providing a haven for the lost boy?"

"You're putting a lot on my shoulders."

A graceful hand gripped Seth's wrist. "We didn't know if Riley would have a mate—too much is unknown about those who are turned so young. And then you appeared, so much sooner than we ever dared to hope. You're our miracle, and we'll cherish you accordingly." Amusement laced her tone. "Being what we are, our affections sometimes come with a bit of a bite."

With that, she released her hold and rose from her seat,

pressing a kiss to Seth's hair before gliding out the door. Seth gave in to temptation and let his forehead fall to the table.

Holy. Fucking. Shit. How was he supposed to ever catch his breath with people like this?

It wasn't like the lawyer thing had been any great wound—the guy had clearly been a douche—but it was hard not to have one's expectations shaped by little things like that. Seth had adjusted his accordingly, and finding out he'd been interacting with paranormals for literal years without realizing seemed to confirm that he was the opposite of anything special.

And now these three were throwing wrenches into all of it, confusing the worldview Seth had built. Acting like he was extraordinary just as he was. Acting like they were *glad* to have Riley shackled to him by the hands of fate.

Seth stood in a rush and began searching the kitchen cabinets.

He needed to bake about his feelings or he was going to combust.

By the time Seth had laid out all his ingredients, Riley had returned.

Seth smelled him before he saw him. It was like the rich, earthy scents of the forest had come to invade his kitchen.

Not *his* kitchen, of course. The moms' kitchen. Which happened to be suspiciously well stocked with everything a human baker might want or need.

Sneaky, tricky, high-handed vampires.

"I know you're there," Seth said when the scent had permeated but Riley had yet to show his face. It was kind of impressive, actually, because Seth hadn't heard the front door open or any footsteps in the hall.

Maybe he'd find out he was talking to himself after all. Olfactory hallucinations or something.

But then Riley stepped into the doorway, the picture of hangdog regret.

"You shouldn't lurk," Seth told him archly. He immediately regretted it. Whatever secrets Riley might have kept, Seth couldn't bear for Riley to look so horribly wounded again.

But the hangdog expression must have been mostly for show because Riley shamelessly stepped into the kitchen, like Seth had invited him in warmly rather than scolded him on sight. "What are you making?" Riley asked. "Cake?"

He sounded hopeful, and Seth raised his brows at the audacity. "No. You haven't earned any cake." He cleared his throat, waving at his ingredients. "I'm making orange rolls."

Riley perked up in an instant, like Seth using his favorite flavor meant the beginnings of forgiveness. Oh God. Maybe it did.

Ugh. Seth was so weak for this sneaky boy.

"Can I help?" Riley asked.

Seth shrugged, turning away before his face could betray him. He wanted to look crushing, but he probably looked more like he *was* crushing. "If you like."

He pulled up the recipe on his phone. Seth had made cinnamon rolls a bunch of times for his old bakery in Seacliff, but the ingredients were slightly different with this variation. Orange zest and juice in the batter, more orange juice in the icing. He'd found a manual juicer in the cabinet, and oranges on the counter, so he was making his own juice. He didn't want to consider that he might be trying to impress the moms. They were vampires; what did they care if he used store-bought juice?

Plus, they'd kidnapped him. One heart-to-heart with Sybil and he kept conveniently forgetting that.

Anyway. The orange rolls were going to be delicious, was the point, and Seth would get to redirect some of his aggression into kneading bread dough.

He turned to grab his first mixing bowl and yelped when he ran into a warm, hard obstacle. Riley was standing right beside him. Lurking. "Jesus!"

Riley only grinned at him, the lost puppy act well and truly set aside. "What's first?"

"Getting you a bell." When Riley's smile didn't falter, Seth shook his head. "We're mixing our yeast."

They got to work.

Riley was a good helper. Of course he was. He was always attentive, homed in on Seth like a fox with a rabbit. It translated well in the kitchen. The second Seth asked for an ingredient, Riley had it in his hand, fingers brushing lightly against Seth's palm or wrist with the exchange.

And Riley—pretty predictably—seemed very pleased to have an excuse to stand right next to Seth, or directly behind him, breathing on Seth's neck in a way that should have been annoying but only left Seth red-cheeked and flustered. Twice, Riley had to correct Seth when he almost put in the wrong measurements. *Twice.*

Could he even call himself a baker?

But still, even with him suffocating under the weight of sexual tension, the familiar pattern of putting ingredients together did help lift Seth's mood a bit. He found himself releasing some of the turmoil of the last twenty-four hours, the stiffness in his frame slowly loosening.

Could he do what Riley had suggested? Let go of *we're meant for each other* and focus on *do we even want each other*?

The problem with that question was, of course, that the answer was a resounding freaking yes.

Because once Seth let go of the constant refrains he'd been using to protect himself—*We're just friends; he's too young; he has an ancient monster inside him who feeds on blood and wants to claim me for a consort*—then it was just...Riley.

And Riley was beautiful, and he smelled like the woods after the rain, and he was...standing very, very close. Always. It wasn't fair, since his very presence shot little bits of electricity into the air, heating Seth's skin and setting his nerves alight.

Good assistant or no, Riley made it very hard to focus.

Seth poured the dough from the mixture onto the flour-dusted counter, clearing his throat. "Riley?"

"Yes?" Riley answered from directly behind him, his nose practically pressed against the back of Seth's head.

Had he been sniffing Seth again?

"Don't you wish you'd gotten to...experiment more? Before meeting me?"

Riley didn't even take a pause to think. "No."

"Why not?" Seth asked as he began kneading the dough.

"I guess partly because...desire isn't like that for me. I don't think about fucking random people. I don't think about abstract body parts or, like, isolated acts. I think about you. Your skin and your scent and what's under your clothes. I think about how it would feel to touch you. To slide into you."

Seth's lower belly tightened without warning, and he let out a harsh breath. His voice when he spoke came out huskier than he would have liked. "That's...intense."

Riley's sigh ruffled Seth's curls. "I know. You hate it?"

Seth wanted to lie, but he couldn't meet that raw honesty with anything but more of the same. "No, I don't hate it. I'm uncomfortable with how much I like it. I don't know what it says about me."

"It says you're my match."

Ugh. Seth slapped the dough against the counter. See? Kneading was *great* for aggression. "Does it? Or do most people thrive off attention? Especially from someone who looks and acts like you?"

"How do I look and act?" Riley asked, all guileless innocence.

Punch. Knead. "Beautiful." *Punch. Knead.* "Otherworldly."

Riley had the gall to sound affronted. "Otherworldly's a copout. You already know I'm a vampire."

"Okay. You act like I'm the only thing you see or care about." Seth could feel Riley's grin, and he refused to look back and be charmed by it. "That's not healthy," he pointed out. Why did he have to keep telling people this? Wasn't it obvious?

Riley huffed. "I. Don't. Care. My life hasn't been healthy. It's been weird and confusing and sometimes sad."

God, he kept tugging at Seth's tender heartstrings. And he knew it, the little sneak. Seth focused on his dough. He was going to cross the line into overworking it at any moment, but he was afraid to stop and have to face Riley for real.

"You think I'm beautiful?" Riley asked after a moment.

Seth let out a wry laugh. "You don't?"

"I don't know. I think I'm...off-putting. People stare. In town."

"People stare because you're hot. And you can get away with off-putting when you're hot. It's called pretty privilege."

"Pretty privilege." Riley brushed his fingers softly against the back of Seth's neck, and Seth tried and failed to control his shiver. "That's what you have?"

Seth's cheeks went hot. He finally lifted his hands from the dough, releasing it from his torture. "No. I mean, I get by, but you—" He coughed. "It's different."

And then Riley's hands were on Seth's hips, turning him to face Riley. He was so close, his dark eyes filled with molten heat. "No, it isn't," Riley said softly, his gaze drifting down to Seth's mouth. "I can't look at you without wanting to kiss you."

"You're a special case," Seth told him. The words came out in a whisper.

"Seth?"

Seth blinked up at him. "Yes, Riley?"

"I'm going to kiss you."

Seth sagged in place. This was why he shouldn't have turned around. He was weak. So weak. "Okay."

Riley's mouth came down to claim his. Seth's hands were useless, covered as they were in sticky dough, and Riley took full advantage. He crowded Seth back against the counter, hips pressing into him, cupping Seth's face as he directed him exactly where he wanted him.

Riley shouldn't have been this good at kissing already. It was ludicrous, the way he could make Seth's knees give out like this, the counter and Riley's broad body the only thing holding him in place.

It was the hunger that did it. The mix of appetite and restraint, the way Riley licked into him with abandon while holding his face so damn gently. He kissed Seth like he was starving for him, and Seth's body flooded with arousal.

By the time Riley broke away to kiss at Seth's upturned jaw, Seth was so hard he ached. He couldn't seem to catch his damn breath. "If—If you were still wooing me," he panted, "what would be next?"

Riley nuzzled his nose against the line of Seth's neck, making his way to a tender spot below Seth's ear. "I'd be trying to get you into my bed," Riley murmured, pressing a hot kiss to Seth's racing pulse. His erection was digging into Seth's hip, and it was only the dough on Seth's hands that stopped him from sliding his hands into Riley's jeans and grabbing for it. "I'd be on my knees begging to fuck you. I feel like I've been waiting an eternity. Forever."

It hadn't even been a month since they'd met, but Seth couldn't bring himself to snark about the time discrepancy. It *had* been forever, hadn't it? He needed—God, he just *needed.*

"We—" Seth let his head fall back, giving Riley more room to work with as he sucked and nibbled on Seth's neck. "We have to let the dough rise for—for a couple hours."

Riley made some sort of hum of acknowledgment, pulling the neck of Seth's T-shirt away so he could lick at Seth's collarbone.

Seth shouldn't have let his guard down. It had served a purpose, protecting him from the intensity of Riley's desire. Now it was like staring directly at the fucking sun, and Seth was melting. Dizzy and hot and melting, like icing left out too long in the heat.

He licked at his lips, chasing Riley's taste. He couldn't stop the words from leaving his mouth. "Take me to your room, Riley. You don't have to beg."

17

RILEY

Riley endured a mini eternity waiting for Seth to wash the dough off his hands.

He tried to be patient, but he knew he was hovering, breathing hotly against Seth's neck as he seemed to have a habit of doing these days. He couldn't help it—Seth smelled the sweetest there, right at the back of his neck, his orange scent so tart and rich it made Riley's mouth water.

Maybe Riley would have been able to help himself if Seth had seemed to hate it, but if anything, it was the opposite. When Riley stood so close—their bodies almost touching, his breath blowing against Seth's skin—all the little hairs on the back of Seth's neck stood up, his heart raced, and his ears turned the prettiest shade of pink.

Seth wanted Riley. He might not have *wanted* to want him, but he did. And if that was all Riley had to work with—a certain fondness and base attraction—he was going to take full advantage.

He realized he might be slightly hindered by his own inexperience, but he was a quick student. He'd been homeschooled for obvious reasons, and he'd always gone above and beyond the curriculum. If nothing else, the quest for knowledge was a way to pass the time as well as expand his constricted world.

And now Riley was going to fill his entire world with his mate. He was going to learn and memorize and worship everything that made Seth sigh and moan and harden. He was going to fucking ace it.

Seth finally turned from the sink, and Riley stepped back to make room. Not *too much* room though. He could sense Seth preparing to retreat, to grow shy where he'd just gotten bold.

So Riley did what he knew would make Seth laugh if nothing else: Riley threw him over his shoulder.

Seth *did* laugh, a gasping sound of amused disbelief that turned into a faux outraged giggle as Riley headed toward the stairs, one arm banded around the back of Seth's thighs. "What are you—"

"You wanted to see my room."

Seth slapped a wet hand against Riley's lower back. "Your *moms*."

But Riley had heard his moms leave the house ages ago. They were either roaming the woods or walking into town. The majority of the rooms in the house were soundproofed—none of them wanted Riley to hear what two vampire moms in desperate love got up to—but the privacy was still appreciated.

So Riley ignored Seth's half-hearted wiggles of protest until they were safely closed up in his room, and then he set his mate down on his feet.

He expected another slap or maybe a wagging finger, but instead, Seth grabbed Riley's face, pulling it down to his level. "Let me see your eyes."

Riley blinked brown eyes at him. "You thought it was my vampire taking over and abducting you?"

"It crossed my mind."

Riley frowned. He wasn't sure if he liked the implications of that. "I'm just as obsessed, you know. It's not all...it."

That was probably the wrong thing to say, considering how Seth had freaked out about the mate thing. And he did seem poised to say something argumentative in return, so Riley took quick advantage of their position and pressed a kiss to Seth's open mouth.

It was incredibly gratifying, the way Seth went immediately limp, melting into Riley as he gasped into the kiss.

Yeah, this was totally the way to go about things. Riley was just going to seduce Seth over and over until he forgot all his reservations. The voice inside Riley seemed to like that idea too, purring its approval as Riley licked into Seth's mouth, pressing his knee against the hardness between Seth's thighs.

By the time they broke apart, Seth's hands were fisted in Riley's shirt and his eyelids were drooping, his pretty lips slack and reddened. He gazed around Riley's room absently, as if looking for an anchor. "You have a lot of books."

That was true, but Riley didn't feel like going through an inventory of his possessions right this second. He kissed Seth again, backing him up to the bed while Seth was pliant and occupied sucking on his tongue. Riley lifted him with two hands on his ass, then followed him down to the bed.

"We can just kiss," Riley murmured, brushing his lips against Seth's jaw, down his throat. Licking at Seth's pounding pulse. Riley could do that without fear now. He had a new confidence in his own self-control—a new belief that the voice wasn't going to ruin everything if he let go—and it was almost as heady as Seth's eager kisses.

For once, Riley and his voice were on the exact same page: keep Seth happy, do whatever he wanted, don't let him run.

Riley hummed, sucking on that tender spot, loving the way it made Seth groan. "We could kiss for hours and hours."

"And you'd be—" Seth arched up, his hands now twisting into the hem of Riley's shirt. "You'd be okay with that?"

Riley went back to nibbling Seth's jaw. He liked that there was the faintest hint of stubble there. Seth was usually so meticulous about shaving. "Yes."

"I wouldn't." Seth tugged Riley's shirt. "Do you have lube?"

The question shot a jolt of electricity straight to Riley's dick. He groaned. "Yes."

"What about condoms?"

Riley paused his nibbling and raised his head. "I'm undead. I can't give you anything. But if you'd prefer them—"

Seth let out a slow breath, but Riley didn't miss the way his hips bucked up. "No. That's... Oh boy. Okay."

Oh fuck. This was happening. Riley was going to fuck Seth, and he was going to do it bare.

He swallowed. Hard. "But we have to get naked."

Seth arched his brows. "We do?"

"Yes," Riley told him, nodding frantically to make it extra clear. He hadn't seen Seth fully naked yet, and he was going to start ripping fabric if it didn't happen soon.

Seth gave him a soft smile. "I like naked."

The smile dissolved into an equally soft laugh as Riley immediately tugged Seth's shirt off, wrestling with his wayward limbs and making sure Seth's soft pants and underwear were quick to follow.

Riley tossed the bundle to the floor, then rose onto his knees, straddling Seth's bare calves, and drank him in.

Seth said he liked running, and Riley could see the evidence of it. There was strength in his thighs. In his arms too—probably from handling dough like he did. And while he was slim, his muscles were still covered by a soft layer that Riley wanted to lick and nibble at. His skin was noticeably paler where his clothes covered, with sparse curly hair on his chest and a thatch at his groin that was darker than what covered his head.

Riley had already known he loved Seth's cock, all pink and slim and ruddy at the tip. He was gratified that it was standing at attention for him, leaking precum onto the soft swell of Seth's belly.

Seth lay surprisingly still under Riley's intent perusal. Riley could hear Seth's heart hammering, but he didn't cover himself, although a dark blush spread from his cheeks down his neck.

"You too," Seth finally commanded, and Riley stood only long enough to shuck off his clothes, climbing back to straddle Seth's calves again afterward.

For some reason, it was *Riley's* nudity that had Seth covering his face. "Jesus," he moaned.

"Can we do it like this?" Riley asked. He had to swallow hard again—so much naked Seth, and Riley was almost on the verge of drooling. "Facing each other?"

"We can, but for the first time, it might be easier—" Seth made a little turning gesture with his hand, then rose onto his elbows. "Do you want to open me up yourself?"

Riley had to grip the base of his cock hard to keep from embarrassing himself. "Yes. Yes, that."

"Get the lube."

While Riley did what Seth asked, Seth turned over onto his belly, tucking a pillow under his hips. Riley's mouth went dry as he fell newly in love with the line of Seth's spine, the way it drew the eye down to the fleshy globes of his ass, the strong muscles in his legs.

Riley also had a suspicion this position wasn't just for ease, that Seth was creating a little distance between them where he could. But that was fine.

This wouldn't be the last time they did this. Only the first.

Riley set the lube down on the covers and crawled between Seth's spread legs. He let himself pet and stroke to his heart's content, running his hands up and over Seth's shoulders and back, loving the way Seth's muscles tensed and then relaxed under his hands. He moved his touch down, down, over Seth's hips and ass, spreading those lush cheeks, fixating on what was revealed.

It was so small here. So tender. How was it supposed to take him? Just the thought of it had Riley's cock bucking. He gave himself another squeeze and then set his throbbing erection right there, on that soft, soft skin. He rubbed gently back and forth, moaning quietly at the feel of it. He was going to be inside there soon. Gripped by that tight sheath. Surrounded by Seth.

"Having fun?"

The question shook Riley out of his fog, and he realized he was squeezing Seth's cheeks around his cock like that was the endgame of this whole experience. He might have been embarrassed, if not for the throaty, husky rasp of Seth's voice. He liked Riley rubbing on him.

"Yes," Riley admitted. "I really am."

But he drew back and grabbed the lube. He squirted some on Seth's crack ("Jesus! Warn a guy!"), then squirted more on his fingers. He pressed on that hole lightly with his fingertip, rubbing careful circles. He teased and cajoled until it softened for him, his fingertip going in easily. The rest of his finger followed, and it was unfathomable, wasn't it, that Riley was going to feel this tight heat around his dick soon?

"Okay?" Riley asked, his own voice about an octave lower than usual.

He heard Seth's hard swallow in the silence. "Have you done this before?"

"You know I haven't. I've just...thought about it. A lot."

Riley went back to fingering his perfect Seth open. He was careful. He was slow. It wasn't hard to take his time. It was fascinating, the way Seth arched and shuddered under his touch. It was like looking at a work of art, the lines of his back and the tension in his shoulders.

"Okay," Seth told him, either after a few minutes or an eon, Riley wasn't quite sure. "Riley. *Okay.*"

He glared over his shoulder at Riley. Seth's curls were mussed —he'd been rubbing his forehead against his folded hands while Riley explored—and his eyes were even glassier than before.

Riley grinned at him, withdrawing his fingers. He'd gotten up to three.

Seth scowled.

Riley's grin fell. "Did I do it wrong?"

"Only if you consider the fact that I'm about to come all over your bedspread. And I'm not—I want to wait. So—" Seth glared pointedly at Riley's dick, which was bobbing in front of his stomach like it was begging to be noticed.

Ah. Seth was impatient. Riley cocked his head. "I thought you'd be nicer in bed."

"And I thought you'd be bumbling."

And just like that, Riley's grin was back. "Did you really?"

He shuffled closer, his knees coming up behind Seth's spread thighs. He notched his cock to Seth's entrance and stopped there. He let his hips rock a little, the head of his cock teasing at Seth's hole and then glancing off. Even that much felt amazing.

"Riley *fucking* Beauchamp."

Grinning like a loon, Riley pressed in.

Fuck. *Fuck.* There was nothing like it. Nothing in this world. It was so tight, the constriction, and Riley could *feel* Seth telling his body to let him in, the muscles relaxing and allowing Riley inch after inch. Seth was almost silent underneath him, other than a quiet, hitching breath and a soft, throaty moan.

Riley's groan was less discreet.

But fuck. It was heaven. Fucking heaven.

Riley bottomed out, and he lowered himself, pressing the length of his body against Seth's back. He tucked his arms under Seth's shoulders, hugging him close.

If Seth had been hoping for emotional distance in this position, he might be disappointed. Every inch of their skin was touching, Riley's breath caressing the back of his neck. Riley pressed a kiss to the crook of it, where it met Seth's shoulder.

He forced himself to stay still, to resist the urge to begin rutting furiously. "Is that— Is that better?"

Seth let out a long, noisy breath. "*God.* So much better." He turned his head, and he was no longer scowling. There was Riley's friend again, all warm and open and trusting. "Are you doing okay?"

"I'm so okay," Riley told him, his voice thick. "I've never—"

Seth pressed their lips together, his kiss firm but sweet. "I know, baby. Do you want me on my hands and knees?"

"No." Riley shook his head. "Like this. I want to be touching."

He drove his hips back, then returned in a stuttered glide. Seth moaned louder this time, and Riley nuzzled his head into the crook of his neck. "Is it good for you?" he asked breathlessly. "Like this?"

Seth slid his hands under Riley's palms, curling their fingers together. "It's good. Don't stop."

Riley didn't stop. He widened his knees, pressing Seth's legs even further apart and pushing them up the bedspread, using the leverage to move over him without losing an inch of contact. Their breaths mingled, and the air was filled with buttery orange, tart and sweet and perfect.

Seth moaned again. And again.

Riley's new favorite sound.

Eventually Riley found it within himself to unclasp one of his hands from Seth's, moving it down to slide under Seth's hip, palming Seth's cock and letting it rub against his hand as he fucked them back and forth.

Seth's body was hot under his, slicked with sweat. It eased the glide, and yet Riley wanted to lick it off him, but he also wanted to stay exactly like this, his body covering Seth's like a blanket, fucking and sliding like they'd somehow merged into one being.

How did people survive this? How *had* people survived this? How had anyone had Seth in this way and then let him go afterward? And how was Riley supposed to let him out of this bed ever again?

It was impossible to fathom. They'd have to stay here forever, locked together. Riley would suck and kiss and lick Seth back to hardness again and again, and he'd fill him again and again, and they would—they would—

Riley didn't feel the change take over. He was too focused on the way his blood was heating, his balls drawing up tight. He was fighting the inevitable conclusion as hard as he could, trying to hold back, trying to let this last as long as possible. He finally gave in to the urge and licked the sweat off Seth's neck, groaning at the salty flavor. And then—

Sweet. So sweet. Salty skin and hot blood. Their mate was clenching, gasping, bucking under them. Sweat-slicked and perfect, hot release covering their fingers. Their mate. Their love. Theirs.

Riley came back to himself with his bloody lips still pressed against Seth's neck.

Seth, who was chanting, "Oh fuck, oh fuck, oh fuck," over and over again.

He wasn't chanting in fear. It was pleasure. Pure pleasure. He'd come on Riley's fingers, and his blood was in Riley's mouth, and he was still shuddering, shivering, his orgasm extended into something his mortal body hardly seemed able to take.

Riley licked on instinct, closing the bite. He could still taste the perfect orange-tinged copper of Seth's essence, and Seth's inner muscles were squeezing Riley's cock like some sort of pulsating vise.

That was it. It was too much to bear. Riley drove in once. Twice. He pressed his hips down as hard as he could, and his whole body shuddered as Seth milked him, taking everything Riley had to give. He lost himself. Not to the change, for once, but to pure sensation. The world narrowed and expanded at the same time, turning Riley inside out within it.

By the time he came back to himself for a second time, Seth was still shuddering. Or no, his shoulders were shaking. Oh fuck. Was he crying?

"Seth?" Riley asked. He regretfully withdrew from that perfect warmth. Otherwise, he was going to get hard again inside Seth and scare him off. "Baby?"

Seth raised his head from where it had dropped. He wasn't crying. He was laughing. "Jesus Christ."

It wasn't exactly reassuring. Was this some sort of breakdown? Had the bite been too much for him? Had Riley been too rough? "What's wrong?"

"First time," Seth gasped. "Your f-first time." And he started laughing again. Cackling almost.

Riley could only stare at the side of Seth's face. His spent cock was pressed against Seth's ass cheek, and Riley idly wondered if he should, like, take it away.

But then Seth rolled over underneath him. He was *glowing*, looking so flushed and happy and sated. He lifted a hand, cupping Riley's cheek. "What am I going to do with you?"

He'd liked it, Riley fucking him. He'd liked it a lot.

The elation was like a drug. At least, Riley assumed it was—he'd never gotten to try any drugs before. But he'd take a hit of giddy, fucked-out Seth any day.

Riley grinned down at his mate, light as air. "You're going to keep me."

18

SETH

Seth woke up from a short sex doze to find arousal already pooling low in his belly.

His breath hitched as he came back to full awareness. He was naked and warm and lying on his back, a large form hovering over him. Broad hands petted at Seth's hips while a determined nose and lips and teeth nuzzled into tender skin.

Riley really seemed to like mauling Seth's neck. It must have been a vampire thing. Not like Seth was complaining. Not when every one of Riley's desperate touches sent a tingle down Seth's spine, his dick twitching in interest.

Seth let out a sigh, and the hands on his hips drifted to Seth's thighs, spreading them open and lifting them to wrap around Riley's lower back.

Right. Riley had wanted face-to-face.

Seth's breath hitched again, his cock filling like he hadn't had the orgasm of his life only a little while ago.

Riley nibbled on Seth's shoulder, and Seth's hole clenched

around nothing, like it was already aching for Riley's girth. Jesus. It had been some time since he'd been dicked down, but Seth didn't remember being this desperate for it. He shouldn't even want it again so soon. He was tender down there.

Not that he was *too* sore. Riley hadn't been rough earlier. No, he'd been...thorough. Very, *very* thorough. He'd taken Seth in strokes that were short but deep, his hips barely lifting from where they'd rested on Seth's ass. As if any inch of space between them had been considered an inch too many.

It had been deeply sensual in a way Seth hadn't known how to guard against, and that was without considering the bite that had forced him into shooting his load without warning.

Seth had been expecting frantic and rushed and to have everything over too quickly. It still would have been hot—Seth was too far gone on Riley not to take the inexperience for what it was and enjoy the hell out of it anyway. But Riley had flipped the script entirely and been slow and thorough and overwhelming.

Tricky fucking vampires.

Had Riley been aware of the hungry noises he'd made while fingering Seth open? The little grunts and murmurs of appreciation, like getting his fingers into Seth was some sort of gift for the ages?

And now Riley wanted more.

That was fine. Seth did too. And as Riley sucked on that tender spot beneath Seth's ear, Seth opened his mouth to tell Riley to stop teasing and give him exactly what he craved.

But before he could, Riley finally lifted his head from Seth's neck, and Seth saw it.

The curtains in the room were drawn, their surroundings dim even with the daylight outside, but Seth could still make out the Not-Riley of it all. Black eyes. Fangs.

Seth tensed, his gasp of surprise covered by Not-Riley's deep, approving hum. Like Seth had been pleasing him, lying there pliant and soft and willing while he tortured Seth's neck.

Was—was this allowed? Riley was touching him, but it was the *other* Riley, and he clearly planned for more than touching. He was equally naked and hard against Seth's hip, rubbing against Seth in a way that made his intentions unmistakable.

Sure, Not-Riley had taken over for a second there while they'd been boning, but he hadn't *initiated* anything. Was this different? Worse somehow?

But the vampire part of Riley was still a part of Riley. That was what Riley had said. Even if it was disjointed and separate in a way it wasn't supposed to be. So not *Not*-Riley, but...Vampire Riley. Or just...Riley.

Seth reached up and cupped Riley's jaw, trying to gain some insight by staring into those black eyes. He pressed a thumb to one of Riley's sharp fangs. "You want me too, hm?"

The rubbing continued, except for now Riley shifted the angle of his hips so that their hard cocks were rubbing together.

Seth shivered with the new, delicious pressure against his hardening dick.

That seemed to be an affirmative.

"I hear you made things pretty rough for Riley growing up." A blink of those black eyes. Seth pressed the other fang, keeping away from the sharp tip. "But you were hungry, weren't you? Hungry and trapped in a body too young for you."

Black eyes drifted closed, as if to savor Seth's touch. Were his fangs sensitive? Did it feel as good to sink them into Seth's skin as it felt to receive their bite? Riley opened his eyes slowly and then treated Seth to another determined rock of his hips.

Seth licked his lips. "Should I let you?"

It was hard to admit to himself how much he wanted to. How much he was drawn to this other side of his sweet friend. But how could he not be? It was like seeing all the alarming intensity in

Riley's nature distilled into an even higher potency. The kind of presence that had Seth's hair standing up, the kind that made him hyperaware of every one of his breaths, his movements. The kind that shouldn't have been erotic but really, really was.

Riley spoke, his voice that deeper, rougher version of himself. "Not. First."

It took Seth a minute—it was hard to think clearly with this unspoken, slow frotting happening—but he got there eventually. "You mean I already gave Riley this first?"

Riley nodded.

"And now it's your turn?"

Riley nodded again.

Seth laughed in disbelief. "Jesus, that's presumptuous."

Riley ducked his head back into Seth's neck, and one of his fangs grazed the tender skin there. He did it with enough pressure to draw a bit of blood, and it sent a jolt of pleasure straight down Seth's spine. He was leaking precum now, the slick substance easing the glide between their cocks.

And then Riley huffed and licked the blood off Seth's neck, soothing the sting.

He lifted his head, staring down at Seth with a new quirk to his lips.

For a creature so hungry, the gesture was surprisingly...playful. Like something the other Riley might do.

Seth, for his part, had no idea what the hell he was doing. And without the benefit of knowledge, he needed to go with instinct.

This part of Riley had been...squashed down over the years. Riley had been fighting himself—fighting this part of himself—for obvious and probably valid reasons, given his age for most of it.

But maybe that was why the voice squashed Riley down in turn. A form of protection or a form of retaliation—either would make sense. But whatever the reason, Riley was older now, and both sides of him needed to get their acts together. He didn't need to be separate anymore, and the fractures in his nature were hurting him.

And there was one thing both sides of him wanted equally.

Seth just couldn't believe *he* was that thing.

All the tension and hyperawareness that came from being covered head to toe with Not-Riley had Seth's whole body trembling now. He wished he could say it was from fear. That would be the smart emotion to be feeling. So sensible, fear.

It wasn't fear.

Seth reached out blindly across the bedspread with his free hand. He found the little bottle of lube and spread some on his fingers, then reached between them and gripped Riley's cock, covering him with it.

All the while, Riley stared down at him hungrily, a low, rumbling sound emanating from his chest.

Seth lifted his chin. "A kiss first."

Riley didn't wait for further permission. He lowered his head and claimed Seth's mouth, swiping his tongue inside like he'd been doing it all his vampire life.

The hunger was the same, Riley and his vampire both. They both kissed Seth like they wanted to consume him. They both had that aggressive need to take everything Seth offered and then grasp for more.

They were two parts of the same whole. Seth could feel it. He was on the right track.

He arched up, wrapping his legs higher as he tilted his hips, leading Riley wordlessly where he wanted him to go. Riley growled again, shifting so his cock lined up with Seth's hole.

Seth moaned at the stretch as that fat head sank into him, all his sensitive nerve endings set alight once more.

God, it felt good. It shouldn't have felt this good, not when everything else was so confusing.

Riley pushed in mercilessly, and when he'd bottomed out, he

dropped onto his elbows. Once again they were pressed together completely, bare skin touching bare skin. Riley drove his hips back and punched in again, and Seth couldn't help the tortured sound that escaped him.

Good. So, so good.

Riley broke their kiss, licking at Seth's lower lip. "More," he growled.

More what? More fucking? More blood? More kissing? *He* was the one who'd stopped the kissing. But he was staring expectantly at Seth's mouth, like he was waiting for something.

He wanted more noises. More of Seth's moans.

Seth dug his heels into Riley's ass and wrapped one arm around his neck. "Do it again, then."

Riley grinned, his fangs gleaming, and then he was driving that thick cock into Seth again and again in a relentless pace.

Seth hoped the moms were far, far from this house right now because he couldn't help the sounds escaping him. The punched-out moans that kept pitching higher and higher. Riley was just so *deep*, completely ruthless as he carved Seth out and filled him up with only Riley, Riley, and more Riley.

Seth desperately shoved a hand between them, cupping his cock. He didn't have the strength or focus to stroke himself, but he let friction do its work, Riley's perfect fucking stomach muscles flexing against the back of his hand.

Seth's eyes fell closed. His back arched.

"Seth."

The sound of it was different from the rough rasp Seth had been hearing since he'd woken up. Softer. More familiar.

Seth opened his eyes. Pure black stared down at him, but still —that was *his* Riley, wasn't it, peeking out from behind the shadows?

And then Seth blinked, and that other Riley was gone. Vampire Riley growled, grinding into Seth with new determination. Seth's body rocked on the bedspread, his arms and legs trembling with how tightly he had them wound around Riley's back.

"Oh fuckkk," he groaned.

And then he was no longer fit for thinking about anything. Or for speaking words that made any sense at all. He was pure tension, a tight pressure that kept building higher and higher and higher until it broke and Seth shattered.

"*Ungh*!"

And then there were teeth in his neck again, but Riley wasn't drinking Seth's blood. He was shivering, his big body pressing Seth down into the mattress as he just...held Seth's throat in his jaws as he came.

It was proprietary. Possessive. Animalistic.

Seth's eyes shut once more, and he let himself fall away.

SETH WOKE AGAIN to find Riley staring down at him, his brow furrowed in concern. His eyes were a deep, dark brown. "It knocked you out."

Seth licked dry lips. His brain was mush. Too many sex endorphins had turned it into soup. "My orgasm?"

"My stupid voice."

Seth stretched in the bed, wiggling to work out the soreness in his lower back. The movement brushed his chest up against Riley's. They were both still naked. That was both wonderful and way too tempting. "I think you need to be nicer to each other. Don't call him stupid."

Riley made a noise of disgust. "It's very smug right now."

"*He*," Seth corrected. "He's a part of you, Riley."

"A very smug part of me."

Seth tried to push the mushy soup of his brain into action.

And of course the first thing it went for was guilt. "Was it— Was I wrong, letting him touch me like that? Should I have stopped it?"

He and Riley hadn't discussed fidelity at all, much less the finer nuances of fidelity when there was a vampire alter ego involved.

But Riley was already shaking his head. "No. You're its—" He swore, correcting himself. "*His* mate too. It—*he* would probably riot if you held yourself back for my sake. It wouldn't be pretty."

Riley scanned Seth's face with his usual intensity. He had his hands planted on the mattress on either side of Seth's head. Nothing felt sticky, so he'd probably cleaned them up again while Seth had been dozing. How thoughtful.

"Was it good?"

Seth coughed at the question, although he probably should have been expecting it. "You're both, um, very...sensual creatures."

Riley's frown morphed into a delighted smile. "It *was* good. You liked it."

Embarrassment made Seth scowl. "Why are you proud of that?" Hadn't Riley been pissed just two seconds ago? Did Seth's glorious orgasms make that much of a difference to his split-personality-induced jealousy?

"Dunno." Riley nuzzled his nose against Seth's hair, breathing in deeply. "I just like making you feel good, I guess."

"Well, mission fucking accomplished." Seth fought for enough space to reach for his phone, checking the time. "We need to get the dough."

Riley kept on nuzzling. "Let's stay in bed."

"You can't keep me hostage in your bed, sexing me up until I agree to be your mate."

Riley lifted his head, and his immediate, guileless blink told Seth he'd been right on the money with that one.

He pushed gently at Riley's chest. "Up you go."

Even if Seth was tempted to let Riley continue with his evil plan, it was the middle of the day, and Seth wouldn't be able to look the moms in the eye if he and Riley disappeared completely for a sex sabbatical. Deflowering their son was bad enough, and somehow Seth had managed to do that twice.

With a beleaguered sigh, Riley rolled to the side. "But you'll sleep here tonight?"

"I'll consider it."

He would—technically—but Seth was also not above trying to convince Riley to let him leave. Seth had a life to live. And he wasn't creating distance between them anymore, was he? Definitely not physically, as their multiple, mutual orgasms attested to. So maybe it was time for this house to let Seth go.

After he finished his rolls, of course.

Seth eyed the pile of clothes on the floor with distaste. He'd already slept in those things. "Do you have any sweats you could lend me?"

"Yeah." Riley padded over to his dresser, still completely nude. God, he was handsome. And that was a good butt. A *really* good butt. He'd need to keep that butt to himself, or Seth was going to be agreeing to a monthlong kidnapping just to stay and ogle it.

Riley came back with gray sweats and a black T-shirt. Seth accepted them eagerly. Clothes would be good—a fabric barrier to his own horny thoughts.

Speaking of. Seth cast a sideways glance at Riley's bobbing erection. "Does that thing ever go down?"

Riley shrugged. "You look good in my bed."

Well, then. Seth cleared his throat and stood, getting dressed as quickly as his shaky legs would allow. Apparently he needed to get back to running to improve his endurance if he was going to keep up with his young, supernatural lover.

Or let him turn you.

Nope. No. Nuh-uh. Seth was not giving that any brain space. He was still trying to come to terms with the *destined lovers* portion of the mate thing—he didn't have any room for the *one-day-becoming-a-vampire* part.

What if turning into a vampire ruined his palate? He'd have to switch from pastries to blood sausages.

He and Riley made their way to the kitchen, and Seth was grateful for the lack of vampire moms in attendance. He needed to get his wits about him before attempting any semblance of chill after what had just happened. Twice.

Hadn't Seth started this day off determined to cling to normalcy? Since when had his normal routine included getting ravaged by impossibly beautiful monster-men?

Seth punched the air out of his dough, then floured the counter and started rolling it out. Baking. Baking was normal.

But if Riley had been hovering before, he was now completely incorrigible. He kept wrapping his arms around Seth's waist as Seth mixed the filling, or pressing kisses to Seth's neck, shoulders, and ears as he cut the rolls to size.

Seth came *this* close to giving in and abandoning the orange rolls in favor of more debauchery. Instead, he made Riley sit at the kitchen table, where Seth could keep an eye on his shamelessly horny ass.

Riley sat meekly enough, although he kept biting back a grin, so he couldn't have been too chastised. "My moms said your grandma taught you to bake?"

"Mm." Seth had somehow managed to pop the rolls into the oven despite the distraction, and now he was filling a bowl with simple icing ingredients. "Yeah, she was amazing in the kitchen."

"What about your parents?"

Seth shrugged. "They weren't as interested. They...I mean, they're great, I love them, but they didn't always...get me, early on. They kept buying me toy cars and action figures for every holiday and wondering why I would hardly play with them. And then we'd go to my grandma's, and she'd take me into the kitchen with her, and everything smelled amazing, and she had these frilly vintage aprons." Seth smiled at the memory. "She'd let me choose one for both of us, and we'd put them on and make something delicious. Plus, she had some of my mom's old toys, and she and I would dress up the dolls and stuff while we waited for our creations to bake. I was well fed there, in more ways than one. I still use her recipes."

Riley's dark eyes were soft. "She sounds amazing."

"She was." Seth ignored the familiar pang of loss and set his icing aside. They had a few more minutes for the rolls to finish. He glanced around the beautiful kitchen. He could imagine his grandmother here, poking through the cabinets and testing out all the high-quality vintage appliances. "She would have loved this kitchen. The whole house."

"I wish I could have met her." Riley ducked his head suddenly, his gaze dropping to his folded hands. "Do you—do you think she'd have liked me?"

God, he was cute. It was ridiculous that he could be so bashful after turning Seth inside out hardly an hour before.

Seth scoffed, although he couldn't completely hide his smile. "Are you kidding? She was totally weak for a pretty face. She would have flirted with you shamelessly, tried to steal you away."

"I wouldn't have let her."

Riley sounded so fierce about it that Seth had to laugh. "You wouldn't have let my elderly grandmother seduce you? Your loyalty is unmatched."

Riley lifted his head again to grin at Seth's teasing, but his next words were solemn, with that perfectly serious Riley edge to them. "You have no idea."

19

RILEY

Riley still couldn't believe he got to do this. It felt illicit. Stolen. A dream he was going to wake up from at any moment.

"I'm pretty sure my back is very, very clean now."

Riley hummed, maneuvering Seth under the showerhead to rinse off the soap Riley had been so carefully working into every bit of naked skin he could reach. "That icing got everywhere."

Although, true, it hadn't exactly gotten on Seth's back, way under his shirt, but it didn't hurt to be thorough.

"That's because you kept distracting me."

Riley grinned. Guilty as charged. He hadn't been able to help himself. Because for someone who'd worked so hard to keep distance between them from the beginning, Seth was endearingly susceptible to Riley's new methods of distraction.

He'd put Riley in a time-out at the kitchen table, sure, but as soon as Seth had been pouring the icing over the rolls and Riley had asked for a taste—first from the mixing spoon and then from

Seth's finger—Seth had gone all flushed and bright-eyed and had let Riley steal kiss after kiss after kiss. He'd tasted like sugar and oranges, and he'd let Riley back him into the counter and—

"You're not putting that thing inside me again today. I'm too tender."

Riley glanced down. He'd been rubbing his erection against Seth's plush cheeks while reminiscing under the hot spray. Oops.

"I won't," he promised.

But that reminded him. Seth didn't have to stay tender. Riley could fix it.

He dropped to his knees on the shower tile.

"What are you— Oh!"

Riley grabbed Seth's hips, keeping him still as he tongued at Seth's hole. He leaned back to tell him, "My saliva has healing properties."

"H-How convenient."

Seth didn't seem to have any other comment, so Riley went back to work. He was pleased when Seth placed his hands on the wall and pushed his ass out at an angle for him. That was helpful.

Riley hummed. He'd helped Seth wash here too—soaping and rubbing and dancing his fingers over furled skin until Seth had swatted him away and told him he was being a horny menace—and Seth tasted like clean skin and soap.

Riley was getting water in his nose, but he didn't care. He liked being here, pressed against Seth's soft flesh, his tongue sweeping circles around that place no one else was allowed to touch.

Riley wrapped a hand around his cock, stroking himself as he pressed his tongue in further. Deeper. Hopefully it was okay if he touched himself, as long as he wasn't trying to put "that thing" back inside Seth again.

Seth didn't seem to mind. He was moaning now, grinding himself back into Riley's mouth. It must have felt pretty good. Riley used his free hand to keep Seth's cheeks open and jerked himself with enthusiasm. It didn't matter that he'd taken Seth twice already—just being here, tasting him, was enough to make Riley desperate to come.

"Ungh. Fuck. *Fuck.*"

Seth's swearing sounded almost pained. Riley forced himself to withdraw and lean away again, gripping his own cock hard at the base to try to hold steady. "Should—should I stop?"

"No! No." Seth arched his spine at an even deeper angle. "Don't stop. Jesus. I'm gonna come."

The little whine in his voice went straight to Riley's dick. He was desperate. Desperate for Riley and what he could give him.

Riley's balls drew up tight, and he growled, planting his face back between Seth's cheeks and sucking hungrily at that perfect, soft entrance.

Seth keened, and Riley could hear him stroking himself too. He really wanted to come, didn't he? Fuck, that was hot. Too hot.

Riley groaned as he lost control, heat erupting from the base of his spine through his cock, spilling over onto his fist. He shuddered, tonguing and sucking through his orgasm until Seth stiffened with a strangled yell.

For a long moment, there was only the sound of the shower and Seth's desperate panting.

"Feel better?" Riley asked. That had been the point, right? Healing any soreness? He'd lost track, but he was pretty sure he'd started with very noble intentions.

Seth let out a breathless chuckle. He was slumped against the shower wall now, that teasing arch gone from his spine. "You'll have to wash my front too. I don't think my knees will hold."

Riley didn't stop grinning until they were out of the shower and Seth dropped his bomb with zero warning.

"Time to take me home, don't you think?"

Seth was already in a fresh pair of Riley's sweats, and he was searching through Riley's shirts for something acceptable. He looked so cute with Riley's waistband rolled over three times that it took Riley a second to hear him.

His stomach immediately dropped. "What?"

Seth turned, hands on his hips. "Riley. I have a life. A business. I know you want things settled, but that takes time, and you can't keep me holed up here all the while."

Riley stood there, at a loss for words. Of course Seth was right. Of course he couldn't stay here forever. Even Riley's voice wasn't protesting, for whatever reason.

Oh fuck, was Riley's *voice* the sensible one?

Because for the first time, Riley understood Wolfgang, who'd turned and sort of kidnapped his mate at their first meeting and then figured the rest out after. Riley finally *got* it. He really did.

Riley wanted Seth to be his. Now. Always. He didn't want to wait. He didn't want to let him go back to town and the life he was making, where Seth might decide vampires and their nonsense weren't worth the pain.

But that wasn't right. And convenient as it had been, what Wolfe had done wasn't right either. To be a good mate, Riley had to consider what *Seth* wanted.

And Seth wanted to go home.

"Can I come with you?" Riley asked, searching for any solution that might stop that sinking feeling from taking over his whole being. "Can—can I sleep over?"

Seth tapped his foot, considering. Riley tried to look as appealing and nonthreatening as possible. He didn't exactly know how to do that, so it mostly involved standing very still and keeping his eyes open wide. He might also have been pouting a little, but Seth was probably used to that by now.

"You can come," Seth finally said. "But I will be *sleeping* tonight. I wake up very early and—"

"And you get grumpy if you don't sleep," Riley finished for him, fighting back a massive grin.

"Exactly." Seth cocked his head. He was still staring at Riley, and Riley wasn't sure about the odd look that suddenly gleamed in Seth's eyes. He looked…devious.

"You can come with me to the bakery too," Seth said after a moment. "And we're going to start something. Maybe a book club."

"A book club?"

Seth nodded, a little wicked smile quirking at his lips. "Yeah. You like to read, right?"

"Yes?"

"Good." Seth tugged on one of Riley's shirts. "That's settled."

Riley's pout was no longer a maybe. "But…why?"

"Because you need to be around people," Seth told him. "You need to make friends. Have interests that aren't me and…me."

"But I like you."

Seth turned away, rifling through Riley's sweatshirts now. "Maybe Violet can help," he murmured. "She seems to be well connected."

He wasn't even talking to Riley anymore, was he?

"Violet?" This was getting worse and worse.

"Yeah." Seth dug deeper into Riley's drawer. Riley wished he could see his face, since the back of his neck was giving nothing away. "I'm gonna see if she wants a job. I can stay open later on the weekends, get my prep done while she finishes out front. And I'll have backup in the event of any more…accidents."

Hadn't they just been in the shower, coming their brains out while they discovered the wonders of Riley's tongue in Seth's ass? How had things devolved so quickly? Riley stepped forward, determined to get things to make sense again. "*I'm* your backup."

Seth waved a hand. "You're my boyfriend, not my backup."

Riley froze in place.

"I…am?"

"Yeah. We're dating, aren't we? I don't let just anyone eat my ass in the shower while they hog all the hot water."

If Riley had been human, he would have drowned in all that hot water, but he let that slide to focus on the important part.

"We are? We're dating?" The sinking feeling finally stopped spreading through Riley's body. It was replaced by a new warmth in Riley's chest. He was being given a lifeline, wasn't he?

Before Seth could speak, Riley answered for him. He couldn't have Seth changing his mind in the next three seconds. "We are," he said hurriedly. "Yes. Boyfriends. I'm the boyfriend. *Your* boyfriend."

"Okay, boyfriend." Seth shot him a glance as he held up a sweatshirt for perusal. "Go get your moms to fix my car."

MAMA SYBIL SET her book on her lap with a frown. She and Mama Daphne were curled up on the living room couch together, taking turns reading out loud. On a different day, Riley might have joined them with a book of his own.

"I still think it would be better if he were leaving with a claiming bite."

Riley crossed his arms. "Leaving as a vampire, you mean."

Mama Sybil raised an eyebrow at Riley, as if to say, *Well? What of it?*

Riley frowned at her. "I'm not doing that to him. Not against his will." He'd decided he wasn't going to be a Wolfgang. He was going to be a Riley. And a Riley respected his mate's wishes, even if his mate's wishes involved horrible book clubs and hiring sullen goth teenagers instead of devoted boyfriends.

His mothers didn't say anything. Mama Sybil's eyebrow stayed arched.

A standoff.

"Fix. The. Car." Riley waited a long moment, the tension in the air growing thicker with each passing second, then added, "Please."

Mama Sybil opened her mouth, and Riley steeled himself for a scolding. Maybe she was going to tell him he had to turn Seth right away or be locked in the attic. Not that they'd ever locked him in the attic—or anywhere—but there was a first time for everything. And the whole mate thing had everyone on edge in a new way.

But then Mama Daphne cleared her throat and laid a placating hand on Mama Sybil's forearm. "Already done, Riley darling."

Riley split a suspicious look between the two of them. "Really? Already?"

"Of course!" Mama Daphne told him. She almost sounded hurt that he didn't believe her. "You two are getting along so well, after all. And you're taking him home yourself, yes? Like a gentleman?"

"Yes." Riley straightened, then told them, "We're boyfriends."

Mama Sybil looked suspiciously close to rolling her eyes, but Mama Daphne made an approving noise. "How wonderful! I knew you'd charm him." She tilted her cheek toward him. "A kiss before you go."

Riley leaned down and kissed both his mothers on the cheek —Mama Sybil huffed but accepted hers otherwise graciously— then went to fetch Seth.

Seth came down the stairs in the sweatpants and sweatshirt that were a size too big for him, his own clothes tucked inside his tote bag. He looked so cute in Riley's clothes. Riley wanted to squeeze him, lift him off the floor and rub his cheek against those curls, but he'd wait. Seth was weird about Riley manhandling him in front of his mothers.

Seth approached the couch, standing solemnly in front of

Riley's moms. They'd remained seated at his arrival, and Riley had a feeling they were trying to be less intimidating rather than purposefully rude.

"Thank you for the hospitality." Seth managed not to sound sarcastic, which was pretty impressive, considering. Maybe it was all his customer service training.

Mama Sybil's smile gleamed in the afternoon light. "Oh, anytime, darling."

Seth narrowed his eyes. "I left a plate of orange rolls for you. I hope you enjoy them. Riley helped."

Mama Daphne leaned forward and reached out a hand, patting at Seth's hip. "What a darling! Drive safe on the roads. Precious cargo and all."

And that was that. No threats. No fangs. Everyone on their best behavior.

Suspicious.

Seth waited until he and Riley were outside the house before breaking and asking, "Am *I* the precious cargo she's referring to?"

Riley only grinned.

It was a comfortable drive through the woods. Seth played one of his more soothing playlists loud enough to fill the car. He didn't seem to be in the mood for chatting, but Riley didn't mind. Seth had a lot to think about, and Riley was just excited to get back to Seth's house, to be inside Seth's space again. Excited for Seth to sleep in Riley's arms and take Riley to work with him the next day.

Riley would be so good tonight too. He wouldn't wake Seth at all, no matter how much he might want to roll him over and sink into him again.

We're letting him sleep, he reminded his voice.

It didn't answer. It—*he'd* been quiet, Riley's voice, emanating a silent smugness ever since he'd taken over in Riley's bed. Smug because he'd fucked Seth, and Seth had liked it. Or maybe because he'd bitten Seth again, and Seth had liked that too.

Whatever. As long as Seth was happy, the stupid voice could aid in Riley's seduction attempts as much as he wanted. Riley had spent too many years battling him and losing. He wasn't going to risk trying to subdue his vampire again only for the bastard to snap and do something all three of them would regret.

Seth made the turn into town, and instinct had Riley swiveling his head toward the coastline. There was a white van parked on the side of the road, near a spot on the cliffs where a little trail wound down to the water. And a group of humans in hazmat-looking suits making their way along it.

Seth slowed the car as they drove by. "What do you think they're doing?"

Riley didn't know, but he recognized one suited lawyer among the scattered humans. But why would Mr. Perkins be out with the scientists?

"They're from that research institute," Riley told Seth. "The one in the suit came by the house before you arrived, asking to study the forest on our land."

Asking to study the wildlife, more specifically. Riley hadn't forgotten that bit.

"Then what are they doing out in the water?" Seth asked. "You think they study both ecosystems? Forest and ocean?"

"I don't know." Riley cracked his window and tried to scent something—exactly what, he wasn't sure—but the briny ocean air made it hard to smell anything but seaweed and salt.

Careful, his voice warned, breaking his previous silence.

Riley didn't need the warning though. He might not have been able to scent something specific, but he could recognize danger when it was right in front of him.

"I don't like them," Riley said.

Seth patted Riley's knee in a placating gesture, driving on past the van on the cliffside.

Maybe Seth thought it was Riley's sheltered upbringing that

was making him suspicious, but Riley didn't think that was it. He was wary of humans but not *suspicious* of them. At least not usually.

And the lawyer had set Riley's hackles up with a single conversation. Even his moms had been unsettled by Mr. Perkins's visit. That wasn't something Riley would be forgetting anytime soon.

Not now that Riley had a mate to protect.

20

SETH

Seth punched and rolled and kneaded and mixed, working the last dredges of his bad mood out in the kitchen.

Riley had been true to his word last night—he'd let Seth sleep wrapped up in his arms without so much as a stray nighttime boner brushing against Seth's ass.

But with no bakery prep done, Seth had needed to wake up earlier than usual, and venturing into the frigid, dark morning had been even more unpleasant than usual when it had meant leaving the warmth of Riley's hold.

Seth had set Riley up in the front with a tea and his book. Seth knew better now than to let the menace stay in the kitchen when there was so much work to be done. Those kisses of his were hazardous to Seth's attention span.

But after the fifth instance of Riley poking his forlorn head in the door, asking if there was anything he could do to help, Seth finally caved.

He stopped arranging his unbaked pear-and-walnut Danishes

with a sigh. "C'mon, then. Scrub your hands and you can brush these with egg wash for me."

Riley looked absurdly pleased, like Seth had offered him marriage and babies and not a bunch of raw pastry dough to cover with yolk.

And despite Riley's tendency for distraction, it turned out having another set of hands was useful after all. After finishing his task, Riley took care of all the smaller annoyances that took time but no skill to manage. He removed trays out of the oven and set pastries on their cooling racks. He organized Seth's dirty mixing bowls and set the worst of them to soak.

There was even time for five minutes of making out and heavy petting before Seth had to shove Riley away and set up his display case.

Violet was the first to show up, barely two minutes after Seth had flipped the "Open" sign.

"Don't you have school?" Seth asked. He didn't sound as stern as he would have liked. The familiar, cheery sound of the bell ringing over his bakery door had put him in a weird, giddy state.

"What time do you think high school starts in the morning, old man?" Violet asked, arching a brow. She definitely dyed her hair black—her eyebrows were practically blond. Or maybe she bleached her brows and kept her hair natural? What was it the kids did these days?

But anyway, she was right, it was only just after six. But how unnatural for a teenager to wake up so early by choice.

Violet shot Riley a suspicious glance and marched up to the counter. She was wearing her heaviest boots today, so the effect was pretty impressive. Her gaze ran over Seth like she was checking for hidden wounds. "Thought you were bones in the woods by now."

This girl. Seth cocked his head. "And how fast do you think bodies decompose, young lady?"

"Touché."

Seth grinned at her. He had a strange urge to give her a hug, but he'd probably be treated to a kick with one of those monster boots if he tried it. "You wanna work here?"

Violet crossed her arms. "Yeah. Weekends?"

"Mm-hmm."

"I want to learn how to make brioche buns."

"Eventually. You're starting up front."

Violet nodded and held out her hand. Seth shook it.

Riley spoke up from his table. "I'm the boyfriend."

Violet shot him an unimpressed look over her shoulder. "Good for you."

Seth set her up at a table with a black coffee and a plain bun, although he added one of the pear Danishes so she could start getting a taste for his other flavors. He'd started to think maybe she was allergic to fruit, but she accepted it with a gracious nod.

A few other regulars showed up shortly afterward—no Luke and Colby yet, but it wasn't their usual day. Seth's sign had claimed he was ill, apparently, and everyone was touchingly concerned over his health.

It wasn't quite like back at Seacliff, where Seth had known everyone so well that a lie like that wouldn't have held in the first place. If nothing else, Seth would have had Matty's demon husband busting down his door the first day he was closed, looking for key lime tarts to feed his beloved.

But still, it was...nice. Seth could sense it, like a shift in the air—this could be the start of a real community, if he let it.

After closing the bakery, Seth went into the back to give Benny a call. Seth had left him in the lurch after their last talk, and now that he was feeling seminormal, the guilt was eating Seth alive.

"Seth! I've been, like, worried."

Seth's stomach sank. "You have?"

He hadn't had any missed calls from his cousin, so he'd been convincing himself his silence wasn't that big of a problem. But then again, Benny was the type of person whose worries didn't stick in his head for long. They were like passing clouds, easily drifting away on the wind.

"Yeah. Helio said I dropped a bomb on you."

"Oh. Well, I talked it out with Sascha though. And then I was..." Seth coughed, lowering his voice even though there wasn't anyone but Riley out front. "Slightly kidnapped?"

"Ohhh." If anything, Benny sounded even more chill than before with that news. "Private island?"

"Um. No. A cabin in the woods."

"A magic cabin?" Benny asked. "Did it give you an Xbox?"

Seth held the phone away from his face, as if that might give him a clue what Benny was talking about. When that didn't work, he pressed it back to his ear. "No. Just—just a regular cabin. Nicely decorated though."

"Sweet. Did you bargain your life away? 'Cause they might hold you to it. It's not so bad though. Dream sex and whatnot."

"Did who—? What?" Seth shook his head. "Benny, it was vampires. I'm someone's fated mate, so they claim."

Seth hadn't been planning to share that particular bit of information, but the confusion was working as a sort of torture device, and he couldn't keep his mouth shut.

"Ah. Congrats." Benny let out a long sigh. "No magic villas though. That's a bummer."

Seth loved his cousin. He really did. But he was going to get a migraine if he kept this conversation up. "Well, I—I should get back to closing."

"Sure thing. But, Seth? If you need help, we'll be there. You don't have to do anything you don't want. Helio's good with bargains—he can get you out of it." Benny's voice hardened as much as Seth had ever heard it. "You've got, like, backup."

"Thanks, Benny. Love you, dude."

After more mutual affirmations of cousinly love, Seth hung up.

But Benny's words lingered in his brain. Because that was right, wasn't it? Seth had backup. *Supernatural* backup, at that. He'd known that, in the back of his mind, after his talk with Sascha.

And he'd let himself get kidnapped anyway.

What did that say about him? That he had a big, fat crush on a vampire, probably. And that he was maybe more of a pushover than he'd thought. He should probably work on that. Otherwise, how would he even have a hope of holding his own in this strange new world?

"Everyone gets to be your backup but me."

Seth turned to find Riley in the kitchen doorway, a sulky frown on his handsome face. Apparently his supernatural hearing had let him eavesdrop on both sides of Seth's conversation. "I'm strong enough," Riley insisted, as if Seth had been about to say otherwise. "I can protect you."

Seth let out a tired laugh, rubbing a hand over his face. The early start to the day was catching up to him. "Protect me from what? You?"

That was the problem, wasn't it? Seth didn't know what or who he even needed protection from. He didn't know enough about Riley's world. He didn't know enough about vampires. He'd never even seen Riley feed.

Riley's sulk took on a stubborn cast. "I'm trying. I am. I—I want you to have everything you want. I want to be the one to give it to you."

"And if I want space like before?"

Riley winced, but then he nodded. "Then I'll leave. And I won't come back until you tell me to."

Seth waited a long, long moment, but Riley didn't take back his reluctant words. Seth sighed. "Put your puppy dog eyes away. You can stay the night again." He turned away to start his closing duties, then whirled back. "Actually, I have an idea."

"No."

Seth paused in the act of placing a blanket over the corner of his couch. He'd thought it might be a good way to prevent things getting too messy. "What do you mean, no?"

"I mean *no*," Riley told him. "I don't want to risk it."

Seth frowned down at the blanket in his hands. "But you've done it before."

"That was just nibbling. It wasn't—it wasn't *feeding*."

Seth turned. Riley was standing across the living room, looking unexpectedly distraught. His hands were fisted at his sides, his brow all furrowed, his mouth twisted like he might actually burst into tears.

Seth had waited until they were home to tell Riley he wanted to practice being vampire food. He'd only waited because he thought it would be kind of a fun surprise—he hadn't actually thought Riley would object.

But apparently Seth had upset him deeply. He should have realized. This was a sore subject for Riley, and Seth had just sprung it on him with no warning.

Seth dropped the blanket and went over to Riley. He grabbed his broad hands, slipping his own between Riley's fingers and his palms, forcing Riley to unclench his fists. "Can you explain to me the difference? Isn't it just a matter of taking a little more than before?"

"I've just—" Riley's gaze darted away, over to Seth's window. "I've never *fed* from a person. Not—not fully. The bites I've given you were slips. What if this time I slip and I *drain* you?"

"You won't."

A muscle in Riley's jaw clenched and released. "How do you know?"

"Because you don't want to hurt me." Seth squeezed Riley's hands, trying to transfer his conviction by sheer force of will. "And he doesn't either. I know it."

"So let's not do it at all." Riley's lower lip jutted out the tiniest bit, his gaze still on the window. So, no tears, but a predictable pout. "I thought we were gonna focus on being boyfriends for a while and forget the rest."

Had Seth said that? Probably. But there was going slow and there was straight-up denial. Seth was a fan of the former, not the latter.

"Well, my *boyfriend* is a vampire. I wanted to slow things down, not stick my head in the sand completely." Seth pressed a kiss to Riley's chin, then his cheek. "Riley. Baby. You want me to turn eventually, right? Isn't that how the mate thing works?" Riley gave a reluctant, stilted nod, and Seth pressed on, "That would mean one day I'd be feeding off people. I want to know what that entails. And it's for you too. What if—what if one day we're stuck somewhere without enough wild animals for you? Somewhere without a blood bank we can access. If you can, you need to learn how to feed off people. And that starts with me."

Seth had been thinking it over all day, in an abstract sort of way. He hadn't decided on the bite until that moment in the bakery, but he'd been thinking about vampires in general. About what it actually might mean to be one. About how long he could be expected to stay human if Riley and his moms were intent on him becoming otherwise.

Riley's gaze had drifted away from the window, down to the pulse in Seth's neck, and he was watching it, his lips parted.

Poor, hungry boy. He wanted this. He was just afraid.

"Baby," Seth said again. Riley's gaze leaped up to his. "It'll be okay," Seth soothed. "I'll make sure of it."

Riley swallowed. Shook his head. Then once again, he gave a short, stilted nod. "If— If he takes too much, yell. Yell for me and I'll—I'll hear you. I know I will."

Before Seth could even agree to his terms, Riley's face shifted, the black taking over his eyes and those cute fangs peeking out from between his lips.

Seth almost took a step back, he was so surprised by the quick change. Not-Riley smirked, like he realized Seth had wanted to retreat. Like he was amused by that tiny hint of subconscious fear not even Seth's almost bottomless trust in him could entirely quell.

Seth narrowed his eyes, annoyed to be caught out like that. "You're going to behave?" he asked.

Riley's answer was to claim Seth's lips in a hungry kiss. He wasn't afraid to involve tongue and teeth, somehow managing to dominate Seth skillfully without drawing blood. He walked Seth backward and pressed him into the couch, growling into Seth's mouth.

That was a maybe, then.

Seth released Riley's hands, his arms coming up to wrap around Riley's neck. He let himself be lowered until he was half-reclined on the couch, let himself go limp and give in to Riley's desires.

He was about to finally come up for air, to beg Riley to focus—there'd been a point to bringing the vampire out, hadn't there?—when Riley's hand came up to Seth's throat, tilting his neck to the side.

Seth let his head fall where Riley wanted it, their kiss finally ending. His breaths were coming fast, both in response to what had just happened and in anticipation of what was still to come.

Then Riley's voice was in Seth's ear, speaking in a low, gravelly croon. "Don't be afraid, little human."

Seth wasn't afraid—not exactly. But maybe Riley was showing him what it would be like if he *was.* If he was a regular human meeting this beautiful, eerie version of Riley in some back alley. If a random seduction took a strange turn without warning.

Would Riley compel him, if that were the case? Would Seth, if he were in Riley's shoes?

Before he could come up with an answer, sharp teeth were sinking into Seth's throat, a hot slice that burned and then tingled.

With the other "slips," as Riley had called them, the two of them had been in the midst of sex, and the pleasure from the bite had been chasing the tail of other, more familiar threads of desire.

Now it caught Seth off guard. The force of it. The way the teeth in his neck seemed to be connected straight to his dick, and how with each pull Riley took of his blood, that connection strengthened. Seth was hard and aching before he even realized he was turned on.

Jesus. Was he going to come in his pants?

Riley was taking steady, deliberate gulps, focused on his task. Seth's head had gone a little light and floaty, but not like he was losing enough blood to be concerned. How did a vampire know when to stop? Instinct? Practice?

If the latter were the case, Seth was totally fucked.

He probably should have considered that before suggesting Riley chomp into him like a blood-filled donut. He also probably should have asked how much blood a vampire *needed* from a feed before he'd jumped into this. Was Seth going to need to go to the hospital after?

But then the fangs were coming out of his neck, and Riley was licking at the bite in long, soothing strokes. Seth might have thought it was another seduction attempt from the vampire half of him, but then he remembered the healing aspect of Riley's saliva. He was making sure Seth didn't bleed out from the bite.

Riley drew back, and that black gaze settled on Seth. "Forget now," Riley growled.

Was he using compulsion? But Seth wasn't forgetting anything, even though his eyes were locked with Riley's black pair. So maybe Riley was just…telling him what would come next?

"Then you make them forget," Seth repeated.

Riley nodded.

"Thank you."

Riley's lips quirked at the corners. "Pretty mate," he crooned. "So sweet. So brave." He kissed Seth again. He tasted like blood—Seth's blood—and yet Seth moaned into it, pressing up with his hips to get some sort of friction. He was still so hard. What did vampire victims normally do? Go home and jerk it with no idea why they'd suddenly become so horny they might burst?

In the middle of the kiss, the humping and the groaning, Riley made a noise, and Seth somehow knew without looking that his boy was back. He whimpered. Thank God. He was ready to explode.

"Touch my dick," he begged. "Please, Riley."

Riley immediately shoved his hand into Seth's pants, gripping Seth's tortured cock.

"Oh God," Seth groaned.

"It felt good?" Riley asked, kissing fiercely along Seth's jawline, his throat. Could he still taste the blood there? Was there a copper tinge to the salt of Seth's skin now?

"It felt good," Seth told him, pressing up with his hips again. "So, so good."

Riley rewarded him with the steady, firm glide of his hand over Seth's erection. "You didn't want *him* to do this?" he asked, pausing at the top, his fist cupped around the sensitive head.

"Want you," Seth moaned, arching up into that teasing touch. "Want you to touch me."

He could feel Riley's grin against his neck as he started jerking Seth for real. It didn't take long for Seth to finish, not after everything that had come before. Riley had barely gotten into the rhythm when Seth cried out, spilling over his hand.

Riley licked it off his fingers afterward. "Every part of you is so sweet," he said. He didn't sound like he was trying to be seductive but like he was pointing out a fun fact. "So delicious."

Seth groaned, covering his face with his hands. "You're going to be filthy, aren't you?"

Riley's answer was to tug Seth's hands away and kiss him again, licking the taste of Seth's own cum into his mouth.

That was a yes, then.

Seth sighed into the kiss, wrapping his arms around Riley's neck and letting his filthy boyfriend seduce him once more.

He supposed there were worse crosses to bear.

21

RILEY

Riley was on Seth's couch again.

This time, they weren't sitting cross-legged facing each other, slimy face masks covering their features. This time, Seth was pressed into Riley's side, his warmth like living sunshine against Riley's body as they watched a show where absurdly kind British people competed in baking.

Riley had tried to tease Seth about failing to separate his work from his home life—"Really, you bake for work and then watch baking for fun?"—and Seth had practically hissed at him like a cranky cat. "It's different. This is *self-care*."

Apparently, Seth really liked his show, and that was not to be questioned. Lesson learned.

Seth really liked his show, and he also really liked Riley's bite. Actually, he'd liked not just Riley's bite but Riley *feeding* on him, draining Seth's blood to keep his own flowing in his undead veins.

And then, because he was perfect in every way a person could be, Seth had let Riley bring him to completion and then fuck between Seth's clamped-together thighs, the blanket Seth had placed to catch stray blood catching Riley's spend instead.

And now, with them cuddled together on this couch, for once in Riley's life, he was...sated, some of that relentless hunger inside him finally eased. How could he be anything but full? Seth kept *feeding* him, over and over. With his care, with his body, and now with his blood.

Riley had taken human blood from its source, and he hadn't hurt anyone doing it.

Seth had even asked for it himself because he trusted Riley—both Riley and the monster inside him. And even though Seth was freaked out by Riley's claims of fate, he was working hard to wrap his head around it all, to better understand Riley's world.

And Riley owed him another truth for that. His worst truth. A glimpse at the cost of his horrible hunger.

It wasn't fair to keep Seth in the dark any longer.

Riley rested his head on Seth's curls, allowed himself one more moment of peaceful warmth. He spoke the words quickly, like if he hesitated too long, they wouldn't come out at all. "I know my moms and I said I haven't fed on any humans before you, but that's not totally true."

Seth paused his show immediately, seeming to sense that something important was underneath Riley's quiet statement. "What do you mean?"

Seth shifted in place, and Riley could feel Seth's gaze searing into him as he waited for Riley's answer. He knew he should turn to face his mate, but he couldn't bring himself to do it. He kept on staring at the laptop screen, that frozen image of someone piping meringue onto a tart.

"The first time I got away from the one who turned me, I made it all the way back home," Riley told Seth. "My mom was there—my birth mom. She'd had the police looking, I think, but they weren't at the house then. It was just her. And I was so—" Riley swallowed, blinking too quickly as his eyes started burning. "I was so *relieved* to see her. I thought everything was going to be okay now that I was home. She grabbed me and held me so, so tightly, kneeling on the living room floor. And I—she smelled—" Riley's voice grew thicker, something solid blocking his throat. He forced the words out anyway. "I was so hungry. *So* hungry. I bit her. I—I drank."

"Oh, Riley," Seth whispered, soft and quiet and so concerned. He slid his hand into Riley's, letting Riley grip his fingers tightly.

"I think because I was a child, or maybe because we're blood-related, my bite didn't...feel good, the way they usually do. So she was scared. She hurt. And the only reason I didn't k-kill her was that she fought me off. My vampire strength didn't match an adult's yet, and she—she grabbed the nearest lamp and smashed it over my head. I was so scared but still so *hungry*. So I ran, and then...he caught me. Again."

Seth didn't say anything this time. He only squeezed Riley's hand, his warm, calloused palm a lifeline Riley didn't think he could do without.

"My moms...they thought I might forget, in time. And I forgot a lot—too much—but I remember the look in her eyes when she was brandishing that lamp, holding a hand to her bloody neck, yelling, 'What *are* you?' over and over." Riley stroked his thumb over the little burn scars on the back of Seth's hand, made himself say the final words. "So that man took me, but *I'm* the reason I couldn't go back."

And then Seth's other hand was cupping Riley's face, gentle fingers brushing his cheek, wiping away tears Riley hadn't realized had fallen. "Riley, you know that's not true."

Seth's green-brown eyes weren't recriminating. They were... they were so soft and concerned that they were almost loving. Like Riley could see now what it would look like to be loved by Seth, and it was so beautiful it hurt. "Your human mother... Sweetheart, she wouldn't have been able to keep you safe. She wouldn't have known what to do, how to manage the changes you were going through. It's horrible, and it's tragic, and I'm so, so sorry, but it's not your fault. You *were* taken from her, baby. That's not on you."

And then Riley was falling into Seth's shoulder, crying in a way he hadn't since those early days, when he'd been so young and scared and lost, knowing he wasn't going to be found ever again, not by the person he loved most in the world.

He'd let the vampire part of him take over a lot in those early days. He'd trusted his strange new moms to watch over him, and he'd let go. He'd hunted for hours and hours in the woods, safe and secure in that blank, nothing state in the back of his own mind.

It had taken time and patience for his moms to draw him out, to coax him into inhabiting himself again. And even though they'd managed it, part of him had always wondered if he'd ever feel whole again.

But he *did* feel whole, wrapped in Seth's slender, strong arms, letting his tears soak Seth's T-shirt. He was a person, wasn't he, even after all that had happened? Maybe a broken person—an unnatural creature with long, jagged cracks running along his center—but a person nonetheless. His moms had done their part, and now Seth was helping hold those broken bits together by sheer stubbornness and kindness and bravery, and all Riley had to do was let him.

Those gentle fingers that had brushed Riley's cheeks now stroked through his hair. "I'm sorry if I pressured you into biting me before you were ready," Seth said. "I get a little single-minded sometimes, but I should have asked. I shouldn't have just...bossed you around."

Riley was too tired and worn out to pretend to be normal about anything. He sniffed back tear-induced snot and told Seth, "You can boss me around all you want. Tell me what to do, tell me when to do it. Because you might not be mine, but I'm all yours." Riley burrowed deeper into Seth's hold. "Every single part of me."

ONE OF THE mysteries of Seth was that he could be so generous and so cruel all in the span of twenty-four hours.

"But I don't want to go back," Riley told him. "I want to stay here. With you."

Seth met Riley's eyes in his vanity mirror as he straightened his cloth headband. This one had a yellow-and-orange checkered pattern, like a tablecloth made out of sunshine. "I'm not banishing you, but you need to pick up some of your own clothes and check in with your moms." Seth turned, assessing Riley's outfit with a skeptical gaze. "My pants are definitely too short on you."

Riley looked down at the sweats he was wearing. Sure enough, he was flashing some ankle. He huffed. "I don't care."

"You look like a dork."

"So what?"

Seth only laughed, then began rummaging through his tote bag, presumably checking to see if he still had the keys and lunch he'd packed only a few minutes before.

Seth had a system in the mornings, and it wasn't a lingering one. He didn't eat breakfast at home, instead waiting to snag one of his own pastries at the bakery during prep. It unsettled Riley in a vague way, like he knew he should have been insisting Seth sit down and eat something hearty to prepare for the day. But it would have been pointless, since Riley didn't know how to cook anything, anyway.

And Seth didn't shower in the mornings either. He only splashed water on his face and dressed in a hurry. He said there was no point to showering when he was just going to get all sweaty and covered in flour at work anyway. He waited until he got home at the end of the day. Which meant Riley couldn't offer to wash his back either.

So basically Riley didn't have *anything* to offer when it came to Seth's routine. Instead, he was being shooed away like a pest.

Tote bag thoroughly inspected, Seth came over and placed his hands on Riley's shoulders. Even though he'd laughed at Riley and told him he looked like a dork, Seth's gaze wasn't dismissive. It was warm. Considerate. "You feeding on me was kind of a milestone," he said softly, giving Riley's shoulders a gentle shake. "Don't you think you should share that with your moms?"

That was reasonable. Sensible. Riley should graciously agree and make a dignified exit.

"It's Violet's training day," he pointed out instead.

Seth laughed again. "Yes, yes, it is. And she doesn't need you pouting at her the whole time she's there."

"I wouldn't pout."

"You would."

Riley scowled. "Don't bake any orange cakes with her."

Seth's eyebrows went up to his hairline. "I wasn't planning on it. I'm just going to be showing her the basics so she knows a little more about what I offer. And she's already run the register. We'll go over closing duties and the little nitty-gritties. It'll be boring."

It didn't sound boring to Riley, not if Seth was doing it.

He didn't know why he was being so clingy, other than the obvious answer that it was in his nature. True, he was a little extra raw from his confession last night, but most of those sharp edges had been soothed by watching Seth sleep.

Maybe it was the unsettled mate bond tugging at him. There was this fear, underneath the peace Seth brought him, this sense that at any moment, all this could end.

Who was to say that Seth wouldn't disappear from Riley's life as quickly as he'd arrived? Riley had come to depend on him so fast, and everything was still so uncertain. Seth was human—not only could he leave; he could *die.*

There was no reason to think he would, but the possibility was always there, hovering in the darkest corners of Riley's mind. Was it any wonder Riley felt a little unhinged about it all?

Seth planted a firm kiss on Riley's scowling mouth. "You can come back tonight. I'll make us dinner."

Riley stole another kiss before asking, "Really?" He couldn't help how hopeful he sounded.

"Yes, really. I told you I wasn't banishing you." Seth wrapped his arm around Riley's as they headed out the door. "Do you want to take my car? You can drop me off at the bakery first."

That was...nice. Domestic, really, sharing a car like that. Some of the tightness left Riley's chest, even as he shook his head. "No. A run through the woods sounds nice."

"Ugh." Seth threw his head back. "It really does. I should go on one soon."

"We can run together."

Seth wrinkled his nose. "But you'll be all composed and perfect, and I'll be all ragged and sweaty."

Riley nodded, pleased with that image. "I like you ragged and sweaty."

Seth gave him a swat, but his cheeks flushed a very revealing pink.

Riley rode with him all the way to the bakery, kissed him senseless at the bakery door, and then went on his way. He wasn't exactly feeling light as air, but he was slightly less disgruntled than he might have been.

It wouldn't be the worst thing in the world to have a bag of his own clothes and some spare books at Seth's. And yeah, Riley's moms *would* want to hear that he'd fed successfully. Mama Daphne probably had some wonderful gift she'd been saving for the occasion. Or maybe she'd want to redo his bedroom to celebrate.

So Riley ran through the woods, relishing the rush of cold, damp air. It was comforting, the familiar scents and sounds of the forest. And Riley was full from Seth's bite, so he didn't need to terrorize the local woodland creatures. He could just enjoy it, taking his place as one of them.

He was momentarily distracted when he smelled something strange along the road, a kind of briny scent with an odd edge to it he couldn't categorize. But it was too saturated with car exhaust and motor oil to make out clearly. Maybe someone had been hauling a catch of fish.

His moms' cars were back at the house, just like Riley knew they would be. His belly clenched with nerves as he got to the front door. Would they be disappointed he'd let Seth out of his sight already? Would they think he'd been reckless to bite him so soon?

But it wasn't Riley's moms waiting for him on the living room couch this time.

Instead of the two women he loved most in the world, it was two grown men, sitting close together. One was blond and blandly good-looking, the other too sharp-cheeked and dead-eyed to be considered classically handsome. Not to mention the horrible checkered suit.

Riley scowled at the two of them. "What are you *doing* here?"

"Now, Riley," Wolfe drawled, placing a possessive hand on Eric's knee as he smiled a smile that didn't reach his eyes. "Is that any way to greet invited guests?"

22

SETH

Seth was more out of sorts than he should have been as he prepped his pastries for the day.

Even with the soothing playlist blaring from his portable speaker, the kitchen felt quiet. Empty. Seth should have been grateful to have a moment to himself, but he missed his pouty vampire lurking in the corner and making puppy dog eyes at him. Seth even missed the way Riley watched his every move, like if he dared to blink, Seth might disappear in an instant.

Instead of disconcerting, the attention had come to feel... grounding. A tether so strong Seth couldn't slip away even if he wanted to.

And he didn't want to, did he? Not even close.

Seth had meant what he'd said to Riley when he'd told him to skedaddle—even a hot-as-fuck vampire looked ridiculous in Seth's too-short pants. Riley had needed to go home and get some clothes that actually fit him.

But Seth had also convinced himself he needed a moment of breathing room to come to terms with an alarming fact: he was falling for Riley. Falling *in love* with Riley. And it was happening too fast—*way* too fast.

But Riley had opened his heart up to Seth last night, offered it to him by telling him about what was surely the worst day of Riley's life, and what was Seth to do but accept the bruised, battered offering?

He could keep pretending they were just dating, that flirtation and attraction were slowly building into something more. But the truth was that there was nothing slow about the way he was falling hard for this vampire. This man who was barely more than a boy. A boy who'd been so lonely and so scared and who had so much love he was aching to give.

Seth wanted to take all that love and give him even more in return. He wanted to hide away Riley's heart with all its cracks and bruises and exchange it for his own, all soft and coddled and bright from a life well loved and so far well lived. He wanted Riley to know it was okay to want so badly and hunger so deeply, and that Seth would do his very best to make sure that aching emptiness never hurt him again.

Seth needed to tell him, of course. Riley seemed to be under the impression that Seth needed to *learn* to care for him, as if that hadn't been happening almost against Seth's will since their very first encounter.

Riley deserved to know it didn't take time and effort to love him. It wasn't difficult at all. He wasn't a monster or a burden. He was...

Well, he was Seth's, just like he'd said. And while Seth had never given himself away to someone before—had never placed his heart completely in another person's hands—he knew Riley wouldn't take the responsibility lightly.

And neither would Seth. Because there *was* a responsibility to loving Riley. He'd been through so much, Seth's poor boy, and he deserved to experience some of the good life had to offer.

And Seth was going to give that to him, whether Riley thought he wanted it or not. Friends. A community. People who weren't his moms or his boyfriend to care for and be cared for in return.

Seth was still smiling when Violet arrived at the bakery, about forty-five minutes before opening. He gave her a tour of the kitchen and explained the basics of his process, what he'd be doing in the back to prep ahead of time while she worked the register.

Then Violet helped him open the front, and he explained what tasks would need to be completed during closing. He took the information he needed from her so he could start paying her officially. His old boss had showed Seth the processes and paperwork required to hire someone already, back before he'd left Seacliff. She'd been insistent he wouldn't be able to do it alone for long. It seemed she'd been right.

Violet lingered in the bakery after the haphazard training, sipping black coffee behind the counter while Seth served his first customers.

There was one he didn't recognize, a man in a black suit who watched Seth with an intensity that had Seth wondering for a moment if the man was an incredibly poorly disguised health inspector. And then he remembered he *had* seen this guy before, on the cliff with the crew in hazmat suits the other day. Maybe exclusively socializing with mysterious scientists had affected his people skills. The man wasn't even the most socially awkward of Seth's customers, so Seth brushed off the uneasy feeling and sent him out with a cheery smile.

Seth waited until the bakery was empty again to make his move.

"What do you think about a book club?"

Violet took a contemplative sip of her coffee before answering. "Here?"

"Yeah. Once a month, maybe."

"What kind of books?"

Seth shrugged. He wasn't much of a reader, honestly. That was more Riley's thing. Seth was just going to be the evil genius using Riley's hobbies against him to force him to socialize. But that seemed like too much of a mouthful to admit at the moment. "Not sure."

Violet gave him one of her discerning looks. "I want veto power."

"You'll come?" Seth asked with surprise. He hadn't taken her for the book club type. He knew she read—she must, if she wrote so much—but she didn't seem like a joiner.

"If it's not too lame."

Seth absently greeted one of his semiregulars, a quiet guy somewhere in his early twenties who usually came in a few times a week. He had sleepy brown eyes and wore anime shirts and kept his tightly coiled black curls cropped short.

"You think other people will come?" Seth asked Violet under his breath. "I want Riley—I mean, I want us *both* to socialize a little."

"I can get you Luke," Violet told him, her tone the same as if she were telling him she could procure him a particularly rare cut of meat. "He's my uncle, you know."

Seth did *not* know. He gaped at her. "What?"

But Violet was already moving on. "And Mr. Evans. He teaches PE and coaches, like, football or something stupid at the high school. I have dirt on him."

"You have *dirt*?" Seth asked, unable to help the shrill edge to his voice. "Should—should I be concerned?"

"Not for me," Violet said ominously. She arched her brows. "You know who I mean, right? Big, gruff, has a beard."

Seth's lumberjack regular, she meant. He *was* gruff. Seth wouldn't necessarily classify him as rude, but he definitely wasn't chatty, and he'd never officially introduced himself.

"Okay, yeah, I know who you mean. Who else?" Seth asked eagerly. Against his better judgment, he was kind of getting into it now. Who wouldn't be fascinated by the mysterious connections of this teenager?

Violet turned sharply to their customer. "Hey. You." The guy froze in the act of quietly perusing the pastries, his sleepy brown eyes going wide and alert. Violet scanned him up and down. "Wanna join our book club?"

Seth had apparently forgotten to go over some of the basics during training—mainly that no one should be addressing any customers as *Hey You*.

But the guy didn't act offended, although he stayed frozen for another long moment before answering, "Um...okay?"

"Perfect." Violet gave him a sharp nod. "We'll put up a sign on the board. Look for it or I'll find you where you live."

"Oh my God," Seth muttered. He hastily put three of the giant cookies the guy had been eyeing into a bag. "On the house. I promise it'll be fun."

Violet's shell-shocked victim took the bag and left without another word. Seth probably should have asked for his name, if only to find out to whom he needed to address his apology letter.

He sighed heavily, casting a sidelong look at his new protégé. "You didn't have to resort to blackmail with that one?"

His sarcasm was completely lost on Violet. Or maybe she just didn't care. She only shrugged, downing the rest of her coffee in one gulp. "He's too new. Only moved here a couple months before you."

Seth thought of other newcomers in town, the man in the suit coming to mind. "Hey, what do you know about this research institute?" he asked. "Any news there?"

"No. But they've made their way into my fanfiction." A savage light entered Violet's eyes. "Hannibal has them over for dinner."

THE REST of the day passed as quickly as it could with a certain vampire's noticeable absence. Luke and Colby showed up later in the morning, and Violet immediately pounced on Luke.

Seth was quickly learning that once she set her sights on recruiting for something, she was merciless.

Luke had seemed hesitant about the book club until Violet had told him she'd get her mom to babysit Colby, and then he was all for it.

"Anything for a night with grown-ups." He had given Seth a hopeful look. "Am I allowed to bring beer?"

Seth had shrugged. "As long as I'm not selling it, it's cool under event rules. I may need to get a permit, but I'll check."

A little booze probably wasn't the worst idea anyway. They were going to be a motley crew, and a little social lubricant never hurt.

As Seth closed down his bakery, the first twinges of real excitement ran through him. He was getting into this idea, not just for Riley, but for himself.

Seth was a social creature by nature, and with all his focus on Riley, he'd been letting his well run a bit dry. Interactions with his customers were great, but they weren't enough on their own. And, to be honest, it had been so long since he'd had to work for this kind of community that the challenge was a bit of a thrill. He wasn't guaranteed friends and companions here due to a lifetime spent in the same town—he had to *earn* them. And that was nothing if not a worthwhile endeavor.

By the time he got home, Seth was still riding high off the anticipation, even though he hadn't heard from Riley yet. Maybe his new vampire boyfriend was still sulking at being made to leave this morning.

Seth eyed his running shoes, waiting so hopefully by his front door. It wouldn't be the worst idea to get a little run in. He was getting woefully out of the habit, and the longer he delayed, the harder it would be to get back into it.

The sky was gray, and the air was cold, but there was no sign of rain, so Seth suited up in as many layers as he could tolerate, stuck his wireless headphones in his ears, and went out the door.

On the other side of his house from his one neighbor, there was what looked to be a game trail leading into the woods. Seth had no idea where it ended—it was possible it was going to dead-end and leave him short a decent run—but now seemed as good a time as any to find out.

He'd been trudging along for about ten minutes, trying not to be disheartened by how heavy his breathing had already gotten, when he felt it. A...presence, maybe. The sense that someone was watching him, raising the hairs on the back of his neck.

Seth had a good idea who it might be.

"I know you're out there," he called softly.

Nothing.

When Riley didn't answer his taunt, Seth stopped, stepping to the side of the trail to catch his breath while he waited for whatever kind of game this was to reveal itself. He took out his phone from his pocket to pause his music.

Seth frowned down at the screen. That was odd. There was a text from Riley, one he'd missed while jogging.

Delayed. I'll be over in the morning. Promise.

Seth hadn't realized Riley was such a stoic texter. He'd expected more exclamation marks, maybe a few emojis thrown in here and there. Definitely multiple hearts per text, at the very least. But then, Riley hadn't had a lot of practice communicating with anyone, had he?

But that wasn't the odd part. Seth's frown deepened as he reread Riley's message.

Because if Riley was stuck with his moms, who or what had Seth just called out to?

Seth peered through the trees around him, not sure what he was even looking for. Were there mountain lions here? Bears? Should he have looked up wild animal safety before going off on his own in the woods?

But he didn't find any clues from looking. Every now and again, a shadow in the dense foliage had his heart skipping a beat, but in the end, there was nothing. No one.

Maybe Seth was imagining things. Maybe he'd gotten so used to being watched by Riley that he was making up the sensation in Riley's absence.

Still, if Seth turned around right now, that would be a good, twenty-minute run right there. He could call it a day without being too ashamed of his athleticism. Maybe once he got back to his street, he'd head down the road a little bit, get some steps in while civilization still surrounded him.

Maybe it was silly to be so spooked by nothing, but it didn't hurt to be cautious, right?

Seth didn't restart his music. Instead, he popped his headphones out of his ears and put them in his pocket, leaving him free to catch the sounds of the forest. He wanted all his senses on alert, just in case. He turned and started back the way he'd come.

The lack of music meant Seth caught the sound immediately when a twig snapped behind him.

Seth whirled around, but before he could see what had made the noise, there was thick fabric covering his face, blocking his mouth and nose.

He panicked, trying to thrash out and dislodge the cloth—he couldn't *breathe*—but strong arms had already wrapped around him, trapping his arms by his side.

Seth was aware of harsh breathing coming from somewhere. A chemical scent that burned his throat and his eyes as he hyperventilated into whatever was covering his face. His stomach roiled. His hands went numb.

And then, nothing at all.

23

RILEY

"I still don't understand why this couldn't be a phone call," Riley said. "Or why I have to be here for it."

Wolfe cocked a brow at Riley over his pretentious glass of wine. Wolfe always brought his own bottles every time he visited, as if Riley's moms didn't have an amazing wine cellar of their own.

Snob. Rude-ass snob.

"Are you always this childish?"

Riley scowled back at him. "Yes."

Eric cleared his throat, giving Riley a placating smile while Wolfe toyed with Eric's fingers with his free hand. "Your moms are concerned about your new neighbors. And Wolfe has always been..."

"Uber paranoid?" Riley supplied helpfully.

"Cautious," Wolfe countered. He set his glass down, tapping neat, blunt fingernails on the dining room table. "I knew you'd be trouble."

"Careful, Wolfe, darling," Sybil drawled. To the untrained ear, she might have sounded unconcerned and uncaring, but Riley recognized the dangerous note in her voice. "That's my son you're speaking to."

She and Mama Daphne were on Riley's side of the table, while Wolfe and Eric sat across from them. Riley would have preferred they all convene on the covered porch—it was less claustrophobic when he could see the forest around them—but Wolfe had been wary about "prying eyes and ears."

Like Riley had said. Uber paranoid.

"Your *son*"—Wolfe stressed the word almost sarcastically, as if he hadn't been the one to basically facilitate Riley's pseudoadoption in the first place—"is an anomaly. And anomalies gain attention. You believe it to be a coincidence that they've set up here? At your doorstep?"

A twinge of guilt hit Riley, deep in the pit of his stomach. He hadn't considered that if something shady was going on, it was probably his fault. Had he really drawn attention to himself? He'd tried to be so careful. He'd been forest-bound for almost a full decade, for fuck's sake.

He looked around the table helplessly. "How would they even know about me?"

Mama Daphne spoke up, her tone gentle as could be. "There's one human witness who wasn't ever compelled to secrecy."

Immediately, Riley knew who she was referring to. His eyes burned. "My mo— My, um, human mom?"

It had taken almost a full year for Riley to tell Mama Sybil and Mama Daphne what had happened between him and his mother —the bite and the terror and the anger—but eventually he'd let them know, afraid if he'd kept it to himself any longer the aching wound inside of him would fester. And he'd been young, and still so scared, and he'd wanted a little comfort.

Like Seth, they'd reassured him that he hadn't been at fault, that his mother couldn't have been expected to know how to manage his transformation. But the memory was still painful, and now it had come back to haunt him in a whole new way.

"It's possible she told the authorities about what happened on your return." Mama Daphne placed her hand over his, squeezing gently. "It would have been in an effort to find you, darling. No doubt she regretted very deeply driving you away."

Riley swallowed hard, willing his eyes to stay dry. He wouldn't cry in front of Wolfe. He *wouldn't.*

He wished Seth were here. If Seth were with them, there would be something delicious on the table to go with Wolfe's snobby wine, and he'd be right there, on Riley's other side, giving him strength without even trying. He wouldn't put up with any of Wolfe's little digs either.

Tomorrow, Riley reminded himself and his voice both. *We'll see him tomorrow.*

"What are we supposed to do, then?" Riley asked. "Knock on their door and ask if they're planning to do any evil research on innocent vampire children, current or former?"

Wolfe shrugged one shoulder. "If needs must. In the meantime, a bit of casual reconnaissance." He narrowed his eyes at Riley as he toyed with the stem of his wineglass. "You're aware that if you'd turned your mate already, we'd have one more ally in the area."

Riley stiffened. He knew he was being baited—they had an entire den in Colorado at their disposal, if Wolfe really needed it—but he couldn't help his reaction. "Seth doesn't need to be a vampire to be an ally."

"To be a useful one, surely."

A low growl left Riley's throat, and Eric spoke up quickly. "Hey, Riles, have you gotten any comics from Colin recently? I'd love to see them."

Wolfe tutted, sliding a look at his mate that was so hotly

possessive it made Riley want to gag. "Tenderhearted," Wolfe murmured fondly.

Eric shrugged, although there was a new flush on his cheeks. "Colin's art is cool, and he hardly ever shares."

It was blatant misdirection, and Eric wasn't even pretending to be subtle. But it was also an olive branch to get Riley out of the room, so he took it. He nodded to Eric, and they left the table and went upstairs to Riley's room.

"Your mate's a pain in the ass," Riley told him as soon as they were inside.

"Yeah," Eric agreed easily. "But he wants us all to be safe."

"He wants you and *him* to be safe," Riley corrected before heading over to his bookcase and pulling out Colin's latest comic.

"For him and me to be safe, everyone has to be. So it works out." Eric grinned down at the cover of the comic Riley had handed him, which had a fictionalized and much cooler version of vampire Riley on it, all black eyes and bulging black veins. One day—whenever he finally decided to release them to the public—Colin was going to be famous for those things.

Riley collapsed back onto his bed, holding himself up with his elbows. He let Eric rifle through the first few pages before he couldn't hold it in any longer. "Why'd you forgive him so easily? I've heard the story of how you were turned."

If Eric was surprised by the question, he didn't show it. He didn't even glance up from the comic. "Because I needed him."

Riley thought of Seth, bright and charming and open with everyone. He thought of Seth's full life, how he'd already made a place for himself inside their insular little town within a month. He sighed. "I don't think Seth needs me."

Eric made a vague, noncommittal noise. "You might be surprised. I was a successful doctor and reputed man-whore. No one would have thought I needed someone like Wolfe. But I did."

He ran a finger over the panels of the comic with a distant look in his eye. "I really, really did."

"And he needed you back?" Riley asked. He knew it was true—he saw the way Wolfe looked at Eric, the rare and out-of-character affection he gave his mate—but it was still hard to fathom Wolfe really *needing* somebody.

Eric laughed. He had a good laugh, actually, bright and hearty. He was a little less blandly handsome when he laughed. Riley could almost see the appeal.

"Oh yeah," Eric said on the end of a chuckle. "He'd be full psycho without me." He finally tore his attention from the comic to give Riley a look. "Want can be a kind of need, you know, if it's strong enough. You don't have to be saving him from misery for him to love you."

Riley shrugged and rolled onto his belly, resting his chin on folded arms. He wasn't sure about that, really. Being a vampire's mate came with a lot of baggage—it was kind of lose-lose in a lot of ways, wasn't it? Saving someone from abject misery would at least be a concession prize.

TECHNICALLY, Riley had his driver's license.

They hadn't compelled anyone to give it to him either. He'd passed the written *and* the practical, even though he'd been terrified to sit in an enclosed car with a human that long. He'd been afraid he was going to cut the test short by draining his instructor. But he hadn't, and now he could legally drive and everything.

He still preferred to go by foot.

Going by foot meant going through the forest, deeper than where the road could reach. And the forest meant familiarity. It was soothing.

And Riley needed a bit of soothing.

Eric and Wolfe were apparently staying at the house in the non-Seth guest bedroom because, to quote Wolfe, "This tragic display of coastal decline possesses no hotels of any caliber."

There had been more discussion of the mysterious institute last night, but all of it had been speculative and pretty pointless, in Riley's opinion. It had all had major "this meeting could have been an email" energy.

Seth had taught Riley that one.

Seth, who hadn't answered Riley's text. Was he annoyed that Riley hadn't come back right away? That would actually be kind of gratifying. Annoyance would imply he'd *wanted* Riley to return quickly—that maybe Seth had missed him, even if it was only for the night.

Riley had certainly missed Seth. He could even almost smell Seth's sweet orange scent out here in the woods, taunting Riley with the night they'd lost to Wolfe and his paranoia.

So maybe Seth was frustrated with Riley for flaking, or maybe he just wasn't a big texter. Riley knew Seth made phone calls to the people back home, but overall, he wasn't on his phone as much as some modern humans seemed to be.

But that was fine. Riley knew where to find him. That was the benefit of his boyfriend owning his own business.

It was past opening, so Riley wasn't going to get alone time with Seth in the kitchen. Which meant he wasn't going to get to live out the new fantasy he had of pushing Seth back against those chrome counters and dropping to his knees, maybe even managing to get Seth's cock all the way inside his mouth this time. Maybe all the way to the back of his throat.

Mmm.

But it was too late for that, so Riley would be a good boy and sit at his table with his book while Seth spread sunshine to all his customers indiscriminately. Riley had his backpack with some spare clothes too, so he wouldn't be booted out right away either.

No doubt Wolfe would be a pest and call Riley back at some point, but Riley would take all the time he could get before then.

Riley skipped the bakery's back door—Seth kept it locked when he was up front—and headed around to the main street. He frowned as he approached. There weren't any lights on inside.

It was dark. Closed.

But it wasn't a Monday. And Seth was never late opening the bakery. Never ever.

Riley glared at the other figure lurking beside the front door. "Where is he?"

Violet didn't even flinch at the dark growl in his voice. She remained leaning against the wall in her black peacoat, arms crossed. "He didn't show up this morning. I thought maybe he'd been taken hostage again." She gave Riley a cool once-over. "But if you're looking for him too, I guess that theory is out."

Riley didn't know how she knew where Seth had gone the last time the bakery had been unexpectedly closed, and he didn't fucking care. He turned on his heel. "His house, then."

"I checked there when he didn't show," Violet called from behind him, stopping him in his tracks. He turned to face her and saw for the first time the furrow of concern on her brow. "I thought maybe he'd gotten sick for real. His car was there, but he didn't answer, and I was loud. Really loud."

Riley would check, of course. He wouldn't trust some random teenager's word, new employee or not. But a creeping sensation of dread was already building, crawling along his spine.

If Violet was to be believed, then Seth was missing.

Missing while some devious institution had everyone's hackles up. Missing at the same time Wolfe had shown up at Riley's door, bitching about abnormal vampires and unwanted attention. Missing right when Riley had come to depend on him, and on the future they might have.

Seth was Riley's. Fate had said so, and Riley had accepted that decision without a drop of hesitation. But fate could also be cruel, Riley knew. Tricky.

Riley had heard enough stories to know that the path to becoming mates wasn't always a smooth one.

People got hurt. *Seth* could get hurt.

And if he got hurt—if he got so much as a scratch on his lovely skin—it would be because of Riley. Because he wasn't smart enough, strong enough, *whole* enough to protect Seth the way he deserved.

Riley didn't feel the change coming on. He didn't lose himself to it either. He didn't retreat for even a second to that vague, nothing place at the back of his mind.

No. For the first time in his life, Riley could feel the voice at the front of his mind *with* him. Not pushing him back. Not taking over. Standing beside him, ready to do whatever needed to be done.

Find. Our. Mate, it growled.

Yes, Riley agreed.

He was only vaguely aware of Violet in the background, her low, awed chuckle. "Holy fucking shit," she whispered. "This is so much better than serial killers."

24

SETH

Seth's head was aching, pounding with a brutal force he'd never felt before.

He moaned, bile rising in his throat as he shifted on his bed. Had he been drinking last night? He felt sick. Like, really sick. He couldn't remember the last time he'd partied hard enough to feel anything close to this. He'd definitely been much younger and much, much stupider.

It wasn't just his head or his stomach either—he was physically shaking, his muscles trembling like he had a bad case of the flu. He didn't feel feverish though. Actually, he was freezing.

There was only cold air brushing his skin, so he reached down to pull his blanket up over himself, but his fingers grasped at air.

Seth grimaced. He really didn't want to open his eyes, but it seemed like he had to. He was cold and nauseous, and he needed to be wrapped in a blanket burrito stat.

He forced his eyelids open, immediately shutting them tight again.

Ugh. His overhead light was *way* too bright. Like, practically fluorescent. He should change the bulbs to something warmer. He would, as soon as he didn't feel like death warmed over.

Okay, second try.

Seth opened his eyes. Kept them open by sheer force of will.

And immediately wished he hadn't.

The bile was back in his throat. Because this wasn't Seth's bedroom, and it wasn't his bed. This...Seth had no idea what this was. All he could see were white tile floors and harsh lighting and what looked to be a glass wall in front of him. There was a little slot in the door, close to the floor, about the length and width of a large laptop. And there was a hallway beyond it that was just as bright and sterile as whatever room Seth was in.

He glanced down, wincing at the sharp pain in his head with the movement. He was wearing a...hospital gown? He had his underwear on underneath, so at least there was that. But this didn't look like any hospital room Seth had ever seen, unless he was in special isolation for something horribly contagious.

But when had he even gotten sick?

This didn't look like a hospital *bed* either. Seth was on some sort of cot, lying on top of a thin, lumpy mattress with a thin, scratchy blanket covering it. He peered over the side and saw a tin cup of water on the floor next to him.

He should probably drink that, but he didn't know if he could keep it down.

Also...*should* he drink that? Who'd even given it to him? What was—

Running. Seth had been running. He'd been in the woods, and he'd heard something? Felt something? He'd thought it was Riley, but it *hadn't* been Riley, and then Seth had been...drugged? Had he been *drugged*?

"Ah, Mr. Carter. You're awake."

Seth looked up from the water on the floor to find a man in

front of the glass, wearing a black suit and glasses. Seth had seen him before, right? At the cliff and then...at the bakery. And now he was here, talking to Seth through some sort of intercom.

All of which explained exactly nothing.

There were a million things Seth could ask—or yell—but he settled on, "Where are we?"

The suited man waved a hand. "Our top-of-the-line research facility. Welcome." He made it sound like Seth had *asked* to be here. Like maybe he'd signed up for a tour of the place and just wandered into this room all by himself.

The oddness of it all made Seth want to scream, but if he opened his mouth wide enough, he'd probably only vomit.

He sat up slowly, moving in tiny increments until he was perched on the edge of the cot with his feet flat on the ground. The floor was freezing against his bare feet, but apparently they hadn't shelled out for the grippy socks to go with the gown. Seth tugged the blanket up around his shoulders. He couldn't seem to stop shivering.

"Why am I here?" he asked, his voice wavering more than he would've liked.

"Because we need your assistance."

Seth was tempted to go into a lecture about the polite ways to ask someone for help—ways that definitely did not include chloroform or its equivalent—but he opted for sarcasm instead. "You're looking for lunchtime catering? I don't bake under duress."

The suited man gave a small, mirthless smile, like Seth's attempt at humor was beneath him to acknowledge. Seth supposed it hadn't been his best work. "Oh, nothing so taxing as all that, I assure you."

The suited man gestured to someone outside Seth's line of sight, and a man in a long white lab coat and goggles appeared. He was holding a small plastic bin filled with medical supplies.

The suited man pressed some button, and the glass door slid

partially open, forming a door to Seth's room. The lab coat guy walked through, and the door shut again behind him.

Seth didn't even think to make a run for it. He just sat there like a dummy. Not that he was sure his legs would hold him, anyway.

"Now," the suited man said briskly. "Mr. Brown here is going to draw some of your blood. If you struggle in any way, I'm afraid we'll have to sedate you again."

For a brief moment, the rising fear and panic threatened to pull Seth under. His breaths sped, and his sluggish heart stalled and then jump-started, racing in his chest.

What. The. Fuck?

He forced himself to slow his breathing as Mr. Brown approached. Panicking wasn't going to help him right now. Neither was any attempt at fighting—not at this moment, when Seth was so weak and so sick. And he'd rather they take some of his blood than drug him again.

What the hell did they need his blood for anyway?

So Seth sat still and frozen while the scientist or lab tech or whatever he was poked Seth at the crook of his arm, taking five vials of blood. Seth's skin felt extra sensitive and tender, and the poke *hurt*.

A few minutes later, with a new Band-Aid on his arm, Seth watched Mr. Brown—and that was an alias, wasn't it?—walk away. Seth's stomach churned. It should have felt the same as any other visit to the doctor, maybe, but it didn't. It felt so much worse.

Seth looked to the suit. "I don't know what you're thinking, but I'm just a regular guy."

The suited man's brows rose over his glasses. "Oh, I think we both know that's not entirely true."

But Seth *was* regular. He was human. Healthy. The only thing remotely unusual about him was...

Riley. His connection to Riley.

Seth's fingers clenched around the blanket on his lap. "What exactly do you study here, Mr....?"

The suited man smiled that same small smile, the one that didn't reach his eyes. "Apologies for my lack of manners. I'm Mr. Perkins. I'm a lawyer, although I believe you'll find my duties at this facility are varied. Much oversight is needed, as I'm sure you can imagine."

Seth couldn't imagine a fucking thing. He could barely process what was happening around him. He was trying to take it all in, but it was like the data wouldn't compute in his brain.

He could see that there was another room across the hallway, behind Mr. Perkins. Another cell, identical to Seth's. It was empty, but Seth could hear...noises coming from somewhere. They were muffled, but there was definitely activity happening in this building. Machines whirring and...maybe someone was growling? It was hard to distinguish, and Seth's head wouldn't stop pounding, which didn't help.

"Don't worry, Mr. Carter," Mr. Perkins said. "You'll be in the best of hands."

It was the least reassuring sentence Seth had ever heard in his life.

"For how long?" he asked, hating how his voice cracked on the last word. "H-How long will I be in your hands?"

"Why, until Mr. Beauchamp comes for you." Mr. Perkins's glasses glinted under the fluorescents as he tilted his head. "Of course, we won't be able to let you go right away. He'll need incentive to cooperate. And mating bonds are so little understood, you see. Especially unconsummated ones. We must take advantage of what falls into our laps, mustn't we?"

And then Mr. Perkins hit some button, and the intercom connection between them shut off, and he just...walked away.

Leaving Seth alone. In a cell. With no idea what came next.

Seth called after him. When that didn't work, he *yelled* after him. He eventually worked himself up to screaming like a fucking banshee, but there was no answer, and no one else came. So Seth choked back the last cry and sat there, shivering in his horrible blanket.

The situation was bleak, wasn't it? Whoever these people were, they seemed to have a lot of funding—nothing about the facility Seth had seen so far looked second-rate, other than his shitty cot —and if they knew about mate bonds, then they had to have some basic understanding of vampires and what they were capable of.

They were going to use him to lure Riley. That was what they'd said, and that was what made the most sense with Seth's... predicament.

And it would work, wouldn't it? Riley would come for him. There was no question in Seth's mind, not an ounce of doubt in his heart.

And Riley would be captured, and it would be Seth's fault.

Hot tears formed in his eyes. He couldn't help it. Seth wanted to be brave and stoic in the face of danger, but he'd never been so scared in his life.

Had he really been put out by his little "kidnapping" at Riley's gorgeous cabin? That had been nothing. A family vacation with no warning and a little bit of attitude.

This was...something else.

This was Seth being Riley's weakest link and evil assholes taking advantage of that fact with no remorse. This was Seth putting Riley in danger by virtue of his existence and his fragile fucking mortal body.

With that thought, Seth made himself stand on shaky legs and walk the perimeter of the room. It was relatively small, maybe seventy square feet total. Other than Seth's cot and cup of water, there was nothing in the room except one of those prison-looking toilet-and-sink combos coming out of the wall. And, of course, a camera staring out ominously from a corner of the ceiling, the red light blinking to let Seth know he was being watched at all times.

Gross.

The air in the room didn't give anything away, not that Seth was even sure what insight could possibly be gained that way—he wasn't a goddamn detective. But it was stale and tasteless, with no discerning scents making their way through.

Seth walked up to the glass wall and peered around as best he could. There were more rooms along the opposite wall, besides the one directly across from him. He didn't see anyone—or any*thing*—in any of them until the furthest one away, where he could just make out the corner of the glass. There, Seth thought he saw something, a shadow or maybe a flicker.

"Hey!" Seth called as loud as he could. "Hey! You!"

There went his customer service etiquette out the door.

But the shadow or flicker didn't respond, and Seth didn't see it come back to its glass wall again. Maybe he'd imagined it. Or maybe it couldn't hear him. Mr. Perkins had been using the intercom to talk to him, and Seth couldn't make out any of the muffled sounds of the building now that it was shut off.

Was his room soundproof? Seth wasn't claustrophobic by nature, but he couldn't help the cold clutch of fear in his belly at the thought. He tried banging on the glass wall, not sure anymore if he was testing its integrity or just giving in to panic. It wasn't actually glass; that was for sure. It was something different, something that had the slightest flexible give under his slaps. But whatever it was, it had to be strong, if other cells here were hiding supernaturals.

And they were, weren't they? That was what this research facility was meant for. It was meant for creatures like Riley. To steal them away and tear out their secrets.

Seth's nausea took the moment to remind him fiercely of its

existence, and he stumbled back to his cot, collapsing on it as he tried to swallow down his bile.

As it stood now, Seth wasn't strong enough to fight his way out. Which meant waiting. Looking for opportunities. Getting as much information as he could out of his captors.

Seth drained the water cup after all. If it was drugged, it was drugged, and Seth couldn't afford to let himself become even weaker by way of dehydration. He already felt the irresistible pull of sleep, anyway. Whatever they'd used to subdue him when they'd captured him, it was gnarly stuff, and he needed to sleep it off before he threw up all over his hospital gown.

He wasn't sure if they'd give him another.

He lay down fully, pulling the scratchy blanket up over him.

Please don't come, he begged, sending his thoughts into the ether. He was under no illusion that he and Riley had a telepathic connection, but maybe if Seth thought hard enough—if he really begged with all his might—Riley would sense it.

Please, please stay away. Don't let them get you. Stay safe. I couldn't bear it if you were hurt.

Seth wished he hadn't sent Riley away yesterday. Wished he'd gotten one last day with his sweet, sulky vampire before everything turned to shit.

But then again, if Riley had stayed, he might have been caught too.

No, it was better he hadn't been there.

Maybe if Riley let it go—if he let *Seth* go—the facility would lose interest in him over time. And then what use would they have with boring, mortal Seth?

Seth ignored the niggling suspicion at the back of his mind that told him it didn't matter if he was boring or not. They'd taken him, and there was no way they'd let him go after he'd seen what they were capable of. He would either escape, get rescued, or die here, alone and scared and with a blanket that hardly deserved the name.

Seth drifted off to what sounded like whale song coming from the floor below. But that didn't make any sense, so it must have been his fatigue and despair making him hallucinate.

At least it was a pleasant hallucination, kind of soothing in its absurdity.

Seth would take every bit of soothing he could get.

25

SETH

Seth had no idea how much time had passed when he woke again. There was no real way to gauge time of day in this place, as there were no windows anywhere, and the overhead lights were the same level of harsh brightness as when he'd fallen asleep.

Seth had the sense—which could be completely wrong, what the hell did he know?—that they were maybe underground.

His captors had dropped food through the slot while he'd been out, though, as well as water in a little plastic pouch. The tin cup he'd had before was gone now. It disturbed him that he hadn't woken up, even with someone else in his room, close enough to retrieve it.

After barely a moment of hesitation, Seth rose from the cot and grabbed the meal. His nausea was much better, and his head ached a little but was no longer pounding. Food and water should help the rest.

The tray tasted like typical bad hospital food—some oversalted, vaguely meat-like main dish with bland sides of indeterminate vegetable origin. The water tasted like the plastic surrounding it, and presumably they'd forgone the cup so they could avoid opening the door more than they needed to.

When he was done, Seth reluctantly peed in the prison toilet, sending an arch look over his shoulder at the camera as he did so.

If they were going to act like perverts, he was going to treat them like perverts.

No one came to see him right away, which wasn't exactly surprising. He doubted he was much use to them until Riley arrived.

If Riley arrives, he reminded himself. *Not when.*

Seth paced to pass the time, periodically pressing his hands against different parts of the white walls, as if there might be a secret latch to freedom his captors had maybe just forgotten they'd included in their grand design.

At least it was better than doing nothing.

Seth tried very hard not to think about Riley. He tried not to imagine Riley scared and worried and running straight into danger with no thought to himself.

Riley would go to his moms first, right? They'd talk some sense into him. They'd claimed Seth was precious, but surely he wasn't any more precious than their own son. Maybe they'd snap Riley's neck again and flee the state before he woke.

It hurt Seth's heart to think that, but it would be better than the alternative. Riley couldn't ever be in this place. He'd had too much taken from him already, too much of his life stolen by hunger and fear. It just...

It couldn't happen.

At some point, Seth heard the whale song again, which meant it hadn't been a hallucination after all. And it definitely seemed to be coming from underneath his cell.

Seth crouched on the hard, cold floor and bent over, placing his ear against the tile. The sound was higher-pitched than any whale song Seth had heard before, but there was the same looping, haunting quality to the calls.

Seth pounded his fists against the floor, then cupped his hands around his mouth to call, “Hey! Down there! Can you hear me?”

There was the briefest pause, and then the song started up again. Maybe Seth had only imagined the break.

He pounded his fists again. “Hello?”

But the song didn’t stop a second time. Seth wasn’t sure why he was hoping it would, other than that it would be nice to have another creature acknowledge his existence in this fucked-up place. He knew the cameras were capturing him trying to communicate, but he didn’t give a shit. They must have been expecting him to try *something*.

“What exactly are you hoping to accomplish?”

Or maybe not.

Seth sat back on his heels. The lawyer was back, either in the same suit or another identical one. Really, how the hell was Seth supposed to gauge the hours down here?

Seth pointed to the floor. “Who are you holding down there?”

He was expecting abject denial, but Mr. Perkins only said, “I think you mean *what* are we holding down there?”

Seth scowled at him. “No. I mean *who*. Just because they’re creatures doesn’t mean they aren’t people.” He was really guessing at the creature part—for all Seth knew, they really did have regular whales down there—but the lawyer’s next words confirmed it.

“I think you’ll find that’s exactly what it means.”

Was that a clue? Was all this because of some anti-creature prejudice? Some drawn-out punishment for their existence? Seth still had so many questions.

He supposed he might as well ask them.

He cocked his head, placing his hands in his lap. “You know, I consider myself very pro-science, but aren't there supposed to be ethics committees you answer to? Some sort of oversight? None of this feels very ethical to me."

"Perhaps if we were funded by the NIH or NSF, that might hold true."

Seth narrowed his eyes. "Who *are* you funded by? The government?" Was this some sort of top secret Department of Defense thing?

Mr. Perkins's lips curved into a small smirk, like he knew very well Seth was pumping him for information but wasn't threatened by it in the least. Possibly because he knew Seth was never getting out of here, so he'd never have the chance to reveal any of what he'd learned. "God, no. Think of the red tape. The thing is, Mr. Carter, that there are many wealthy parties extremely interested in the long lifespan of the supernatural. The anti-aging aspect alone would entice almost anyone, don't you think?"

Seth stared at him blankly, the words taking longer to process than they should have. "You're telling me you're working for youth-hungry millionaires?"

He couldn't help the disgust that leeched into his voice. He was trying to keep Mr. Perkins talking, which meant not offending him right out of the gate, but really? Kidnapping and threats and spy cams to watch Seth pee all in exchange for what—anti-wrinkle serums?

"Oh, exponentially more wealthy than that," Mr. Perkins told him mildly. "You scoff, but eternal life, eternal youth—the search for these things has been driving fanatics through the ages. Not all of us have an easy ticket like some."

Easy ticket? Was he talking about the mate bond? Clearly Mr. Perkins had never been wooed by a half-feral recluse with obsessive stalker tendencies. There was nothing easy about it.

Except for the fact that Seth had fallen for it within weeks.

Maybe it *had* been easy.

"Too bad your particular ticket couldn't protect you better, Mr. Carter." Mr. Perkins shook his head in false pity. "I'm afraid he doesn't have the strength to deserve these gifts he's been given."

Seth stared at him, aghast. "Gifts?" he echoed incredulously. "*Gifts*? He was turned against his will. As a *child*. He's been through enough without you poking and prodding him."

Seth stood slowly, his hands clenched at his sides as heat flushed through his body. He was surprised he wasn't melting the floor where he stood. He approached the glass with slow, careful steps. He felt the need to rattle this man, to wipe that unconcerned little smirk off his lawyer face.

Seth placed his hands on the see-through wall and lowered his voice to a low croon. "You think Riley is the only supernatural I know? You're wrong. Dead wrong. I have connections you couldn't even dream of. I'm the fucking Godfather of supernatural beings. And when they find out you've taken me, they're going to bring down a wave of destruction on this place the likes of which you've never seen. So stay. The fuck. Away from him."

Seth had never spoken like this in his life. He had no idea where it was coming from, other than remnants of old TV shows he'd watched once upon a time. But it had the effect of finally putting a little wariness behind Mr. Perkins's dead eyes, so Seth was grateful for the inspiration.

It didn't last long though. Mr. Perkins's expression quickly shuttered, and he tutted at Seth, meeting him threat for threat. "Are you aware how rare a vampire turned in childhood is, Mr. Carter? The fact that Riley aged to adulthood? Fascinating. There's so much to be learned. We'll be running tests on your Riley for decades upon decades. He won't be seeing the light of day in this lifetime or the next."

The heat of Seth's momentary triumph was replaced by cold chills and a sour taste in his mouth. He could see it too clearly:

Riley, captured and contained, trapped in this place longer than most humans lived.

Seth swallowed past the bile. "How do you sleep at night?"

He hated that he asked, but he couldn't help it. He genuinely wanted to know.

Mr. Perkins didn't even flinch. "He's a beast. An animal. They all are. I don't turn a blind eye to what we do here—I enjoy it." He followed that disgusting confession up with a nod to Seth. "You, on the other hand, are human. We will try to make you as comfortable as possible for your stay. And if one day it's necessary to complete the mate bond for further study, we'll attempt the most humane conditions possible."

"He was human once too."

"A human who, within hours of turning, tried to drain his own mother? Some might say he was a monster all along."

And with that, Mr. Perkins broke the intercom connection and walked away.

And all Seth could do was watch, even as his muscles tensed and twitched, his futile rage burning higher and higher, hotter than his body could contain. For the first time, Seth wished he wasn't human after all. He wished he had claws and teeth and fucking dragon fire, if that was a thing.

But he didn't. He was helpless. So helpless.

It wouldn't happen again. Seth might have been bullshitting the lawyer just now, but he would *make* it true. No more sitting on the sidelines. No more getting left in the dark. Seth might not have been a fighter, but so what? He knew *people*, and he would use that however he could. He would protect himself. He would protect Riley.

Eventually someone came to draw his blood again. Seth let him, although he was surprised his blood didn't sizzle in the tubes with how fired up he was.

He still couldn't tell how much time was passing while he was stuck in this cell. It felt like days, but that was probably the boredom talking. Things dragged when there was nothing to do.

At one point the lights flickered, and Seth heard hurried steps and murmured voices. Which, if he could hear them at all through the soundproofing, must have meant they were louder than murmurs.

What would happen to him if the power turned off? Would that see-through wall open for him? Or would he be locked inside in the dark?

Seth could guess the answer, and it wasn't the one he wanted.

Some time later Mr. Perkins was at the door again. He didn't look quite so smug or unconcerned anymore. There were tight lines around his mouth and a vein pulsing in his forehead.

He looked pissed, actually.

"Tell me what other supernatural entities you know."

Seth was sitting cross-legged on his cot, where he'd been counting the ceiling tiles. It had been as boring as it sounded. He cocked his head at Mr. Perkins's audacity. "Um. No?"

Mr. Perkins stared at Seth, then tapped the glasses covering his eyes. "You see these? Every member of this facility has a pair, or goggles of the same material."

That was true, from what Seth could tell. The two lab coat goons who'd drawn his blood so far had been wearing goggles. Seth had assumed it was in case they accidentally hit an artery and sprayed blood everywhere. Maybe that didn't happen in real life, but it had been his best guess.

Still, why Mr. Perkins felt the need to keep Seth updated on the fashion choices of his institute was a bit of a mystery.

"These protect against compulsion," Mr. Perkins explained impatiently. "A benefit of our research so far. We can't be compelled, and we have tranquilizer guns that can put a vampire down in less than three seconds. Any rescue attempts will be futile, I assure you."

Seth bit back a small grin. "You're really riled up right now, aren't you?"

Mr. Perkins's eyes flashed fire, but before he could respond, a new guy showed up. This one wasn't in a lab coat or a suit. He looked almost like he was military, all dolled up in beige fatigues.

Of course they had a private militia at the billionaire research facility. Why not?

"Sir," the guy greeted Mr. Perkins respectfully. Seth almost expected him to salute.

"What now?" Mr. Perkins snapped. "How can three vampires —two mothers and a *child*—be giving you this much trouble?"

"Sir, there's someone at the door. The, um, front door."

Mr. Perkins turned to face the newcomer fully. "There's someone at the front door of the secret research bunker," he repeated.

"Yes."

"*Subdue* it," Mr. Perkins hissed.

The faux soldier cleared his throat. "Well, sir, she's not an 'it,' is the thing. She's human. One of the local population." He lowered his voice and leaned in, but Mr. Perkins still had the intercom button active, so Seth could hear his every word. "A minor, sir. She said she's writing a school report and has questions for the facility."

Violet.

Seth knew it without a doubt. Violet was here.

What the fuck? Seth's confusion was mirrored by the mystified look on Mr. Perkins's face, although that was soon washed away by the sheer rage that swept over the lawyer's usually bland features.

"You allowed a local *high schooler* to slip onto the grounds? To find the *entrance*?"

It was the first time Seth had heard him raise his voice. It was incredibly satisfying to think Violet was the one who'd made it happen.

Employee of the month, for sure.

As if reading Seth's mind, Mr. Perkins shot him a vicious look and cut off the intercom. He and the faux soldier hurried away.

Seth was really tired of watching people abandon him in his cell.

Worry swirled in his gut. He really hoped Violet knew what she was doing. Seth would never forgive himself if she got hurt.

The lights flickered, same as they had before. Except this time they did it again. And again.

And then Seth was thrust into complete, unrelenting darkness.

26

RILEY

Riley hurried through the bunker's back entrance seconds before the power went out, Wolfe barely a step behind him.

Riley had never been so grateful for his enhanced vampire sight as he was now, rushing down the dark hall and into the stairwell. Other than a few glowing emergency exit signs, there was no outside source of light in this place once someone made it past the first level. If he'd been human, he wouldn't have been able to see past his own feet.

Riley had never really gotten to experience them in any depth, these enhanced abilities he'd gained when his whole life had changed. He'd always been absent in this form, letting the vampire half of him run wild while he hid somewhere safe and distant in the back of his mind.

But he was here now, faster and stronger than any of the horrible humans who inhabited this place, his senses honed beyond what they could imagine. He and his vampire were working in sync, and these people had no chance of keeping Seth away from him.

Footsteps echoed below them, and he and Wolfe froze, waiting to see if they'd come past.

The monster in Riley was urging him to keep going anyway, to lunge forward and bite and claw through anyone or anything that dared stop them. But Wolfe had warned Riley to be cautious. "We don't know what specialized weapons they may have, or what tools they've developed to deal with our kind," Wolfe had said. "We have to be warier than usual."

Riley had agreed. He hadn't *wanted* to agree, but he'd been forced to as a condition of the rescue. Otherwise, his moms and Wolfe had all threatened to incapacitate him and stuff him in some closet while they did the heavy lifting.

"This is foolish," Wolfe growled after the sound of the footsteps trailed off. The humans had been running down instead of up, heading deeper into the bunker rather than fleeing to the entrance.

Riley and Wolfe continued on.

"It was your plan," Riley reminded him.

"*My* plan was to wait for reinforcements."

"Not happening."

Riley wasn't leaving Seth in this place for a single second longer than necessary. It was bad enough he'd run home to tell his mothers and Wolfe in the first place.

Riley hadn't wanted to. Neither had his voice. After they'd broken into Seth's house and found no sign of him—his tote and wallet and car keys all left conspicuously on his kitchen table—they'd both been burning to start a rampage, to rip through the town and surrounding areas until they had Seth back in their arms. Their teeth had ached to tear out the throats of whoever had dared take him.

But Riley had stopped long enough to think about what Seth

would do—what he would want *Riley* to do—and the answer to that had been simple: he'd want Riley to be smart and careful. He'd want him to ask for help.

So Riley had gone home to *tell* someone he was about to start ripping through buildings and tearing out throats, and they'd made. Him. Wait.

Wolfe had made calls. So many calls. He'd located a hacker, some relative of Alexei's he'd met once on the East Coast. And then there'd been *more* waiting as the hacker did what hackers do, somehow finding his way into the research institute's system, narrowing down the exact location where Seth had most likely been taken.

It had involved a lot of assumptions, this plan. Assuming it had been the institute that had captured Seth. Assuming he'd been taken and not...something else.

They knew they were relying on guesswork, but the gut feeling of every vampire in that room was all they'd had to go on, so that was what they'd done.

Finding the location would have been a feat in itself, considering the spot the hacker had identified was actually a second, hidden bunker, separate from the main research facility. It twisted in Riley's gut, the knowledge that he probably wouldn't have found it on his own.

But the hacker had *also* found digital blueprints of the facility, and a way to take over both their main power and the backup generator remotely.

Calling him had been the definition of smart and careful, and Riley had hated every second.

Seth had been *taken*. He was probably scared and sad and maybe even hurting. Riley had needed to be there, stopping it. He'd needed to be killing whoever had touched him, not sitting in his mothers' living room, debating exit strategies.

Particularly since they'd never decided on one.

They'd figure it out though.

Bite them. Tear them. Drain them dry, Riley's voice chanted now.

Yes, Riley agreed.

Out loud, he reminded Wolfe, "If you wanted backup so badly, you could have brought Eric."

"Eric does not risk his safety," Wolfe said, his words clipped and impatient. "Not ever. Bring it up again and I'll snap your neck and leave you to their experiments."

Riley was almost tempted to take Wolfe up on it. Maybe they'd put him in the same room as Seth. At least then they'd be together, the search finally over.

But no, he was too close to give up now.

The hacker had found evidence of a newly occupied room in the facility's records, one that was now on their feeding schedule.

A cell, he'd called it, actually. The word had burned its way into Riley's veins, demanding retribution.

They'd put Seth in a *cell*.

He and Wolfe were headed there while Violet occupied the front. She'd somehow wormed her way into the operation, mostly by way of following Riley to his moms' house and demanding her part.

Riley and his moms had objected; Wolfe had overruled them. He clearly had no issue endangering the local humans, and Riley had been too antsy to act to waste time arguing the point. If Violet wanted to take the risk, so be it.

For their part, Riley's moms had eyes at the main facility, in case the hacker's intel was wrong and Seth was being held elsewhere. They'd make their way inside the second Wolfe or Riley gave word.

But Seth was here. Riley could sense it, even with no sign of him. He certainly couldn't *scent* him. There was no familiar, comforting orange-butter deliciousness in these halls—only stale, sterile air, saturated with cleaning chemicals and disinfectants and despair.

But Riley still knew.

Seth. Seth, Seth, Seth.

Riley and Wolfe ran down yet another set of stairs. It had barely been a minute since they'd broken in, but it felt like hours. In the distance, Riley could hear shouting, the panicked sound of humans stuck in one of the elevators. Good. He hoped they suffocated in there.

He and Wolfe stopped at the third level underground, second from the last in this facility. They ran down the hall, and Riley scanned the opening to every room he could see.

And there.

There.

Riley could see him, if only dimly. Seth was in a hospital gown, sitting on some rickety cot and looking frailer than he ever should. No. No, no, no. Riley's warm, solid human mate should never look so cold and scared.

"Seth!" Riley called, banging on the clear barrier between them.

Seth looked up from where he'd been staring blankly down at his feet. He cocked his head, his eyes unfocused in the dark. "Hello? R-Riley?"

His voice was muffled, even with Riley's enhanced hearing. His cell must have been soundproofed, at least to some extent.

"Tell the hacker to put the power back on," Riley told Wolfe, his hand still on the barrier, as if he could reach through and touch Seth if he only wanted it badly enough. "Now."

"You're aware it will allow *all* the doors to open. He couldn't narrow it down."

"I know."

Wolfe peered down the hall. He had an embroidered pocket square tucked into his bespoke suit jacket, as if he was attending a matinee at the opera and not engaging in a rescue mission. "There could be dangerous creatures contained here. Hungry and enraged."

"We'll manage," Riley said through gritted teeth. "Open. The door."

Wolfe shrugged and pulled out his phone. The hacker had instructed them to embed some satellite software so they'd have service even in the bunker.

Wolfe muttered something into the phone, but Riley wasn't paying attention to the words. His eyes were focused on Seth, who was still on his cot, staring blankly through the barrier, unable to see through the darkness that engulfed them.

Our mate. Whole. Breathing. Waiting.

Yes, Riley agreed. *Our mate.*

He flinched as the lights came on, bright and just as sterile as this horrible place's scent.

Seth was on his feet in an instant, running at the barrier. "Riley!"

The door slid open as he reached it, and then he was in Riley's arms, whole and unharmed and smelling of buttery orange and sharp disinfectant.

Riley tucked his face into the crook of Seth's neck, holding him tightly and breathing him in. He wished he could hold him even tighter. Wished he could hold him so tightly that he merged into Riley's skin, encased in Riley's body, protected and secure and never allowed to leave Riley ever again.

But Seth was tugging at Riley's shirt, pulling back even as Riley tried to get him closer. "Riley! Listen! They can't be compelled—the glasses and the goggles. You have to knock them off if they come. And they have—they have tranquilizers. Good ones. We need to go."

"Are there any other creatures on this floor?" Wolfe asked almost idly, still peering up and down the hallway.

Seth turned to him, distracted and impatient. Then his eyes widened. He blinked, his hand still twisted in Riley's shirt. "I know you."

Riley bristled. Had Wolfe been *stalking* Seth?

Wolfe barely glanced at Seth as he answered, "I doubt that."

"You came into the bakery in Seacliff once," Seth insisted. "Your blond boyfriend got a pecan streusel scone and a maple-bacon muffin. He said you knew Sascha."

Wolfe cocked his head, his gaze running over Seth with considerably more interest than he'd shown before. "Ah, yes. He enjoyed those immensely, my mate. He wanted the recipe for the muffin. You'll give it to him."

"Um."

They were interrupted by the sound of thundering footsteps, and then a horde of humans was spilling from the stairwell into the hallway. Mr. Perkins was securely in the middle of the charge, surrounded by what looked like soldiers, all of them holding guns, probably the tranquilizers Seth had been talking about. One of them was also holding Violet, and Seth inhaled sharply at the sight of her.

Damn it. Riley shouldn't have let her help. He should have realized Seth wouldn't like it.

"This is why I wanted to wait for backup," Wolfe murmured.

Riley ignored him.

"Gentleman," Mr. Perkins announced loudly. "You're trespassing here."

He sounded calm, but sweat was beading on his brow, his heart pounding loud enough for Riley to hear. He was, at the very least, rattled by their presence.

Riley would like to do more than that. He'd like to tear those vocal cords out with his nails, make sure without a doubt that no more slippery, slimy words would ever leave that slippery, slimy mouth.

Yess, his voice hissed. *Rip. Tear. Crush. Drain.*

Riley ignored the bloodthirsty thoughts and shoved Seth behind him. Wolfe stepped forward, stopping immediately when the soldiers all raised their guns higher. Wolfe lifted his hands, as if to show he was unarmed. It almost made Riley laugh.

As if Wolfe needed a weapon.

"Mr. Perkins, I presume? I'm afraid the game is up. Your unauthorized research facility is now known to two major supernatural organizations, neither of which will allow such an atrocity to stand. Any further action on your part would be ill-advised."

Riley almost choked. Two major supernatural organizations? Was the Colorado den included in that? They were barely more than a big, dysfunctional family. They certainly weren't *organized*.

It was weird how Riley had never realized how similar Mr. Perkins and Wolfe sounded until they were in the same room together. Maybe Wolfe had missed his calling as a slimy lawyer.

Mr. Perkins came forward, although Riley noticed he didn't step even an inch past the soldiers. "I'm afraid all I see are two *individual* trespassers. And I would greatly appreciate it if you'd put away the fangs. One wrong move and you'll be unconscious in an instant." When neither Riley nor Wolfe reverted back to human form, Mr. Perkins made a deliberate gesture toward Violet. "And if you'll kindly re-enable the locking mechanisms to our doors, we might allow your protected humans here to leave unharmed."

That explained why the soldiers hadn't shot them all on sight. The hacker was holding their system hostage. Good.

Although, now they were in a standoff, and Riley wasn't sure how to break it.

If Riley and Wolfe sacrificed themselves, taking the tranquilizers head-on, Seth could run behind them and get out the stairwell door. But, for one, that would require Wolfe making a sacrifice on Seth's behalf, which was incredibly unlikely. For two, Seth would have a horde of soldiers following right behind him.

And for three, Violet would definitely get caught in the cross fire. Seth wouldn't like that.

Where did that leave them? They could get word to Riley's moms, have them sneak around the back and come up behind the soldiers. What were the chances of them arriving in time before all four of them were captured?

Seth tugged at Riley's shirt. Riley held him tighter. He was ready to tell Seth that it was all going to be okay, that they'd figure it out. If nothing else, Eric would call for the Colorado den and they'd all be rescued eventually. Riley wouldn't let anyone hurt Seth—he'd make that a clear condition of their surrender.

But Seth wasn't asking for reassurance.

"Riley," he whispered. "Let me borrow your phone."

27

SETH

Seth took the phone from Riley's hand.

For just a moment, in the midst of all the chaos, he was overcome by deep, overwhelming pride. Not for the rescue, exactly, though that was very welcome, especially if they managed to make it out alive and uncaptured. But for the fact that Riley was *here*. Present and accounted for. Seth had been able to tell from the moment he'd run into Riley's waiting arms. Riley's eyes were black, his fangs were out, but he was still undeniably at the forefront, looking out at Seth from that dark gaze, both parts of him united.

My brave, brave love.

Riley had come so far, and *no one* was going to fuck with that progress. No scientists. No lawyers. No youth-hungry weirdo billionaires. No one was taking Riley. Seth would make sure of it.

Mr. Perkins, little weasel that he was, caught on to Seth's movements immediately. "I would stop doing whatever it is you're doing, if you don't want your mate unconscious in the next three seconds."

Seth didn't even pause in the act of punching in one of the few numbers he knew by heart. "You're going to shoot me for using the phone? Good luck getting your prison doors to ever lock again, then."

Violet snorted. None of the soldiers fired.

That was what Seth had thought.

The other line picked up right away. Seth could hear grumbling in the background, like someone was annoyed by the interruption, but his cousin's voice rang out, deep and clear and so, so welcome. "Seth?"

"Benny." Tears of relief pricked at Seth's eyes, and he blinked them rapidly. *No crying in front of the enemy.* "I—I need that backup we talked about. Um, right now?"

Benny didn't hesitate. "Sure thing," he said.

And then he hung up before Seth could tell him where he was or what was happening.

Well, okay. Had that been a hit or a miss?

Mr. Perkins cocked a brow. "By the time your 'backup' gets here—"

And then Benny and Helio were right there, in the bunker, smack-dab in the middle of the two factions facing off in the hallway.

Benny couldn't possibly have looked more out of place, broad-shouldered and golden and noticeably shirtless, wearing the tiniest swim trunks known to man. Helio didn't exactly look suited to an underground lab either, haughty and coldly handsome as ever, wearing some white linen ensemble that definitely belonged at some all-inclusive island resort.

It was the middle of winter—where the hell had they come from?

At their appearance, there was the horrible, cacophonous

sound of a dozen tranquilizer guns firing, but Helio waved a hand, and the shots froze in midair, then dropped uselessly to the floor.

"Seth!" Benny strode over and lifted Seth into a tight bear hug. Seth could feel Riley stiffen beside him, but he didn't protest. No doubt somewhere in his tireless eavesdropping attempts, Riley had figured out Seth and Benny were cousins.

"Is that it?" Helio asked coolly, stopping another round of tranquilizer darts as Mr. Perkins yelled orders at his soldiers. "Can we go?"

Benny ignored the question. Still holding Seth in midair, he turned to face Riley, giving him a beaming smile. He either didn't notice or didn't care that Riley's eyes were solid black, fangs poking out between his lips. "Hey. Are you the ass-eating guy?"

"Yeah." Riley nodded. "I'm the boyfriend."

"Cool. Nice to meet you."

Seth wiggled in Benny's arms, trying to get gracefully to the ground and failing miserably. "Um, Benny, do you think Helio could handle them? The soldiers?"

Benny looked over his shoulder at Helio, and Helio heaved a sigh, waving his hand again. Instantly, the soldiers disappeared from view. Completely. Zero sign of them or their guns.

That...was not what Seth had been expecting. "Where did they go?"

Helio shrugged a careless shoulder. "Scattered throughout the fae realm."

"You can do that?" the vampire Riley had arrived with asked sharply. He was eyeing Helio like he was the most fascinating thing he'd ever seen. Seth was suddenly a little concerned this guy was going to commandeer one of the cells and lock Helio in there for his own experiments.

"This dreary hellhole is full of broken promises, false hopes, and dirty tricks. There's quite a bit of power for me to draw from."

Helio gave Mr. Perkins a condescending nod. "My compliments to the chef."

Mr. Perkins only stood there, wide-eyed and frozen. Without the soldiers holding her hostage, Violet had already run over to their side, standing tall with their faction. Good girl.

Seth knocked gently on Benny's chest until Benny released him to the ground again, where Riley quickly tugged Seth back to his side. "Will they be okay?" Seth asked. "The soldiers?"

"It depends on which of the fae find them first," Helio told him, already sounding bored with the topic of conversation. "*Now* can we go?"

Benny scratched his chest, shrugging at Seth. "We're having island time. He gets cranky if we're interrupted. Are you good here?"

Seth was still a little hung up on the approximately dozen humans Helio had just relocated to *another fucking realm*, but that was kind of Seth's fault for being vague with his instructions, wasn't it? And if this was a sort of tiny, one-hallway version of war, those soldiers had been fighting on the wrong side, right? They'd lost. Now they were facing the consequences.

They were going to take Riley. They were never going to let him go.

"We're good," he told his cousin. "Thank you."

"Anytime, bud." Benny nodded to Riley and gave Violet a little one-sided fist bump. "Sick boots."

He leaned down to press a kiss to Seth's head, but before it landed, he and Helio were already gone again, almost as if they'd never been there at all.

"I love him," Violet whispered in their wake.

Seth didn't know if she was talking about Benny or Helio. Hopefully Benny. Helio was kind of terrifying and definitely not fit for teenage crushes.

Riley's vampire friend gave Seth a considering look. "You have a fae in your arsenal. I thought they were a myth."

Seth shrugged, hoping he gave off the impression of having had even a bit of control of that entire, confusing interaction. He turned to Mr. Perkins. "I told you, didn't I?"

Mr. Perkins bolted.

The other vampire was on him in a second, one arm securing Mr. Perkins around the chest, the other hand tugging his head to the side in a very deliberate manner. "Riley," he offered in a lazy drawl.

Mr. Perkins let out a horrible, high-pitched laugh. "Do you really think it ends with me? You think this is the only facility of its kind?"

The other vampire tightened his hold until Mr. Perkins groaned. "Sometimes it's not for closure," the vampire crooned. "Sometimes it's just for fun." He bent Mr. Perkins's neck at an even harsher angle. "Riley," he offered again.

Riley stepped forward with a low growl.

Before Seth had even made a conscious decision, he was placing a restraining hand on Riley's arm. Riley stopped immediately, cocking his head at Seth. Riley was still united, Seth thought. Still whole and present and in charge of his own autonomy.

Seth knew he didn't have much time. He tried to get his thoughts in order. "I understand you want vengeance," he said slowly. "I know he planned horrible things for you."

"He *took* you," Riley said fiercely, as if that was all that mattered. Not the trap itself, but the bait that had been used.

"I know. I'm not saying he deserves to live. He's cruel and dangerous, and I don't want that decision left up to me. But—" Seth hesitated. The other vampire was watching them closely. Seth lowered his voice. "It doesn't have to be you."

Riley's black eyes gave nothing away. Seth swallowed hard. "You and your moms worked so hard for so long to keep you from doing exactly this. I don't want to be the one that breaks that." He tilted his chin to the waiting vampire. "Let *him* do it. He looks... capable."

He looked more than capable, Riley's companion. He looked cold-eyed and curious and wryly amused, like the life he held was nothing to him and the conversation happening in front of him was only mildly interesting.

"You're trying to tame him," the vampire said to Seth. "But it would be wiser to encourage him. He's already failed to protect you once."

Seth made a low noise of frustration. He stepped forward to face the vampire with the ugly burgundy suit, all Seth's helplessness and frustration coming to a boiling point. "I'm not taming anyone. I'm giving him a choice. Everyone keeps talking about whether he can protect me. That's bullshit. How about this? How about *I* protect *him*. I'm older and wiser, and he's—he's mine. He's *mine*, okay? He said so, and I believe him. *I'll* take care of *him*."

The vampire scoffed. "You aren't strong enough to protect one of our kind."

"I'll fix that." Seth turned to Riley, who hadn't once taken his eyes off him. "It's your choice, baby. I'm not—*you're* not an experiment. You're not a problem to be solved. Do what you think is right. But you don't have to kill him for me. I don't need it."

"You'd turn for me?" Riley asked. There were layers to his voice, gruff and soft at the same time. Like both sides were speaking, vampire and lost boy for once sharing the stage. "For us? Is that—is that what you just said?"

Seth adjusted his hold on Riley's arm. Not because he wanted to restrain him, but because he needed the connection. "I want to stand by you. *With* you. You're not alone, Riley. Not in any of this. I love you—*all* of you. You're mine, I'm yours. We protect each other. We protect our friends."

Riley smiled, slow and fanged and beautiful. "We don't care

about the lawyer," he said, his voice rough and low. "We only care about you."

He made a gesture to the other vampire, and there was a strangled, gurgling scream. Seth barely registered it. Because Riley was kissing him, a perfect, hard press of bruising lips and fangs and tongue.

Seth wrapped his arms around Riley's neck and hung on tight.

He'd done it, hadn't he? Seth had helped end this, in his meager, human way. He'd made the right call, and he'd protected the man he loved. He'd do it again and again if he needed to. He'd call in every favor, every connection he had.

"I love you," Riley murmured, kissing Seth all over his face. "I love you so much. More than anything." He captured Seth's mouth again, lifting him off the ground.

"Ew. Gross."

Seth broke the kiss. Violet. He'd forgotten about Violet.

Oh fuck. She was watching a man get *eaten*. "Look away!" Seth yelled, banging at Riley's chest until he put Seth down.

Everyone kept lifting Seth off the freaking floor today. He wasn't *that* dainty.

"I'm talking about the kiss," Violet said, and Seth finally realized she was facing the wall, away from Mr. Perkins's untimely end. He was kind of surprised she wasn't visually devouring the gore, but maybe writing about bloody retribution and witnessing it in real life were a little different after all. "My eyes might be closed, but I can still hear your mouth sounds."

Seth gave Riley a stern look. A look that said, without a doubt, *What in the fuck is she doing here?*

Riley's black eyes and fangs receded, leaving only a sheepish young man with kiss-bitten lips in their wake. "It was Wolfe's idea."

Seth was going to assume Wolfe was the vampire in the garish suit. The one who had just—from the sound of it—ripped Mr. Perkins's throat out with his teeth. Seth swallowed back bile. "She could have been hurt. She's probably traumatized."

"I'm not," Violet said, sounding cheerier than Seth had ever heard her. "Not unless you two get *really* gross and bang it out on the floor right now."

Seth took a deep breath and gathered the tattered remains of his dignity. "We're not doing anything on this floor," he said, grabbing hold of first Violet's and then Riley's hands. "We're getting out of here."

"And the other staff?" Wolfe asked.

Seth shot him a glance, pointedly ignoring the body now slumped on the tile behind him. "We leave them. The doors stayed unlocked, right? Whoever or whatever was held here on the other floors escaped?"

Wolfe cocked his head like he was listening. "I believe so," he said after a moment. "We have someone who can verify."

"Then leave it, I'd say. I'm not interested in a massacre. If they start up again, we'll deal with it."

"Very well."

Seth had no idea why this vampire was listening to him. Maybe it was because Seth had summoned Benny and Helio's help, or maybe Seth's stupid little speech had impressed him. Hell, maybe he was only mollifying Seth in the moment and would come back and kill everyone in the dead of night.

It didn't matter to Seth. This place was gross and evil, and Seth had done what he could to not make it all worse, but it was time to go.

Seth took one step, and his knees buckled.

Before he could hit the ground, Riley had picked him off the floor, tucking Seth to his chest in a bridal carry. Maybe Seth *was* that dainty, because he didn't protest this time. He was tired and cold and ready to be coddled now. He'd been brave and strong enough for one day.

Wolfe stalked over and held an arm out to Violet. "Young lady." He had blood smeared all over his mouth, dripping down to his pocket square.

Violet took his arm without hesitation. "Let's roll."

28

RILEY

Running was easiest.

Riley knew there was a car somewhere—Violet had driven most of the way to the bunker, and she'd probably left her keys in the engine for a fast getaway. She seemed like the type to think ahead like that.

But sitting still in a moving vehicle that included Wolfgang and Violet as its occupants sounded like a new form of hell after what they'd just been through, so Riley ran with Seth in his arms, leaving the other two far behind. He could faintly hear Wolfe mutter something sarcastic and cutting at the bunker entrance, but Riley ignored it easily.

"These hospital gowns really let you feel the breeze," Seth murmured, his only comment on their method of travel.

He was cold, of course. It was winter in Washington, so obviously Seth was cold, his flesh covered in goose bumps. And he was too pale already from his ordeal, with dark circles under his eyes that had no right to be there.

Riley needed to fix it, but all he could do to help was run faster. He didn't even have the words to answer Seth, couldn't seem to form the sounds needed to apologize for not thinking of bringing a warm blanket or a coat. The adrenaline rush from the rescue had faded, and all that was left inside Riley was a shuddering, desperate need to get Seth *away*.

Seth didn't complain though. He only huddled into Riley's warmth as Riley sped them through the woods.

"We're going back to mine?" Seth asked after a while.

Riley made an affirmative grunt. There. Communication.

"Your place is closer," Seth commented mildly. "And won't your moms want you to check in? You were close to getting captured. I'm sure they're worried."

Seth's considerations were thoughtful. Logical. Riley should agree and change course accordingly.

Riley couldn't seem to access that part of his brain, though, the one that agreed with Seth like it should.

In the bunker, Riley had been running through halls filled with racing human heartbeats, filled with rushing blood that Riley had been given carte blanche permission from his family to take. He would have been allowed to bite and drain and kill without remorse, if that was what it took to rescue Seth and stay free from the institute's clutches.

And yet Riley's only focus—his only drive—had been to find the one human heart in that whole place that beat only for him. To search it out not to harm but to protect.

Riley had even been offered Mr. Perkins on Wolfe's version of a silver platter, and Riley's monster hadn't so much as sniffed at it once Seth had laid his gentle, calloused hand on their arm.

Their whole focus had been on their mate and the promise he'd made.

You're mine. I'm yours. That was what Seth had said.

"Privacy," Riley managed to say now, in response to Seth's concerns.

Riley's house would be too full of people, and every one of them would want to poke and prod and ask their questions. His moms would want to coddle and comfort; Wolfe would want more information about the fae. Violet would...Riley didn't know, actually. But it would probably be something annoying.

"Ah," Seth said. "I see." He paused for only a beat, then asked, "You're not...I mean, are you planning on turning me right now?"

This was where Riley was supposed to act purely human—the moment where he promised he could wait until Seth was 100 percent ready. Until Seth was, at the very least, warm and fed and happy, and not shivering and traumatized from that horrible fucking cell.

But Riley couldn't form the right words, and even though his fangs had receded, it was his voice who answered Seth, "Yes. Right now."

Riley didn't take it back. He couldn't. Seth had promised to protect him, and what Riley needed protection from right now was his own pain and fear and panic. That niggling dread that Seth might get taken from him again. That the next disappearance might be permanent. That Riley might lose the forever he'd only just found.

Riley could feel the weight of Seth's stare, his racing thoughts. But Seth only let out a deep breath, tightening the hold he had around Riley's neck. "Okay," Seth said. "I guess now is as good a time as any."

Riley wanted to apologize. To say he was sorry that Seth had been taken because of him. Sorry that Seth had been fated to be with someone so needy and hungry and impatient. But those words wouldn't come any more easily than any of the others. And an apology might be taken for some kind of regret, and Riley didn't have any of those when it came to Seth. Not when Seth had finally agreed to be his.

Except for maybe wishing Riley had brought a goddamn coat to keep him warm.

THE INSTITUTE HAD TAKEN his mate's keys, but that was fine—Riley had already broken the lock on the front door when he'd come searching for Seth earlier. He'd figure out how to fix it later. Or maybe Seth would come live with him instead and they wouldn't need to worry about it anymore.

But no, it probably wasn't normal for a new boyfriend to come live with the in-laws first thing. If anything, Riley and Seth were probably supposed to have their own place together, somewhere separate from the home where Riley had spent his formative years.

But Seth liked Riley's house, didn't he? He'd said so.

Riley's voice snarled at him, impatient with the scattered direction of his thoughts.

It's time, his voice insisted.

I know, Riley hissed back.

But Seth was still shivering, so Riley headed straight to Seth's bathroom. He turned on the shower, letting the water warm while he carefully removed Seth's hospital gown, then his own clothes.

Seth curled his arms around himself and looked up at Riley with a sweet smile, one that almost hid the fact he was shaking like a leaf. "S-See?" Seth said through chattering teeth. "I'm f-fine, baby. T-Totally unharmed."

Riley wordlessly pressed his fingers to the soft skin at the crook of Seth's elbow. There were two puncture wounds, tiny and healed but nonetheless *there*.

Seth frowned down at Riley's fingers. Then he bit his lip,

peering up at Riley with a look that said Seth didn't know how his next words might be received. "Oh yeah. They took some blood back there."

Riley shuddered with the force of his fury, his fangs lengthening without warning. That they would *dare* do such a thing to his mate. Seth's blood was precious. Unique. Perfect. It wasn't something to be stolen without permission in a cold, unfeeling dungeon with—

Cold fingers landed on Riley's face, and then Riley's head was being tilted until he was looking into Seth's fierce eyes. "*Hey*. It's fine. There's still plenty left."

Riley scowled. "Not. Funny," he managed to say.

"I know. I'm sorry." Seth sighed, looking back toward the shower. "Let's just get warm, okay?"

Right. The spray was billowing with steam now, filling up the room around them. It was time. Riley turned the knob to a less boiling temperature and then lifted Seth over the lip of the tub, only releasing his grip when he was sure Seth's knees would hold.

Riley followed behind him, crowding Seth in the cramped shower. He took Seth's soap and used it on his mate, scrubbing him thoroughly and ridding him of the sterile hospital scent that clung to his skin, freeing the buttery orange perfection hiding underneath.

Seth didn't speak again until Riley was lathering up his hair for him. "I feel a little like a sacrificial lamb. Like you're going to cleanse me, then anoint me with oils, then lay me down on white linens and steal my mortality to the sound of Gregorian chanting or something."

The jokes were Seth's nerves talking, Riley was pretty sure. And what he was saying might even be a reality in an ideal world. Maybe not the chanting—Seth was clearly exhausted and talking nonsense—but the rest of it.

Riley could picture it all: lifting Seth out of the shower, carefully drying every inch of his skin and lathering him in lotion, then finally lowering him down onto clean sheets and biting into him slowly and with great reverence.

But Riley didn't have the patience or the strength of will for all that. Seth was here, in front of him. The shower was too small for them, and Riley barely had to reach to touch the perfect curve of Seth's spine or grab the plump flesh of his bottom. Seth was no longer shivering either. He was warm, and he was whole, and he was *here*.

The familiar lust Riley always drowned in whenever he was in Seth's presence was burning in his belly, and if he wanted to, Riley could forgo his own plans entirely and press down on Seth's shoulders, bending him over until his spine arched in that perfect way. Riley could make use of his untimely erection and press into his mate, take solace in the warm grip of him, revel in the beautiful noises he made when Riley was hitting right where he should.

But even that wouldn't be what Riley and his voice needed.

When Riley didn't answer his teasing, Seth twisted to look back at him. "Oh," he said after a moment, blinking at whatever he saw on Riley's face. "Right now?"

Riley nodded. *Yes. Right now.*

Seth gave him a smile. It was shaky, but it was genuine, with all the familiar warmth in Seth's beautiful eyes. "You're lucky I'm such a badass, otherwise this all might be a little overwhelming."

More jokes but also more truth. Seth *was* a badass. He claimed he was ordinary, but in reality he was strong and brave and adaptable. Riley had never seen anything as wonderful as Seth calmly taking Riley's phone and asking his cousin to come save them.

Seth had such...*faith* in people. In their goodness and their love. He trusted that they would live up to his expectations and that they would be the best versions of themselves, just as he was always the best version of *him*self.

Seth had been doing it with Riley since the beginning, showering him with this faith and trust. He'd done it when he'd bravely come to Riley's home, knowing what Riley and his mothers were. He'd done it when he'd first let Riley claim his body and his blood, despite knowing the depths of Riley's hunger. He'd done it again when he'd asked Riley and Wolfe for mercy for the rest of the institute's staff.

And he was doing it now.

Overwhelming. Yes, that was the word.

Seth's brow furrowed, and he turned to face Riley fully, the shower spray hitting his back. "Oh, baby. Don't cry. We're okay."

Riley hadn't even realized he was crying. How stupid. "I want to be...better for you," he said, his voice thick.

Seth shook his head. "What are you talking about? There is no *better*. I like you just the way you are. Just...keep loving me. We'll figure the rest out as it comes." He stood on his toes and pressed a soft kiss to Riley's lips, then took a deep breath. He tilted his head to the side, baring his neck. "Be brave for me, okay, baby?"

Shouldn't it have been Riley saying that?

Riley swallowed hard. His fangs itched to sink deep and stay forever. "It hurts," he told Seth instead, because he hadn't thought to warn him before. "The transformation."

Riley had vague memories of horrible pain and fierce burning. Of waking up empty and starved and confused.

But his moms had told him tethered mates woke up easier, craving their mates instead of human blood. They'd warned Riley that mates needed consummation rather than destruction.

It had been their vampire version of the birds and the bees.

Seth didn't shy away with the warning. "Most transformations do," he said. Like it was that simple.

Maybe it was.

Riley kissed Seth's neck. His shoulder. The corner of his lips. When he returned to Seth's neck, Riley's voice came up from the depths and stepped in with him at the front of his mind. Together they bit in and drank.

They drank. And drank. And drank.

Seth moaned, swaying in Riley's hold. His burgeoning erection brushed against Riley's thigh. This part felt good for him, at least, Seth's beautiful body all flushed with the pleasure of the bite. Riley wished it could stay that way.

But that wasn't how this worked.

Riley and his voice drank until Seth's heartbeat grew sluggish, his eyes falling closed. They drank until Seth was teetering on that precipice between life and death.

It was the scariest thing Riley had ever done, letting Seth get to that place.

Riley lifted a shaky wrist and bit into it, immediately pressing the open wound to Seth's slack mouth. Riley held it there until Seth jerked, then swallowed. Riley held Seth tight as his mate stiffened and screamed.

It had never been so tempting to let the voice take over, to retreat and let himself hide from the worst of what was happening. But Riley stayed present. He hugged his mate to his chest as the screams gave way to oblivion and Seth went limp in his arms.

For Seth, he was brave.

29

SETH

After what felt like an eternity of freezing limbs, Seth was finally warm. So warm. The perfect temperature, even—not too hot and not too cold.

He probably *should* be too hot, judging by the weight on top of him. He must have been under about a million blankets. How was he not smothered?

But no, the warmth was perfect. And also...internal. Like Seth felt good on the outside but there was also something heating him up from the *inside*. Something kind of glowing and pulsing, sending him feelings of love and wonder, threaded through with weirdly sour strains of worry and guilt.

Seth opened his eyes.

Well, that explained the weight.

"Riley."

Riley lifted his head from where he'd had it buried in the crook of Seth's neck. He was sprawled over Seth, covering every inch of him, Seth's duvet the only barrier between them. Riley's eyes were red-rimmed, and his cheeks were stained with unmistakable tear tracks.

"Seth," Riley whispered hoarsely. "Your—your heart stopped."

It was surprisingly alarming to hear that said out loud, considering Seth felt just fine now. He could hear his heart beating, same as Riley's heart still beat, even as a vampire.

Seth would have liked to cup Riley's cheeks, but his arms were pinned by Riley's weight. He gave what he hoped was a reassuring smile instead. "It started up again though. My heart."

Riley's face crumpled, and fresh tears started coursing down his cheeks. "You were in so much pain. I—I really hurt you."

Seth's poor, sensitive boy.

"Not intentionally," Seth soothed. "You warned me it would happen."

Seth shifted under his covers. He was naked. Presumably Riley had never redressed him after the shower. Riley was naked too. He'd probably had bigger things to worry about than clothing. Like, for example, Seth's heart stopping. But with the sheets and the duvet, there was still too much fabric between them.

Seth needed to feel Riley right on top of him. He needed the reassurance of his touch. Everything was a little too bright, or too loud, or too...intense. The bedroom light hurt his eyes, and he could hear his elderly neighbor in her yard way too clearly, and he could smell the shampoo in his own hair, clogging his nose. It was only that warm pulse inside him that was keeping him from getting completely overwhelmed. Seth kept returning to it, prodding it in his chest. It felt steady. Irrevocable.

That was Riley's love for him, wasn't it?

Had Riley told Seth they would feel each other's emotions once they'd bonded? Seth couldn't remember. It seemed like an important bit of information to impart.

Seth would freak out about that later.

"Come under the covers," he requested.

Riley only stared at him. The tears had slowed down, though, so that was good.

Seth shifted and nudged and pushed and cajoled until Riley was wrapped in his cocoon with him, still on top of Seth but now skin to skin.

There. That was better.

Seth grinned up at him. "Hello."

Riley dropped his forehead to Seth's with a little wounded sound. Poor baby. It had been a lot of change in one day, assuming it was still the same day as when Seth had...turned.

Whatever day it was, Seth was a vampire now. They were bonded. It was done.

Seth had made the decision as hastily as he'd previously been determined not to, and he'd chosen *right.* He knew that now, as certain as he knew anything. He knew it because that love that was pulsing inside him belonged there, just as his belonged to Riley.

Something else inside Seth stirred at the thought, something covetous and hungry.

"Can you feel me?" Seth asked, wrapping his arms around Riley's back and nuzzling his forehead against Riley's. "Inside?"

Riley nodded as best he could, and he was too close for Seth to see his smile, but Seth could feel it anyway. "Yeah. You really like me, huh?"

"I love you," Seth corrected. He spread his legs a little, shifted again.

"And you—you feel okay?" Riley asked. "You're not...ravenously hungry? Aching? Ready to die if you don't bite into someone and drain them dry?"

God, was that how Riley had felt waking up after his transformation? It sounded horrible.

Seth shook his head, liking the way their foreheads rubbed together with the motion. "None of that. I just want to be close to you."

He shifted again, bending his knees a little. There. Now if he could just—

Riley suddenly rose onto his hands, his brow furrowed as he peered down at Seth. Seth blinked up at him.

"Seth."

"Yes, baby?"

"Are you trying to...sneak my dick inside you?"

"Huh?" Seth asked, the picture of innocence. He tilted his hips up, then huffed in frustration. Riley moving had really messed with his angles.

They were both hard though—Seth had felt that the moment Riley had pressed down fully against him—so it wasn't like Seth was exactly *sneaking*. He'd just felt certain that if he could get in the right position, they would just...slip in together.

Seth wanted that. Needed that, actually. Some inner part of him, hungry and alert, was demanding it.

"I just—" Seth wriggled upward. "Um, I feel very strongly that you should be fucking me right now."

He was pretty sure he wasn't the only one feeling it either. He could sense Riley's desire, like a tingly, spicy addition to that wonderful, pulsing love feeling.

"Consummation," Riley said solemnly, like Seth was spouting actual wisdom. He was still holding himself up on his hands though. Too far away. Much too far away. "It's part of it, the bonding. The drain, and the exchange, and then consummation."

Consummation. How lovely. Now if they could just stop talking about it and actually *do* it.

Hands would probably help. Seth had those. He reached blindly and managed to grasp Riley's thick cock in his palm. There. Perfect. Now to just get it where Seth needed it to go.

"Baby," Riley chastised, all faux-stern.

It made Seth grin even as he wriggled. He liked when Riley

called him that. Liked that they had the same pet name for each other. As if they were two halves of the same whole.

Ugh, that was sappy. Seth was going to be embarrassed by that thought later, when the horniness subsided enough to let his brain work again.

"Baby, we need lube."

Seth frowned up at Riley. That sounded like a delay. Even more so when Riley shifted, moving as if to leave the bed.

"*No.*" Seth immediately released his grip on Riley's cock and wrapped his limbs around him as tightly as he could.

"I'm just—" Riley struggled, leaning precariously over the side of the bed with Seth still attached. "The drawer."

Seth didn't free him. He heard the sound of rummaging, and then Riley was moving them back to the center of the bed. He had a bottle in his hand. Lube, presumably.

Riley froze, staring at Seth. "Seth. You have fangs."

"I do?" Seth ran his tongue over his teeth. He did. Sharp little fangs. How fascinating. "Lube your dick up for me," he ordered.

That starving pit in his stomach was growing deeper, its presence inside him getting more impatient by the second. He and Riley needed to be joined. Entwined. Slick skin sliding and empty holes filled. Gasping and thrusting and melting together.

"You want me." Riley grinned at Seth as he pumped lube into his hand, then quickly coated his erection. "You want me so bad, and I can *feel* it."

He moved to put his fingers inside Seth, and Seth slapped his hand away. "No fingers." He tilted his hips up for what felt like the thousandth time. Was he going to have to beg? "Just go."

"But—"

"Go slow. I'll be fine."

Riley hesitated for only a moment before nodding, wide-eyed. "Okay." He sucked in a breath, staring down at where Seth had spread his legs wide, his eyes hot. "Yeah. Okay."

Riley carefully pressed Seth's knees back, tilting Seth's hips at an even higher angle. He kept one hand on the back of Seth's thigh and used the other to notch the head of his cock to Seth's waiting hole. He shifted forward.

Seth bore down and let him in.

Yes. Yes, yes, yes. Seth could have cried, his relief was so strong. This was it. This was what they needed. Even just that fat head slipping inside him was heaven.

It was slow at first, despite Seth's eagerness. He'd never really worked himself open on someone's dick before. At the slightest resistance, Riley would withdraw and push in again carefully, gaining small bits of ground at a time. Seth let him move at his own pace, concentrating on the perfect fullness of the stretch, the slight burn as Riley's cock filled him inch by inch.

Seth kept his eyes on Riley's face. He liked watching the sweet furrow of concentration on Riley's brow. His forest scent was stronger than ever and more nuanced than Seth had ever noticed —damp earth and sharp bark and traces of fog. Seth breathed it in, losing himself in Riley's dark gaze as heat swirled in his belly.

"This is very intense," Riley whispered. The hand holding Seth's leg up was shaking.

"Yeah," Seth agreed. "So intense."

How could it not be, with both of them staring into each other's eyes like the other one would disappear if either of them blinked?

Seth giggled at the thought, some of his feral energy waning now that he was getting what he needed. The sound cut off into a sharp whine as Riley finally bottomed out with one hard thrust, his hips pressed firmly into the vee of Seth's thighs. Seth immediately wrapped his arms and legs around him again, holding him in place.

Oh God. Seth was full. Perfectly, blissfully *full*.

He felt giddy with it. It didn't help that through their new bond, Seth could feel the sharp spikes in Riley's pleasure, his satisfaction at sheathing himself inside Seth. And then there was Seth's own arousal, the hot pool in his belly that had him clenching down on Riley's cock. It was desire layered on top of desire, sharp want and heady lust swirling together. Seth's veins were full of it, his muscles trembling with the force of their joint emotions.

"My mate," Riley rasped, deep and hoarse in Seth's ear. Seth couldn't tell if it was the vampire or the man speaking. It didn't matter. They were one and the same, Seth's loves. Their appetites might have been different, but they were part of the same soul, the one Riley had linked to Seth's own with blood and pain.

Vampire. Man. Monster. Boy. Every part of Riley belonged to Seth, just as every part of Seth belonged to Riley in turn.

Riley groaned, his breath hot on Seth's neck, and then they began to rock together, skin sliding against skin, just the way Seth had wanted. Their joining was desperate and wordless and deep.

So, so deep.

Seth let the pleasure take over. He was babbling, something stupid and sappy with a lot of "oh fucks" thrown in, but he couldn't seem to stop.

He could have come just like that, his cock rubbing against Riley's firm stomach as Riley filled him, but Riley suddenly withdrew and flipped Seth over, impaling him from behind before Seth could even protest the loss. He bore down into Seth again and again, chanting now, the words frantic and fevered. "Mate. My mate."

Seth arched his back, hissing his approval. That was right. Seth was Riley's. He'd given up his mortality, and in return he'd gained this perfect, primal devotion.

Seth wouldn't take the gift for granted. He'd nurture it, protect it, and return it with his own tenfold. He'd be the best mate he could be for this brave boy who'd found Seth in these woods, who'd been as patient as he could bear while Seth adjusted to their fate.

"Love you," Seth moaned. "Love you. Love you."

Riley pressed him down into the mattress, deep and insistent until Seth was flat on his belly, Riley's hands digging into the mattress by his head. The pleasure that had been building without mercy crested, and they shuddered together, Riley's release filling Seth just as his spurted onto the sheets.

It was the most natural thing in the world for Seth to lunge forward and press his lips to Riley's wrist, to let his mouth fall open, to let his fangs slide in, to suck and swallow what flowed out to coat his tongue.

Riley's blood was rich and earthy and decadent, just like the forest that surrounded them. It was his essence, his life force, full of all the strength and power that lay hidden under the beautiful, vulnerable exterior.

"Yes," Riley murmured, letting his weight fall once again over Seth's body, covering him completely. Keeping him in place. Keeping him close. "Take it. It's yours."

Yes, Seth thought, gulping greedily as the new presence inside him rejoiced. *Mine.*

30

RILEY

Riley tugged gently at the curls tickling his chin. "Seth."

There was no answer except Seth adding teeth to the hot, biting kiss he'd been pressing to Riley's neck.

Riley shivered, his hands clenching against the steering wheel. He couldn't help the blood that rushed straight to his dick, especially when Seth's strong fingers found Riley's cock over his jeans.

"Baby," Riley tried again.

Seth lazily soothed the sting of the bite with his tongue, fingers dancing over Riley's bulge. "Mm?"

"We have to get out of the car."

Now Seth pressed a pout to the tender skin he'd been mauling. "Why?"

"Because you need to eat."

Seth set sharp teeth against Riley's neck with obvious intent, and Riley gave up hope on his erection ever going down. "You need to eat *human* blood," he insisted. "You can't only feed on me."

Yes, he can, Riley's voice crooned. *Bite us. Drain us. Drink us dry.*

Riley gave the metaphorical finger to the horny, obsessed creep inside him. *Not fucking helpful.*

He cleared his throat, clasping Seth's wrist and lifting his hand away from Riley's jeans. "Also, everyone's already on the porch. Watching us."

That got Seth's attention. He drew up with a start from where he'd been draped over the console, turning to look out the passenger-side window to the house's porch, where Wolfe, Eric, and Riley's moms were all standing in a group, very obviously staring directly into Seth's car.

Only Eric had the grace to look remotely embarrassed at being caught spying. The other three only looked various shades of smug.

Riley would have liked to be annoyed by that, but the smugness matched his own all too well.

My mate, his very being seemed to purr. *I've claimed him.*

After several...vigorous and thorough rounds of consummation, Riley had texted his moms, letting them know he was going to need to make use of some of their blood stash. Seth had seemed more concerned with draining Riley's cum than draining anyone's blood, but Riley knew his mate would get hungry eventually. And he was going to make absolutely *sure* Seth was never hungry in a way that would cause him to hurt someone. It would cost Seth too much to take a human life—Riley would never allow it.

As Riley's moms waved enthusiastically, Seth's cheeks flushed pink, and he let out a belated, startled squeak, flying back from Riley like his touch was suddenly fire.

It was a reminder that underneath the horny, newly turned vampire exterior, Seth was still Seth. A cheerful, kind, trusting man who was definitely mortified at having been caught molesting his young boyfriend in his in-laws' driveway.

Riley couldn't help his grin.

Seth swatted him in the chest. "Why didn't you *say* something?" he hissed.

"I just did."

"Oh my God." Seth lunged to open the passenger-side door, almost falling out during his escape. Maybe he was still getting used to his new strength and speed, or maybe he was just too embarrassed to get his feet under him properly.

Riley followed him to the porch at a more sedate pace, trying and failing not to look like a proud husband bringing his new bride home.

Immediately, both Riley's moms swept Seth into a three-person hug, cooing and clucking over him like two stylish mother hens.

"Welcome to the family!" Mama Daphne cried.

Eric grinned at Riley. "Congrats."

Riley didn't need to return the smile, because he was already beaming. "Thanks."

He and Seth switched places so Riley could be smothered in motherly affection in Seth's stead. Seth held out a hand to Eric. "Hello again. I hear you like my muffins."

"He's particularly fond of cinnamon rolls as well," Wolfe drawled. "You'll make some for him before our departure."

Eric widened his eyes at Wolfe as he shook Seth's hand. "Um, you don't have to."

"He does," Wolfe said.

"I'll add it to the menu tomorrow," Seth told Eric, completely ignoring Wolfe, which was probably the wisest course of action. "Although, there's a question of whether anyone will come in. I have to be the wishy-washiest small-business owner in town with all these unexpected lost days." He looked around the porch. "Where's Violet?"

"She returned home," Mama Daphne told Seth. "She

promised to, quote, blow up your phone later, end quote. She's a lovely girl."

Riley's moms ushered everyone into the house and toward the kitchen. There was a pot of blood on the stove, simmering on low heat. Riley usually just tossed his in the microwave, but clearly they were going all out for his new mate. As they damn well should.

Seth's eyes widened the second he smelled the blood, but he didn't react otherwise.

Wolfe took a seat at the kitchen table, pulling Eric onto his knee. "Does your bakery have a social media presence? That's how my Eric finds his points of interest when we travel."

The thought of Wolfe and Eric perusing Instagram to find the best local restaurants was too weird and domestic to fathom. Riley pushed it out of his mind immediately.

"Um. Not much of one?" Seth said.

"Riley can help with that," Mama Sybil offered, pulling a large mug from one of the cabinets and setting it by the stove. "He should make himself useful with all the space he takes up skulking at your tables."

Rude. Accurate but rude.

Seth chewed on his lower lip, seemingly lost in thought. He was very pointedly not looking at the stove. Was he disgusted by the thought of human blood? But no, Riley didn't feel that through the bond. Seth was only nervous, just like anyone would be, taking a big step toward an entirely new existence.

"Maybe you and Violet can coordinate," Seth finally said, giving Riley a little grin. "She knows how to grab someone's attention."

That snapped Riley out of his musings. He scowled. "Maybe we should discuss the evil institute we just disbanded instead."

Seth smirked at him, like he knew exactly why Riley was changing the subject. Ugh. One cooperative mission with the local goth grump and now she and Riley were going to be inextricably tied forever, weren't they? Like a female mini-Wolfe, sneaking her way into Riley's family without his permission.

"There's nothing to discuss," Wolfe said coolly. "Cooper pulled all the personnel files already. Between your mothers and Eric and myself, we'll have no trouble keeping an eye on the employees who remain."

"Cooper?" Seth asked with a frown. "Cooper is your hacker? Is that...Cooper Zaitsev?"

"I don't know his surname," Wolfe told him. "Cooper with a bloodthirsty chaos demon for a mate."

"Bracchus," Seth mused. "I know them. And Sascha and Kai? Ivan and Nix? Matty and Night?" Seth rattled off names speedily, his eyes bright with enthusiasm. They were names Riley was vaguely familiar with, via Jay and Alexei, two other members of the Colorado den.

How entwined *were* his and Seth's far-reaching social connections?

"You know all of them?" Seth asked, looking from Wolfe to Riley.

"We're acquainted." Wolfe's eyes gleamed as he smirked at Seth. "Demons as well as fae, hm? How interesting."

Once again, Seth seemed to be either immune to Wolfe's creepiness or determined to ignore it. "I can keep an ear out at the bakery," he offered, although he gave Riley a sidelong look that promised they'd be discussing all this later. "I'll let you know if I hear about anything that might be related to the...captured that escaped." He blinked as Mama Sybil wordlessly handed him the mug, now filled with heated human blood. "Um, thank you."

The whole kitchen held its breath. Or maybe that was just Riley.

Seth raised his eyebrows at them all. "Seriously? With an audience?"

Mama Sybil smiled her meanest smile. "Perhaps we elders will retire to the living room."

SETH TOOK MORE care looking at Riley's room this time around. He spotted Colin's comics quickly. "It's you," he said, grabbing one from the top of the pile.

Riley eyed the vampire on the cover, younger and braver and more vicious-looking than reality. "A version of me."

"Someone from your den draws these," Seth guessed.

It was a reasonable theory, considering no one else would have known Riley well enough to create a fictional version of him.

"Colin," Riley told him. "And then, um, Jay and I read them together."

Seth's brow furrowed as he stared down at the comic. "I know Jay," he said slowly. "Don't I? He and his husband, Alexei, would come to the bakery every day when they were visiting Sascha."

Riley almost laughed. Of course Jay had been getting pastries from Riley's fated mate for literal years with none of them being the wiser. Of fucking course.

"My moms have talked about joining them," Riley said. "When we all age out of our current homes. Live off the grid for a while as a group. It's a small community, but never boring. And they're loyal."

For some reason, that made Seth smile.

Maybe it was part of what had fated Riley and Seth together, these connections between them. Or maybe it was the reverse, and their mutual friends were just a step along the road, pushing them toward each other without their knowing.

There were more important things to focus on now though.

"Are you delaying?" Riley asked Seth, gesturing to the mug of cooling blood in Seth's hand.

Seth shrugged, then set Colin's comic carefully back on its pile. "Maybe."

"Because it makes you a monster?"

Seth laughed, like Riley was being melodramatic. "Because it's human blood. That can be weird enough on its own. You don't have to attach anything extra to its significance. "

It was a marvel, wasn't it, how different Seth's transformation was from Riley's own? It was a little painful to compare—a sharp twist in Riley's gut he might never fully get over—but it was also beautiful. An unexpected gift from the universe, that Seth didn't have to suffer to be his.

Seth's brow furrowed, like he was concentrating, and then black eyes and those sweet little fangs he'd used to drink from Riley's wrist took over his features.

It was strange, seeing those green-brown eyes so dark. Strange but not terrible. Not terrible at all.

Seth took a careful sip. Hummed in thought. Took another. "Weirdly satisfying for a liquid," he said after a moment. "Like a really good soup."

Another minor revelation Riley couldn't even be remotely surprised by: Seth comparing his first taste of human blood to a really good soup.

Riley took a seat on the edge of his bed as Seth slowly finished the mug. Seth set it down on top of Riley's bookcase when he was done. "I did it."

"You did."

Seth came over to the bed, standing between Riley's spread legs. The bed was low enough that it made them the same height, more or less. "A lot of changes in a short amount of time," Seth said mildly. His eyes had gone back to their usual color without Riley noticing.

Riley swallowed. "Do you...regret it?" He didn't think Seth's attitude toward the mug of blood was one of someone devastated and defeated by their loss of humanity, but it didn't hurt to check.

"No." Seth shuffled closer, setting his hands on Riley's shoulders. Riley took hold of Seth's hips, reassuring himself with the familiar shape of him. "You know," Seth began. "I came here because I was feeling...stagnant back in Seacliff. On paper, I should have been as happy as ever, but underneath, I was...aching, kind of. Wanting more and not knowing why."

Riley tugged gently, encouraging Seth to move even closer, straddling his lap. Seth grinned at him after he'd settled, like that was exactly what he'd wanted. His gaze ran over Riley's face, almost as if he was taking him in for the very first time.

"I've always put so much importance on tending to my community, to the people around me, but there's something special about having a person of my own." Seth cocked his head, still smiling. "It's a little selfish, the way I feel about you. The way you're *mine.* I like that, I think."

Riley grinned back at him. He liked that too. Belonging to Seth. Being a part of his private self, a small piece of Seth's sunshine that didn't get given away to everyone else. "What about your voice?" Riley asked. "Has it spoken to you?"

Seth cocked his head in the other direction, his gaze going distant as he thought it over. "Not really. Or maybe it has, and it just sounds like my own thoughts. I feel a...presence, I guess. A part of me that's a little sharper. Hungrier." Seth focused back in on Riley, and Riley could almost see it, that little something darker lurking in the back of Seth's pretty eyes. "It's very drawn to you."

Riley leaned forward and pressed a kiss to Seth's smiling mouth. What a relief, that their obsession might be mutual from now on. Or maybe it always had been, in a sense. Maybe that was why Seth had never truly turned Riley away.

"I've started things moving for our book club," Seth murmured against Riley's lips.

Riley stayed silent, waiting for a clue as to why Seth was changing the subject.

"You don't have to come," Seth told him, drawing back far enough to make eye contact again. "I initially thought...I guess I wanted to give you something more than what you've had. To help you feel like you belong here. Not just in the woods but *here*, with the people that come with it. But I meant what I said before—you don't have to be different than you are. If you want to keep your circle small, that's fine. I'll still be coming home to you."

How funny that Seth claimed his love for Riley was a chance to be selfish, when his love felt like anything but. Riley could feel it inside him, warm and...calming. Like a weighted blanket thrown over the beast inside him, keeping Riley more content than he'd ever been.

"No," Riley said. "I'll try it. I like books, and we'll see how I feel about the people."

He was mostly interested in a chance to see Seth interact with other humans when he wasn't in customer service mode. Maybe that wasn't what Seth had in mind as to Riley's investment in the whole endeavor, but it was what it was.

Seth would always come first. That wouldn't change.

Seth beamed at Riley. "You can help me come up with discussion questions each month. I'm not actually much of a reader."

"We can think of them together," Riley offered, fingers tightening on Seth's hips. "At home. Your home. Where I live now."

They were discussing the future, in their own way, so Riley might as well get this part taken care of. Their bond had been completed, and Riley was no longer content to lurk in the shadows, the lost puppy in the woods.

He was ready to be brought in from the cold.

Seth fingered a lock of Riley's hair, humming again. "Give you an inch, you take a mile."

Riley nodded. "Yes."

"We can pack your stuff tomorrow."

"Tomorrow?" Riley frowned. Was this going to be some sort of wedding night ritual, forcing him to spend their first night as a bonded couple on his own?

"I thought we could stay here tonight. Give your moms some more time to gloat. And you said these room were soundproofed, so..." Seth wiggled in place, the motion rubbing his pert ass against Riley's very interested dick.

Right. Seth was Seth, but he was also a newly turned vampire with all the horny enthusiasm for consummation that entailed.

Riley grabbed harder at Seth's hips, momentarily overwhelmed by the enormity of what lay ahead. An eternal lifetime with his obsession. Mutual love and care. A place for him always, right by Seth's side.

Seth didn't give him time to linger in the overwhelm. He shifted and huffed impatiently, and Riley helped Seth discard his pants, tugging his own down to his knees. He held Seth tightly to his chest as Seth sank down onto him, still lubed and wet from the last time they'd joined together. Seth was perfect. Tight and hot and perfect and *his*. Riley's mate. His love. The man who'd accepted Riley just as he was, and in the process made him whole.

Riley tugged Seth's head down to his, slamming their mouths together and drinking in his moans.

Thank you, Riley said, either to fate or the gods or whoever or whatever had sent Seth to him. *Thank you for this gift.*

Riley would take precious care of him. Of them. He might have been young and lost when all this had started, and he might not have been all that much older now, but Riley knew the worth of what he'd found.

He wouldn't ever forget.

31

SETH

The kitchen countertop was digging into Seth's back, hard and a little painful.

All he could do was arch even harder against it, his hands clutching at the edge. "Fuck," he whined. "That's it. That's so good."

Riley hummed around Seth's cock, and Seth honest-to-God whimpered, the sound breathy and a little broken.

Had he taught Riley that move, or had Riley just figured it out on his own? Seth couldn't remember right now. There was no blood left in his body to operate his brain—it was all down south, sucked there by Riley's filthy mouth.

The playlist Seth had put on earlier had ended at some point, and the empty kitchen was filled with Riley's slurping enthusiasm and Seth's increasingly frantic moans. It smelled like orange and musk and deep forest.

Riley ran his tongue along the underside of Seth's erection, somehow still bobbing without pause, and Seth lost it, hips jerking as he tangled a hand in Riley's hair. "Baby, I'm gonna—"

Riley's answer was a low growl, pushing forward until his lips were pressed against Seth's pubic bone, Seth's cock lodged in the back of his throat.

He swallowed.

"Oh *fuck.*" Seth groaned as his fingers tightened around Riley's strands. The sound was half pleasure and half pain. Maybe those ratios were off. Who the hell knew. Everything was just so wet and so hot and so, so *tight.* Seth could barely breathe as he shot down Riley's throat.

He was left panting and shaking, bent half-backward over the counter as Riley drew off with a wet-sounding pop. Seth whimpered again, oversensitive and overstimulated and satisfied in a way that had him wanting to melt down to the floor.

Riley stood from his kneeling position, looming over Seth now. He bent over and tucked his head into Seth's neck as he jerked himself quickly to completion.

Seth wrapped his hands around Riley's back, tugging him closer. Something dark and hungry inside Seth preened at the slick sound of hand on flesh. *Yes. Come for us.*

Moments later, Riley shuddered with his release, and Seth angled his neck to encourage the sharp slice of Riley's teeth, the lazy draw of Seth's blood.

Even after Riley closed the bite, they stood there for a long moment, soaking in the contact and breathing in each other's scents. Then Riley pressed a kiss to the front of Seth's throat and stalked over to the sink to wash his hands.

Seth blinked after him, still a little dazed. Then he glanced to the clock. He straightened with a start, tugging his pants up. "Oh fuck. They're almost here! You were supposed to be helping me plate the cakes!"

It had started that way, hadn't it? Riley had been helpfully bringing over the cooling cakes while Seth prepped the serving trays. And then in the next moment, Riley had been on his knees, and Seth's pants had been at his ankles, and somehow Seth's dick had found its way into Riley's waiting mouth.

Riley shrugged. He was facing the sink, but Seth could see the quirk of a smile he wasn't even trying to hide. "I got hungry."

"Oh my *God*."

Seth hurried to take Riley's place at the sink, shoving him bodily so he could wash his own hands. He ignored Riley's husky laugh, rushing over to the cakes and grabbing the first. Seth set a cooling rack over the top and flipped it, sighing his relief when it came out clean.

He frowned to himself as he started on the next. "Why did I make two different orange-flavored cakes? What was I thinking?"

Riley came up behind him, wrapping his arms around Seth's waist. "You were thinking that orange is the best and most delicious flavor in the whole world."

Seth laughed, charmed in spite of himself. This fucking kid. "No one thinks that."

"I do."

"You're delusional."

"You're snippy when you're nervous," Riley countered, pressing a kiss to Seth's neck.

Seth frantically brushed the glaze onto his first cake with a pastry brush. "I just want everyone to have a good time."

"Aren't they all coming because of Violet's blackmail? You might be expecting too much."

"Only one is coming because of blackmail." At least, Seth thought that was true. He *hoped* it was true. This was going to be a sad-sack event if it wasn't.

It was the first official meeting of their book club. So far, interactions between the members had been limited to a group chat where Seth had announced the first book—a gothic classic as a nod to both Riley and Violet—which had been met with multiple thumbs-ups and zero actual conversation.

Of course, Seth had seen everyone individually, serving them pastries here and there as they came into the bakery. But there hadn't been much time for book discussion.

In the past few weeks, Seth had gotten back into a routine. He'd reverted back to his regular bakery hours without fanfare, and the town had seemed willing to forgive his repeated absences. (A few regulars may have made some pointed comments about his inferior immune system failing to protect him from the Pacific Northwest's wet winters, but that was neither here nor there.)

Riley and Violet had been taking turns documenting Seth's baked goods and posting them to social media, which had already been serving to increase weekend foot traffic to Coastal Crumbs. They also, for whatever reason, seemed equally determined to document *Seth*, sneaking photos of him in his aprons and headbands and posting those photos almost as often. But the posts seemed to do well, so Seth let it be.

"Pretty privilege," Riley had said to him smugly.

Whatever. Seth was pretty sure it was the headbands that stole the show. (He had a new vampire bat one he was particularly proud of.)

Riley liked to edit and post the photos while curled up in bed with Seth, usually with an ASMR video playing in the background.

It was funny—Seth had always liked living alone. He'd found a certain joy in surrounding himself with people during the day but still having his own space to return to.

It turned out, though, that Seth didn't mind cohabitation at all, if it was Riley he was doing the cohabitation with. When it was Riley Seth was waking up to, and chattering to all day, and cozying up with at the end of the night as Seth scrolled through YouTube videos and Riley read his books. Then it was easy. Natural. Perfect.

They didn't have to sleep as often either, which meant getting to enjoy long walks in the woods late at night, followed by hours of tea and conversation with Riley's moms.

Funny, too, how Seth had been a little scared of Riley's intensity toward him at first. Or, to be more accurate, how Seth had been scared of how drawn to it he'd been. But Seth could understand it now, after his own transformation. Seth had the same intensity inside him, simmering under his skin. A constant pull to his mate, a love that was a little sharper than Seth had grown up thinking love should be.

But that was fine. What was a little bit of sharpness between vampire mates?

They hadn't heard from any escaped paranormals yet, but sometimes he or Riley thought they caught a strange scent, on the coast or in the woods or—one time—in the middle of town. They hadn't been able to follow the scents to anything concrete, but maybe that would come with time.

For now, with Riley's extremely unhelpful presence plastered to his back, Seth brought the two cakes to the front of the bakery. They'd pushed two of his tables together, spreading the chairs around them, and Seth placed one cake on each. He'd also made coffee for those freaks that drank the stuff at night, and Luke was—

Well, Luke was at the door.

Seth let him in, and Luke held up a paper grocery bag with a cheerful grin. "I brought beer! And some wine, in case that's more anyone's thing. My sister said I should. And, um, soda for Violet, because she threatened bodily harm if I left her out." Luke set the bag down on the table and eyed Seth's offerings with a hopeful gaze. "Damn. Something smells good."

"Thank you." Seth shifted on his feet, hyperaware of Riley at his back, emanating smugness. "We've got orange Madeira with a cinnamon-rum glaze and a Harvey Wallbanger cake. That's, um, also orange."

"Fuck yeah." Luke took a seat, grabbing a beer out of his bag and popping the top with the edge of Seth's table. "God, it's nice to swear sometimes. No little ears listening." He gave Riley a belated nod. "Hey, Riley."

Riley set his chin on Seth's shoulder. "Luke."

All in all, it was a promising start.

VIOLET WAS the next to arrive, followed by the bearded, flannel-clad high school teacher, who turned out to be named Trent.

Seth greeted Trent's arrival with a certain amount of wariness —the guy was taller even than Riley and built like he felled trees for a living—but Violet's blackmail victim didn't seem upset to be there. He just grabbed a beer from Luke with one of those silent bro nods and took a seat, setting an earmarked paperback copy of *The Woman in White* onto the table.

Anime Shirt Guy was last to show up. He was, in fact, wearing a different anime shirt tonight, and his name was Zephyr. He gave them each a shy, hesitant smile and claimed one of the sodas, as well as a piece from both cakes.

Double cake would always get Seth's approval, so Zephyr definitely got a gold star.

And then the six of them were all seated, with the inevitable awkward silence that came from a group of people thrust together without much previous interaction. Sure, Violet was Luke's niece, but she didn't seem inclined to break the silence on her own, other than to comment that, "For a book club, this is a total sausage fest."

"Who was in charge of recruiting?" Riley asked, the only word he'd spoken to anyone so far besides their name in greeting. He'd chosen the chair next to Seth's and shoved it so close that their legs were practically crossed over each other.

Violet tilted her soda toward him in acknowledgment. "Touché."

Seth cleared his throat, kind of feeling like he should have a gavel to bang against the table. "So, um, I thought we'd do a little icebreaker, if that's not too cliché? We can keep it easy. Let's all say something fun or exciting or weird from our week."

There were vague sounds of affirmation and a few nods, but no one spoke first.

Oh God, were they going to have to go around in a circle, like some sort of forced grade-school activity? Seth opened his mouth to suggest it, and then everyone was speaking at once.

"I've been hearing singing coming from the coast late at night. Almost every night now. I don't recognize the language."

"I'm pretty sure my house is haunted."

"Becky Simpson tried to edge past me for valedictorian, but she couldn't cut it in calculus."

"Something keeps eating the heads off my chickens."

Well…okay. That last one was from Zephyr, and Seth turned to him. "You have…chickens?"

"Six of them." Zephyr frowned to himself. "Well, four now. Rest in peace, Fluffy and Dumdum."

"What kind of coop do you have?" Trent asked. Trent of the haunted house, according to his icebreaker. He didn't look like the type to believe in that stuff, but maybe he'd just been trying to keep his on gothic theme. "I know some tricks to keep the predators out."

Luke—who'd apparently been getting serenaded nightly in a foreign language—rubbed a hand over his scruff. "Damn. I was thinking about getting chickens as a fun thing for Colby, but not if they're gonna get eaten. He'd never forgive me."

Seth grinned at Riley. Just like that, the ice had been broken.

Riley hooked his pinkie finger with Seth's and then, miraculously, actually focused on the conversation happening in front of him.

Seth poured himself a glass of wine with his free hand as he listened to the benefits of an automated coop locking system. He felt...hopeful. Light. This was the start of something, he was pretty sure. Something small, maybe, but also...real. Like a little reminder that Seth might not have been human anymore, but he hadn't lost his humanity. He could still be part of the world he loved so much.

He knew things would need to change and evolve when he and Riley didn't age down the line, but that would all come later. They had years before they had to worry about that to any extent. And yeah, maybe Seth was going to have a major freak-out coming his way when that finally sank in, but for now, he was fine.

He'd fed on his first human last week, and it hadn't been some horrible, traumatizing thing. It had been pretty pleasant, actually. He and Riley had driven up to Bellingham. They'd gotten teas and taken them to a park, and Seth had pulled someone aside to ask to use their phone. It had been a matter of quick compulsion and a quick bite behind a tree, and then his victim had been free to go, none the wiser. Seth hadn't even felt guilty about it. It hadn't taken much to fill his stomach, and the whole thing was probably more ethical than the majority of the meat industry, if he really thought about it.

Overall, he still felt like himself, especially here and now with cake on the table and his boyfriend at his side, listening to the casual, contented chatter around them. And yes, Seth could hear the hearts beating around him, if he focused, and feel the rush of nourishing blood pulsing in his guests' veins. But he could also hear *Riley's* heart, strong and steady and beating in a rhythm Seth already knew deep in his bones.

As much as he'd hated getting captured by the institute, Seth had also been given time to think in that cell, locked away for hours by himself without a companion or phone. Time to realize he didn't actually need much out of life. He didn't even *want* much. He wanted a community to rely on. He wanted to keep the people he loved safe. He wanted to bake delicious goods for himself and for others. And he wanted Riley, with all his sweet, feral devotion.

Whatever happened, they'd figure it out together. And they would have the help of Riley's moms, the Colorado den, Benny and his terrifying husband, and Seth's demon contingency back home. Even Violet would have their backs, and there was no fucking doubt that girl was only going to grow more intimidating with age.

Seth and Riley weren't alone. They weren't monsters. They were young and in love, and they had whole lifetimes ahead of them.

Seth rested his head on Riley's shoulder. He couldn't think of anywhere else he'd rather be.

EPILOGUE

RILEY

Riley held Seth close as the cool water lapped at their bodies.

"Mm," Seth hummed. He was sitting on Riley's lap with his head thrown back on Riley's shoulder, his face turned up to the sun. "The heat feels so good. It's been horrible back home."

Riley scoffed. "It was only a week."

"A week of gray! In summer!" Seth gave an exaggerated shudder, though Riley could see him biting back a grin. "Horrible."

"It rained here yesterday," Riley pointed out.

"Psh. A summer monsoon. Totally different."

"I didn't realize you were such a desert baby underneath."

"Me neither." Seth let out a happy sigh. "It helps that this vampire body doesn't get overheated."

That was Seth, always focusing on the positive of their respective transformations. He'd even declared that his enhanced senses had made him a better baker and that he was now able to play around with subtle flavors he hadn't had the palate for in his human form.

Riley didn't know about that—he'd loved Seth's pastries before, and he loved them now. But he liked that Seth saw it that way.

They drifted back into a comfortable silence, basking in the shallow lip of the swimming hole they'd found. Or, more accurately, the swimming hole Jamie had given them directions to.

Riley was almost as content as Seth, except he kept having to ignore the niggling, lusty urge to shuck off his swim trunks, lay Seth down in the dirt, and enter him in one smooth glide.

But while the area they'd found was secluded, hikers still came through every now and again, and—as Seth kept reminding Riley on occasions like these—exhibitionism wasn't their thing.

Still, Riley let his hands wander over Seth's sun-warmed skin, nuzzling at his mate's neck. Riley had kissed and licked every bit of skin there a thousand times over these past seven months, but it was still his favorite spot. Although, Seth's hands came in at a close second. Also, his face. And maybe his butt. And his hair.

Maybe the neck favoritism was due to his voice's preferences sneaking in, or maybe Riley would have had a thing for that slender throat even if he'd been human, but there was no way of knowing, was there? Riley was who he was, and so was his mate. Riley's lovely, beautiful mate.

One of Riley's wandering hands managed to find Seth's burgeoning erection under the water. Aha. So Riley wasn't the only one affected. Riley cupped the bulge over Seth's swim trunks.

Seth's lips curled into a smirk, his eyes still closed against the sun's glare. "What are you up to down there?"

"Are you *sure* we're not exhibitionists?" Riley asked, arching up to rub his own erection pointedly against Seth's pert bottom.

Seth laughed. "I guess it depends on how willing you are to let another person see me all flushed and naked and moaning on your cock."

No, Riley's voice snapped at him. *Fuck no. Ours. Only ours.*

"You've got his hackles up," Riley scolded, his pout only half-fake.

Seth's smirk grew even more smug. "I'll kiss them back down later."

Riley reluctantly left Seth's pretty cock alone and went back to holding him tightly on his lap. It was a case of good timing because a few moments later, they heard the telltale heavy tread of a hiker coming in on the path.

"Hand me one of those water bottles?" Seth asked casually.

Riley leaned back and grabbed one, handing it to Seth just as the hiker crested the portion of the trail overlooking their water hole. He was young and sunburned, his face creased in a friendly smile as he gripped his hiking poles. "Hello there! Do you know how much longer to the waterfall?"

"Not much longer!" Seth rose from Riley's lap and scrambled up the hill to stand next to the hiker, pointing a finger in the opposite direction from where the man had come. "Just follow the path through those saguaros. It's faint, but it's there."

"Perfect! Thank you!"

Seth turned to face the hiker, using a hand to shade eyes Riley already knew would be all black by now. "Don't be scared," Seth said, still in his same friendly tone, although his voice had lowered to a slightly deeper, rougher register. "And don't move."

He quickly lifted the hiker's wrist and bit in, drinking in steady, patient gulps as the hiker stared bemusedly at him, his face flushed either with heat or arousal. Seth dropped the hiker's wrist gently back to his side when he was done. "Forget I did that. We gave you directions and an extra water. You'll drink it on your way."

The guy smiled dazedly at them both. "Thanks for the water. Sure you don't need it?"

"Nope!" Seth grinned at him with a mouth full of blunt human teeth. There wasn't a trace of red anywhere on his mouth—he was always a very neat eater. "Have a good swim!"

The hiker continued down the trail while Seth waved at his back.

He was so easy with it, Riley's mate—the hunt and the feed. He'd helped Riley achieve some semblance of the same, but Riley still didn't like hunting without Seth. Riley preferred to drink human blood from the source with Seth right beside him, usually with a hand on Riley's shoulder, ready to pull him back if he lost himself to the hunger.

Some wounds took a little longer to heal—that was what Seth said when Riley was feeling feelings about his dependency.

Case in point: Riley wouldn't be feeding from any humans on this trip. He'd made the decision before they'd left, knowing he would be too wired. Too...nervous. Instead, he'd gorged on an elk before their departure, and he and Seth had an emergency cooler of blood bags stashed back in Tucson.

"We should get going," Seth said, glancing at the position of the sun above them.

"We could stay the night here," Riley suggested, almost succeeding in pulling off an air of innocence. "Camp under the stars. It'd be romantic."

Seth gave him a knowing look. "We don't have to go at all. We could head back to Tucson, spend some more time with Colin and Jamie and their respective devotees."

They'd already spent three days in Tucson visiting the den members that lived there. Seth had declared that he needed face time with each vampire couple Riley knew. And in the fall, they'd be heading back to Seacliff for Riley to meet the demons and their mates.

Seth was convinced that solidarity was the key to their future—building a network of friendship and communication so that if any of them smelled something fishy brewing, everyone would be on alert and available to help.

Whether it paid off or not, Riley had delighted in showing Seth off to the den these past months. It was hilarious how everyone was so determined to be protective of Riley—apparently there'd been a kerfuffle about him bonding while still so young—but the second each of them met Seth, they were charmed out of any hesitation. His wholesomeness seemed to confound them into complacency, as well as the contrast of his deep, sometimes vicious protectiveness over Riley.

It turned Riley into a smug asshole every. Single. Time.

Maybe he should draw on some of that energy now. Confidence was key, right? Riley rose from the water. "No. I want to go."

Seth came over and stood on his toes, grabbing Riley's face in his hands. He pressed a firm kiss to Riley's lips, then another, teasing at the seam with his tongue. Riley opened eagerly. Despite his neat appearance, Seth still tasted like the coppery tang of fresh blood, and Riley licked it out of his mouth with all his usual greed.

Seth smiled at him when they broke apart. "So brave, baby."

But Riley wasn't all that brave. He never had been. He was only...certain. Of himself. Of his mate. Of the fact that, even if the worst happened—even if he broke all over again—Seth would be there to pick up the pieces, to put them back together with his tender, patient care.

THEY ARRIVED in Bisbee at sunset.

Maybe they should have left the swimming hole earlier, after all—showing up for this visit just as night fell really wasn't going to help Riley's case. But, oh well. It was done. They were here.

Seth had typed the address into his phone's GPS, and they followed the directions up the road where the houses stacked along the hills, dotting the desert landscape.

"It's beautiful," Seth said, peering out of the windshield at every house they passed by.

"Mm." Riley tapped his finger on the passenger door. "My moms said a lot of artists end up here. There's—there's a community, I guess."

"Is *she* an artist?" Seth asked. "Was she?"

Riley shook his head. Why his eyes were suddenly burning, he had no idea. He blinked them rapidly. "Not that I remember. Not professionally, at least. She was a phlebotomist."

Seth didn't remark on that particular irony. He continued driving slowly, then parked outside the house that matched the address they'd been given. Seth parked on the street—not in the actual driveway—and Riley was grateful for that bit of distance as he took everything in.

The house was charming; that was the word for it. It was a one-story wooden building painted brick red, with colorful wind chimes hanging over the porch and plenty of cacti in the front yard.

Seth shut the car off.

Riley was breathing too fast, which was stupid because he didn't really need to breathe at all. It was muscle memory, or maybe another way their bodies camouflaged what they were. Another way to hide the monster inside from unsuspecting people who—

Seth's not a monster, Riley reminded himself, drawing in a much slower breath. *And we're the same now. So that means I'm not a monster either.*

Riley's voice was quiet, other than a vague, silent wariness. Maybe he was remembering how much he had fucked up the last time they'd tried to do this.

"What if...?"

Riley couldn't finish his sentence. There were too many horrible ways to end it—how could he possibly choose?

"If anything goes wrong," Seth said, his words slow and careful, "then I'll compel her, and we'll be on our way. It will be very sad, and probably painful, but it won't destroy you. I'm here, and your moms will come as soon as you call them. Whatever happens, you're not alone." Seth slipped his hand into Riley's, squeezing. "I promise. Never again."

Riley swallowed hard. Seth's promises were so easy to believe. He always meant them with his whole heart.

Riley slouched down in his seat and turned his head plaintively to his mate. "I need a kiss first."

Seth smiled. "Okay, baby."

He leaned over the console and pressed a soft, warm kiss to Riley's lips. Then his cheek. The other cheek. Both eyelids, one by one.

Riley kept himself still, soaking in the affection. "And I—I need you to tell me you love me."

"I do," Seth said immediately, his breath ghosting over Riley's temple. "I love you so, so much."

Riley took another breath and let it out in a long, slow exhale. His heart was still beating like it was fit to break out of his chest, but that couldn't be helped. "Okay. I'm ready."

They got out of the car and walked up the drive. Side by side, they climbed a quaint wooden porch up to the door. It took an eternity. It took no time at all.

Riley's moms had found the address. Or, more like, they'd had it for a while, after keeping track all these years. It was a promise they'd made him, when they'd first taken Riley in—that once he stabilized, he could look for her, if he wanted.

Riley hadn't ever been sure he'd be stable enough. Or brave enough. But he and Seth had been making their plans to visit

Tucson, and Riley had...wondered. For the first time, he'd asked his moms to tell him what they knew.

Seth hadn't pushed or said a word about it until Riley had broached the subject himself. And then Seth had said that whatever Riley chose to do, he'd be there at his side.

And now they were here.

Riley knocked on the door.

It took her a minute to answer. Riley's moms had told him that she hadn't had any more children, or ever married. Riley didn't remember enough to know why he hadn't had a father in the picture—he only knew he hadn't. Just his mother. He remembered it had felt like more than enough.

The door opened.

The woman in front of him had dark eyes and dark hair shot through with gray. Riley had forgotten the details of her face, but he knew her instantly. Her nose was strong, and her cheeks were round, although she looked thinner than he remembered. Older.

"Hello?"

It took only a split second, as she looked between them. Then her eyes locked on Riley's face. They widened in shock.

And then she was crying, and Riley was being held tightly by arms he'd never thought he'd feel wrapped around him again. He hadn't expected it, and he was sent back on his heels with the force of it.

"Ohh," she moaned, and there was so much grief in that sound that Riley could hardly bear to hear it.

"I'm sorry," his mother whispered, clutching Riley to her. "I'm so sorry. I didn't mean to yell. I didn't mean to scare you. Didn't mean to—to say—"

Riley carefully—so carefully—reached up and patted her back, this woman he knew and didn't know all at the same time. "It's okay," he said. "I'm here. I'm here, Mama."

She pulled back, placing her hands on Riley's face. She was

pretty, even with those deep grief lines around her mouth and on her brow. She had kind eyes. He'd known that. "Riley. *Riley*. My boy."

Riley's face was wet, his throat thick with emotion he couldn't yet speak. She started pulling him by the arm. "Please. Please come in."

If he'd been alone, Riley didn't know if he could have done it. A strange, overwhelming mix of fear and love and hope and grief had him frozen, his feet stuck to the porch.

But then a hand clasped his, warm and calloused, and Riley felt it—Seth's love, that beautiful blanket that never grew any less comforting, no matter how many times Riley wrapped it around himself.

Just like that, Riley's muscles unfroze.

Whatever happens, I'm not alone.

With his mate at his side, Riley stepped inside the door.

THE END.

AUTHOR'S NOTE

Thank you so much for reading Don't Feed the Vampire! I hope you enjoyed your time with Riley and Seth.

I'll admit I was nervous to return to vampires after some time away from my fanged friends, especially to start off a new series, but Riley and Seth have been in my head for a while now, and I couldn't resist telling their story. I love a case of sweetie pie meets sweetie pie, especially when one of those sweetie pies is maybe half feral and a wee bit obsessive.

Thank you to my patrons (and to Charity!) for being Riley and Seth's earliest readers and hyping me up along the way. And extra thanks for all the orange-centric recipe suggestions!

What's Next?

Luke and our mysterious whale-song "guest" of the institute! I'm excited to leap into something a little different, with a brand new paranormal creature to obsess over.

If you're too impatient to wait, you can read WIP chapters as I write them on Patreon.

If you want to stay in the know, you can sign up for my newsletter for updates and news on upcoming releases. And I can always be reached by email if you just want to say howdy. I love, love, love hearing from my readers!

graebryanauthor@gmail.com

ABOUT THE AUTHOR

Grae Bryan has been reading romance since she was far too young to know any better. Her love for love stories spans all genres, and there's nothing she finds more exciting than all the fictional worlds she has yet to explore.

She lives in Arizona with her family, who graciously share space with all the imaginary men in her head. When not writing or daydreaming or parenting wild children, she can generally be found reading more than is healthy, walking her monster-dog, or cuddling her demon-cat. She loves all things gothic, cozy, lovely, or strange.

Find her online: graebryan.com

Patreon: patreon.com/GraeBryan

Facebook: @GraeBryanAuthor

Instagram: @authorgraebryan

Sign up for her newsletter: graebryan.com/contact

Join her Facebook reader group: Grae Bryan's Reader Den

ALSO BY GRAE BRYAN

Vampire's Mate Series

Roman (Book One) – Danny and Roman

Soren (Book Two) – Gabe and Soren

Lucien (Book Three) – Jamie and Lucien

Johann (Book Four) – Alexei and Jay

Wolfgang (Book Five) – Eric and Wolfe

Colin (Book Six) — Colin, Fox, and Dane

Cassian (A Vampire's Mate Novella) – Blake and Cass

Demon Bound Series

Wreaking Havoc (Book One) — Sascha and Kai

Inviting Bedlam (Book Two) — Ivan and Nix

Calling Chaos (Book Three) — Cooper and Chaos

Unleashing Mayhem (Book Four) — Matty and Nightmare

Novellas

An Unwitting Bargain - Benny and Helio

Contemporary Omegaverse

Overeager (Extra Credit, Book One)

Hot for Teacher (Extra Credit, Book Two)

www.ingramcontent.com/pod-product-compliance
Lightning Source LLC
LaVergne TN
LVHW090554110826
845146LV00001B/120

* 9 7 9 8 9 9 0 5 5 1 9 8 5 *